Alex Delaware Novels

City of the Dead (2022)
Serpentine (2021)
The Museum of Desire (2020)
The Wedding Guest (2019)
Night Moves (2018)
Heartbreak Hotel (2017)
Breakdown (2016)
Motive (2015)
Killer (2014)
Guilt (2013)
Victims (2012)
Mystery (2011)
Deception (2010)
Evidence (2009)
Bones (2008)
Compulsion (2008)
Obsession (2007)
Gone (2006)
Rage (2005)

Therapy (2004)
A Cold Heart (2003)
The Murder Book (2002)
Flesh and Blood (2001)
Dr. Death (2000)
Monster (1999)
Survival of the Fittest (1997)
The Clinic (1997)
The Web (1996)
Self-Defense (1995)
Bad Love (1994)
Devil's Waltz (1993)
Private Eyes (1992)
Time Bomb (1990)
Silent Partner (1989)
Over the Edge (1987)
Blood Test (1986)
When the Bough Breaks (1985)

BY JONATHAN KELLERMAN AND JESSE KELLERMAN

The Burning (2021)
Half Moon Bay (2020)
A Measure of Darkness (2018)

Crime Scene (2017)
The Golem of Paris (2015)
The Golem of Hollywood (2014)

OTHER NOVELS

The Murderer's Daughter (2015)
True Detectives (2009)
Capital Crimes (with Faye Kellerman, 2006)
Twisted (2004)

Double Homicide (with Faye Kellerman, 2004)
The Conspiracy Club (2003)
Billy Straight (1998)
The Butcher's Theater (1988)

GRAPHIC NOVELS

Silent Partner (2012)
The Web (2012)

NONFICTION

With Strings Attached: The Art and Beauty of Vintage Guitars (2008)
Savage Spawn: Reflections on Violent Children (1999)

Helping the Fearful Child (1981)
Psychological Aspects of Childhood Cancer (1980)

FOR CHILDREN, WRITTEN AND ILLUSTRATED

Jonathan Kellerman's ABC of Weird Creatures (1995)
Daddy, Daddy, Can You Touch the Sky? (1994)

CITY OF
THE DEAD

JONATHAN KELLERMAN

CITY OF THE DEAD

AN ALEX DELAWARE NOVEL

BALLANTINE BOOKS

NEW YORK

Published in the United States by Ballantine Books, an imprint of
Random House, a division of Penguin Random House LLC, New York.

BALLANTINE and the HOUSE colophon are registered trademarks
of Penguin Random House LLC.

LIBRARY OF CONGRESS CATALOGING-IN-PUBLICATION DATA
Names: Kellerman, Jonathan, author.
Title: City of the dead / Jonathan Kellerman.
Description: New York : Ballantine Books, [2022] | Series: An Alex Delaware novel
Identifiers: LCCN 2021020940 | ISBN 9780525618584 (hardcover; acid-free paper) |
ISBN 9780525618591 (ebook)
Subjects: GSAFD: Mystery fiction. | Suspense fiction.
Classification: LCC PS3561.E3865 C56 2022 | DDC 813/.54—dc23
LC record available at https://lccn.loc.gov/2021020940

Printed in the United States of America on acid-free paper

randomhousebooks.com

2 4 6 8 9 7 5 3 1

First Edition

To Zev

CITY OF
THE DEAD

1

Four fifty-three in the morning was too early for anything. Alfie had said so to Donny back when it was four eighteen and they were still on the freeway. But at least they'd be early, maybe catch a nap before unloading.

Donny, as usual, had smiled and said nothing. Which was fine with Alfie. If you had to be sharing the cab on a long haul with someone, a guy who didn't talk much was a good deal.

They'd spent the last five days together, hauling a big house full of stuff from Pepper Pike, Ohio, to La Jolla, California. Rich doctor moving stuff from one dream palace to another.

In La Jolla, the guy was waiting for them, smiling and waving like they were old friends. Big beach house, looked like a bunch of ice cubes stuck together. Blue spots of ocean at the end of the property and a whole bunch of bright-green palms.

Like living in a postcard.

But a lot of steps.

Dude ran down them. "Hi, guys, I'm James."

"Doctor," said Alfie, because he'd read the papers the company gave him and knew the rules. Someone has a title, you use it. Even if they're pretending to be regular folk.

"Aw," said James. "Okay, if you insist on formality, call me Teach."

Alfie stared at him. Dude looked more like a . . . Alfie didn't *know* what. Long gray hair and beard, string of beads around his neck, these stupid little glasses with red frames.

But not a hippie or a homeless. Not with the goochy-poochy clothes. *Alligator* shoes. And a *beach house,* for God's sake. Almost as big as the humongous place in Ohio they'd moved the stuff from, that one looked like the White House, a maid in a uniform standing around while they worked, suspicious, nasty eyes.

Loading took a full day. The same would go for moving it into this place.

All those *steps.*

"Teach," said James. "As in teacher."

"Ah," said Alfie. Donny hung back, pretending not to hear.

"I'm a professor," said James.

"Wow," said Alfie, hoping that would cut it short so he could put on his weight belt, scope out the job, and start.

"Virology," said James.

Alfie knew what that meant because his mom had developed a herpes and couple of years ago, he took her to a virologist.

Plus, you could figure it out: virus/virology.

When Alfie didn't say anything, James said, "I specialize in viruses."

I specialize in killing my back to move your shit and your steps aren't going to help.

Dude annoyed him. Why not mess with him?

Alfie made his face innocent. "You do computer cleanup?"

James's lips tightened. So did the rest of his facial muscles, sending little ripples through his beard.

"No, I'm a physician. Infectious diseases and such."

And such. Who says that?

Alfie said, "Wow," with no wow in his voice.

The three of them stood there, then James the Virologist finally regained his smiley attitude and made a big show of running up the stairs.

Reaching the stop, he grinned and stretched. "Glorious day! You guys want something to drink?"

"We're fine."

"Then up and away!"

They'd been driving for a day more than planned due to a brakes thing in Tulsa where they had to spend the night in a motel full of gnats and with what sounded like tweaker lowlifes next door not sleeping and the smell of gasoline everywhere.

Shit trip to California and now they were going to be lifting and hauling and uncrating and moving stuff around all day because people always changed their minds about furniture.

Alfie and Donny *trudged* up the stairs.

When they got inside the house, music was playing loud, piped in through unseen speakers.

James said, "That okay? The song?"

"Sure."

Then he winked.

That's when Alfie started hating the asshole.

The job took longer than they figured because James's wife, a scarecrow blonde with a mouth as tight as a drawstring purse and some kind of accent, insisted on inspecting every single crystal and porcelain thingie and when you do that you find something and sure enough, there were two broken plates and that meant tears, dirty looks, and paperwork.

Combine how much stuff there was, the house being on three levels, plus their mandated lunch and dinner breaks and they didn't finish until six p.m. Meaning they had to spend the night before taking the last haul—a smaller bunch they were taking to another professor in the Westwood neighborhood of L.A. Professors all over the place; company had some kind of deal with Case Western.

GPS said Westwood was a hundred and thirty miles north, meaning at least two and a half hours if they were lucky, a lot more if they weren't, L.A. traffic sucked.

They found a motel better than the one in Tulsa in Anaheim, near Disneyland. Better but not good. One bit of luck: separate rooms so Alfie didn't have to listen to Donny snore. Guy should lose weight, that gut out to here had to mess up his breathing.

But Donny was strong. Stronger than Alfie who was ten years older and not a big guy but even so, stronger than he looked.

Donny, a football guy in high school. Alfie, baseball. Wiry but all sinew. For years he'd been scoring free drinks in bars doing arm wrestling.

Now he hurt all the time.

When they got to Anaheim, they both were exhausted, had a couple burgers, conked out at eight, slept lousy, and were up at two forty-five with coffee and bearclaws from a twenty-four-hour Dee-Lite Donuts across from the motel, you could smell the sugar and fat.

When Alfie finished, he said, "Let's go, now."

Donny said, "Now?"

"This early, maybe we can cruise on the freeway. Better we wait there than sit in crap."

"Lemme pee," said Donny.

"Then we go?"

"Sure."

Good strategy, rumbling along in the dark, the freeway really feeling free.

Alfie said, "Guy was an asshole, no?"

"Who?"

"Dr. Virus. The song."

"Huh?"

"Dire Straits? 'Money for Nothing'?"

Donny said, "That's a good song."

"A great song," said Alfie, "that's not the point. He played it *for* us. Set it up for when we came in. Then he *winked,* dude."

Donny thought about that. "So?"

"Use your noggin. What's the song about?"

"Never listened to the words."

"Oh man," said Alfie. "Okay, here's the deal: It's about guys like us moving stuff into a rich guy's place while they're talking smack about him. Not a virus doctor, a rock star. The guys who're supposed to be like us—did you ever see the video?"

"Nope."

"They're cartoon . . . like cavemen. Like monkeys, got monkey faces."

Alfie made a stupid face even though Donny was driving and not looking at him. "They're basically ape-men talking trash about a rock star with big talent. Probably the guy who wrote the song and plays the guitar . . . Mark . . . whatever. We're talking *hugely* talented."

"The guitar's awesome," said Donny.

"Exactly, dude's a genius, he *deserves* all his stuff. But the moving guys are stupid caveman monkeys too stupid to get that. That's what Virus-boy was communicating to us: I deserve all this but you don't think I do 'cause you're stupid. Assuming on us. Except we do get it, we're not stupid. He didn't give us credit for being human beings who get stuff."

Donny didn't answer.

"You still don't get it?" said Alfie, hearing his GPS beep—"turn right the next block . . . yeah, here . . . man, it's narrow. And dark. Good thing no one's out except maybe a squirrel, you squish a squirrel no one's going to care, they're like rats with better tails . . . you really don't get it?"

"Get what?"

"The song. What the asshole was communicating."

"You say so," said Donny.

Then he hit something.

2

This year's low crime rate got Detective Moses Reed up early. One of those inexplicable drops in bloodshed and mayhem had loosened the vacation schedule at West L.A. station. When Moe was jolted from his bed at five forty-five a.m., the night guys were prepping to leave and the sergeant said, "They could theoretically take it but they'll end up punting to you anyway. And right now, they're basically begging you. At some point, you can cash in on a favor."

Moe said, "No problem." At least traffic would be nil.

Both of the D's he worked with, when he worked with anyone, were out. Alicia Bogomil was vacationing with Al Freeman, a Kobe Bryant look-alike and her new boyfriend. Al was an Inglewood auto-theft guy and a total motorhead. The two of them taking a ride up the coast to Carmel in Freeman's '76 Rolls-Royce that he'd tuned up himself.

Moe's other colleague was Sean Binchy, now using every opportunity to be with his wife and kids since he'd almost been thrown off a tall building a couple of years ago. The Binchys were at a Bible camp in Simi Valley.

Leaving Moe, who was batching it anyway, because *his* girlfriend was a forensic anthropologist spending a few days at a seminar in Chicago.

The L.T. was also in town but no way Moe was calling the boss on what sounded like a vehicular accident. He mixed and drank two glasses of the protein shake, showered, shaved, got dressed, and drove to Westwood.

Thirteen minutes from his apartment in Sherman Oaks. Had to be a record.

The incident had taken place on one of those hilly streets east of the U.'s sprawling campus. Nice houses, nice trees, nice cars.

Not the kind of place you had four a.m. pedestrian-versus-vehicle confrontations.

Three squad cars on the scene. Yellow tape blocked off entry and exit to the street, encasing a hundred-foot stretch where the moving van sat.

One of the uniforms summed up, then pointed. "Those are them."

Indicating two men standing with another officer. One big and heavy, the other midsized and lean.

Moe said, "Where were they headed at that hour?"

"A house four blocks up. They came from San Diego, slept in Orange County, set out early to avoid traffic. Claim they were going slow, saw nothing, just felt impact."

Moe said, "Any signs of a deuce on the driver?"

"No evidence of any impairment at all, Detective, and their logbooks say they had adequate sleep. Actually, they both look totally aware and with it. And freaked out. They estimate they were going maybe fifteen per, felt a bump on the passenger side, figured it was an animal. Then they saw the victim."

"I.D. on the victim?"

"Nothing on him," said the uniform. "Literally. He's buck naked."

Moe blinked. "That's different. Young, old, medium?"

"Looks young. Smallish. To be honest, there's probably not enough intact face for an I.D. Unless you guys have some new high-tech thing. My guess, he's a stoned-out student."

Moe said, "High-tech? If only. Naked, huh?"

The patrolman said, "The sororities on Hilgard aren't far, maybe there was a party and some idiot wandered off and got slammed."

"Worth checking out. Thanks."

Moe left him and walked around to the front of the van. Huge thing, white, well kept. A national company named Armour, Inc., with a muscular arm logo. A slogan below the logo.

We treat your belongings like ours.

Which sounded good on the face of it. Unless you were dealing with a client who was a slob.

Moe took out his flashlight and ran it over the van. Was surprised to find no damage or blood on the hood or the windshield. No damage, period, until he got to the right side and the beam caught a dent just above the bumper.

Lateral impact. Vehicular wasn't his strong point but this was a bit different.

He phone-photo'd the dent. Maybe an inch deep, two, three inches in diameter. Concave. Flecked with blood. For a human head to do that to heavy-duty steel there had to be considerable force.

He got closer to the damage. Cup-shaped, perfect fit for a skull. He pictured the victim, maybe a naked frat boy, staggering around in the dark, too out of it to hear or see the van.

Even with the headlights on? Assuming they *were* on.

No reason they shouldn't have been on, the drivers were pros. Plus, they'd driven a hundred plus miles, no way they could've pulled that off without lights. So, lights on, but the victim hadn't paid attention.

So accidental *was* likely: some poor stoned kid had walked right into a mass of metal, got caught on the head, and flew backward. If Moe's luck held, he could wrap this up and wait for a real case.

Unless, despite what the uniform thought, the drivers *had* been impaired. Or had done something else that made them culpable.

Time to talk to them. The body could wait, it wasn't going anywhere.

Donnell "Donny" Backus had been crying. Huge, baby-faced, kettle-gut guy in his early thirties. Muttonchops, body ink up the neck. What the guys at the gym called soft-strong.

Moe introduced himself, played friendly while checking Backus's eyes and breath and overall body odor. Nothing. Guy was sweating but not giving off anything alcoholic or dope-like. On the contrary, a pleasant, piney shampoo aroma wafted from him. Recent shower; good hygiene.

Alfred "Alfie" LaMotta was dry-eyed, looked more angry than upset. Dark hair, ponytail, fox-featured, wiry build, no tats. His lined, chiseled face was dominated by steady dark eyes. Nothing overtly impaired about him, either, and anyway, he'd been the passenger.

Moe's gut feeling intensified: wrong place, wrong time for everyone.

But you never put on blinders.

He had the two of them go over it again, mostly LaMotta doing the talking with Backus sniffing. Heard the same thing the uniform had related, copied it down in his pad. "Thanks, anything else you can think of?"

Alfie LaMotta said, "Dude has no clothes on. Got to be a nutcase or a junkie, right? Charging into us like that."

Waiting for Moe's confirmation. Moe didn't offer it.

LaMotta frowned. "Sir, we did nothing wrong, this is our worst nightmare. We came here especially early to avoid traffic and people and any kind of hassle. Who'd figure some guy's going to dart out in the darkness? If he'd of been in front of us, we might've even seen him. But from the side? We thought it was a critter. A cay-ote or a deer. We see them all the time. Especially deer, they're the worst. Kill more people 'cause of accidents than bears do. Right?"

Leveling the question at Backus, who sniffed and nodded and shook his head and bit his lip and said something unintelligible.

Moe said, "What's that?"

"I am so, so sorry."

LaMotta frowned. "What could you do, man?"

"Nothing," said Backus. "I'm just sorry. For it happening."

LaMotta sighed and turned to Moe. "My man was a choirboy."

Backus said, "I'd be sorry anyway."

Moe said, "So your destination is four blocks away."

LaMotta said, "Four friggin' blocks north then we unload, go figure. Don't imagine we can get there anytime soon."

"We'll need photos of the van's exterior, photographer's on the way. And if you don't mind, a go-through of the interior."

"What're you looking for? Dope?"

"I'm sure you guys are clean but—"

"No prob, do your thing," said LaMotta, gritting his teeth. "My man here was a choirboy and I drank in high school, put weight on, took it off, and haven't touched a drop since. We do coffee, we're not Mormons, we like our coffee. *Live* on coffee. For the purpose of we don't *need* anything else besides coffee."

Moe said, "Got it."

"You also need to know the company mandates rests and meals, we take every single one, you can check our logs. We slept appropriately, you want to verify, check with the Islander Motel, Anaheim Boulevard. Exactly for that reason—sleeping well, being fit—we sacked out there last night, paid with the company card. You can also check with the twenty-four-hour Dee-Lite Donuts across the street where we got coffee and bearclaws. Kid at the counter had a pizza face."

Moe copied.

Alfie LaMotta said, "You're really going to verify?"

"I like to be thorough, sir."

"Fine. Us, too. We two got the lowest breakage rate in the company. Check that, too. Never had a problem before. *Never.*"

Moe headed for the body, pausing when he saw the coroner's investigator show up in an unmarked compact. Gloria Mendez, suited and gloved, got out carrying her big case, the one that included a digital camera and that dealie you could use to get prints that you emailed. Made it possible for an on-site victim I.D., another step for human progress.

He liked Gloria. Thorough and smart and didn't make mean jokes. They exchanged greetings and continued to the small, cruelly lit, pop-up tent where the victim was.

Poor guy was lying in a strange position, like a piece of paper that had started off folded then released itself but not completely. The lower half, slumped in the street, the upper half lying at an unnatural angle on the breezeway.

Like something tossed aside.

Naked, all right. Pale flesh. Unmarked; where were tattoos when you needed them?

Moe took a closer look, careful not to make contact.

Male, Caucasian or possibly Asian or light-skinned Latino. On the short side, Moe's guess was five-five, six. Slight build, narrow shoulders and hips, not much muscle or body hair.

A youngish body, which fit the stoned-student scenario. Moe imagined making the dreaded call to parents, once proud Junior had been accepted to the U.

The unbloodied hair strands Moe could see were short, dark, straight. The head below the hair had borne the sole visible impact of the collision, leaving the skull caved in, the face turned to something wet and red and pulpy. Slightly more damage on the right side.

Blood had pooled around the face and dribbled down toward the curb. That made sense; open head wounds tended to bleed profusely.

Gloria said, "Obviously I can't I.D. him."

"How about an on-site print?"

"Sorry, the gizmo's on the fritz. What exactly happened?"

Moe repeated the drivers' story.

She inspected the body. Photographed. Lifted the small frame obliquely to peer underneath, said, "No defects on the back," and gently laid the guy back down. "What kind of damage was done to the van?"

"Minimal." Moe described the concave dent, the blood, and took her to have a look.

When they returned to the body, Gloria said, "Guess that would fit with him tripping, lurching forward, and making contact with his cranium. The impact threw him backward. At least he wasn't pulled under, good luck I.D.'ing that . . . poor soul . . . what's your take on the nudity?"

"Given the neighborhood, maybe an impaired student wandering around."

Gloria eyed the body again. "He does look kind of young."

Moe said, "Can't wait to notify the parents."

"Don't envy you," she said. "Every year we get a couple of these, right? Precious things sent away to get educated, only to die of alcohol poisoning or falling off balconies."

Moe nodded. "Not to mention suicides. We had two here last year, both in the dorms."

"Well, one thing," said Gloria. "If he is a student, someone cares about him, so I.D. won't be an issue very long." She took a closer look at the hands. "His fingertips look pretty good so once he's back at the crypt they can take a shot at printing him."

Thinking to herself: *You're right about the notification. Better you than me.*

3

Sunrise was five fifty-nine and as the moon relented, a soft, silver glow settled over the death scene.

Lights had come on inside a few of the neighboring houses but no one had ventured out at six eleven, when Moe released the tape on the north end of the cordon and allowed the van to pass through before resealing the street. The enormous vehicle moved excruciatingly slowly. Alfie LaMotta at the wheel, now, staring straight ahead and looking put-upon.

The big one, Backus, had seemed stricken and Moe wondered if the company provided psych support. Someone like Delaware.

Gloria's comment about balconies had flashed images of Sean's near-disaster a couple of years ago.

On that one, Delaware had done more than get shrinky, he'd actually saved Sean's life. That meant, he told Sean, that he couldn't be Sean's therapist. Something about boundaries and objectivity.

Delaware *had* gotten Sean a referral and at least from what Moe could tell, that was working out. Though to Moe's eye, Sean was different.

Quieter, more serious . . . coming close to dying could do that to you, something Moe never wanted to find out for himself.

Enough pointless remembering, time to do the job. Next step: talk to neighbors. Maybe he'd luck out and someone knew the victim.

Maybe someone's college-aged son. That would be convenient but horrible and Moe would be faced with an on-the-spot notification and all the aftermath that would bring.

He'd never gotten used to notifications, figured he never would. Especially the face-to-faces. A lot easier, as cruel as it sounded, to call someone in Wisconsin or wherever.

He'd give beginning the canvass some time, let people wake up naturally.

A crypt van appeared. Gloria took a few more photos, emailed them to the coroner, and cleared the body for transport. Two stoic drivers zip-zipped the victim into a bag, not working hard to tote the flimsy weight. The clack of the gurney snapped open, assaulting the morning. Up, in, the van drove off. Down came the pop-up but Moe kept the uniforms there to help with the canvass.

He'd start at six thirty. Earlier if someone came out.

At six eighteen, someone did.

Old guy stepping out of a white, two-story Spanish house and standing on his front porch. Overgrown shrubs blocked what was probably a picture window. The neighbor was stooped, bald, wore an oversized gray terry bathrobe. Burgeoning sunlight touched on pale, hairless shins and the veined tops of feet in backless slippers.

The old guy looked around some more, moved forward and corralled a single uniform, said something and headed straight for Moe.

Making good time despite a stiff gait.

Facial expression of someone headed for the complaint desk.

Moe met him halfway. "Sir."

"You're the detective in charge."

"I am, sir."

"Name?"

Moe handed him a card. The old man looked at it but didn't take it. "Mr. Reed, tell me what's going on."

"There was an incident—"

"Obviously." Sour look. "Could you be a trice more specific?" Barking the request, then shrugging as if aiming for some sort of apology. The scowl that lingered on his face fought that.

Moe figured him for the guy who'd lived here forever, thought he owned the block.

Moe said, "A moving van hit someone."

"Someone naked."

Moe tried to hide his astonishment. "How did you find that out, Mr. . . ."

The old guy smiled mirthlessly. "I'd give you *my* card but since I retired from the practice of management consulting longer ago than you've been around, I don't need one." He fingered his own chest. "I am Rainer Gibbs." He spelled both names. "I've lived here for fifty-two years and this is the first time anyone has ever been struck down by a moving van or anything else. Given the nudity, should I be worried about *ahem* social change? Meaning teenage perverts running amok?"

"Mr. Gibbs, how did you hear the victim was—"

"Naked?" said Rainer Gibbs, savoring the word. "From your colleagues, Mr. Reed. Or should I say your subordinates—those forced to wear uniforms rank below you, correct? Whatever their status, they don't modulate their voices. I was in my front room having my tea, heard the commotion, opened a window, and listened. A van, eh? There should be a law against those behemoths invading residential streets."

Be kind of hard to move anywhere if that was the case. Moe said nothing.

Gibbs's eyebrows danced. "In any event, one of your troops said a quote unquote naked d.b. was lying out in the street. I took 'd.b.' to mean 'dead body.' Am I correct?"

Wonderful.

Moe said, "You are, sir."

"Then I might possibly have a—what do you people call it, a lead? Or a clue as it was known in my day?"

"Either way, Mr. Gibbs."

"A clue, then. I might have one. Go take a look at *that* place." Pointing north.

"One of your neighbors."

"No, no, I don't consider renters neighbors. They've got no stake in the game, no pride of ownership. The place is owned by a merry widow—that's another story—who hasn't lived here for years. She *rents* and for the past year or so has rented to *her*. And *she* doesn't act respectfully."

"She being?"

"No idea what her name is. I call her the strumpet. That's probably a word you're not familiar with. In any event, she's got men—women, too, but mostly men—coming in and out. Different people, it's not like she's entertaining. *That* feels to me like a high-end brothel."

Moe said, "Have you ever seen evidence of prostitution?"

"Hardly," said Gibbs. "Would you have preferred me to peep through windows?"

"Not a good idea, sir."

"Hmmph—in any event, Mr. Reed, I complained months ago to you people and was told there was nothing that could be done unless evident evidence of a crime surfaced. Now you've got your evident evidence. A naked person came to an unnatural end. Is that sufficient for you?"

"Which house specifically are we talking about, sir?"

Gibbs pointed. "Three up from mine. The style-devoid structure with the horrid blue siding and the insufficient shrubbery. Want to lay odds I'm right? If your naked d.b. came from anywhere on the block, it was there."

"Thank you, sir."

Gibbs's face constricted. "Is that a sincere thank-you or a get-lost thank-you?"

"Sincere," said Moe, not sure if it was.

He went to check.

Despite Gibbs's architectural critique, the house seemed decent if bland, a two-story traditional with a flat green lawn and a lush planting of birds-of-paradise looking downright avian as it shaded a neat bed of white impatiens. Moe had come to know flower varieties because his mother's new passion was gardening. Probably her twentieth passion in as many years; breeding goldfish hadn't worked out too well when herons discovered her shallow pond.

He did have to agree with Gibbs the Grump about the blue siding.

A welcome mat on a clean concrete stoop said *Nice People Welcome. Good Intentions Tolerated.*

His knock was met with silence. So was his doorbell-push. He felt eyes boring into the back of his neck, saw Rainer Gibbs back in front of his Spanish, arms crossed, watching him.

Obnoxious old coot. The scrutiny made Moe feel he was back in school reciting poetry that made no sense.

Crossing the lawn, he reached the blue house's driveway. A gate blocking entry was unlatched. Moe chose to see it as an omen and passed through.

He'd made it nearly to the house's rear door when he saw the blood.

Spots of blood, what looked like low-impact spatter, already beginning to rust in the sun. Not a huge amount—maybe a dozen specks that continued right up to the door. Someone else might not have noticed.

To Moe's trained eye, enough blood to matter.

He stopped, deliberated, decided.

Time to call the boss.

CHAPTER

4

Milo phoned me just after nine a.m.

Not the typical time for one of his calls. Black skies bring out the predators and the prey, so nighttime's the right time for the killings. Milo feels I might have something to offer.

As I sat stalled in commuter traffic on Beverly Glen heading south, another prisoner of the daylight, I figured something had happened hours ago and he'd been on the scene for a while.

Meaning complicated.

My destination was in a northeast pocket of Westwood that ran parallel to the U. I could've run the three miles from my house on the Glen and had done so many times. But that morning, I'd chosen to run uphill, meaning north, had jogged to Mulholland and back, was stretching out and drinking coffee.

I showered, got dressed, walked to Robin's studio, kissed her, petted the dog, returned to the house and down the steps from the entry landing, and got in the Seville.

Crawling the three or so miles to Sunset, I slogged another westward mile to the U.'s eastern border at Hilgard Avenue, drove a few blocks before hanging a left, crossing two more quiet, leafy streets, and hooking north.

Walking distance from campus and the sororities and religious centers that lined Hilgard, but far enough from adolescent merriment to be quiet. Hilly abbreviated streets hosted two-story houses originally designed to house faculty. Professors emeritis could afford to stick around because they'd bought decades ago. Good luck to any other academic not attached to medicine, law, or business.

The yellow tape was visible half a block away, the activity massed near a boxy structure sided in royal blue.

I was entering the scene with little but curiosity. All Milo had said was, "One of those, Alex. If you're free."

I was because my appointment was booked late in afternoon. One of the child custody cases that pay my bills and allow me to hope I can help some kids going through the dissolution of their families.

I said, "Morning's clear."

"What a pal."

Four black-and-whites were parked in front of the tape. In the distance, several officers conducted door-knocks.

The sole uniform guarding the tape stopped me. Young, arms crossed, almost comically grave. "No entry, sir."

"Dr. Delaware for Lieutenant Sturgis."

"Duck under, sir."

Yellow, numbered plastic evidence markers marked a section of sidewalk and street not far from the entrance to the cordoned area. A second group of markers, larger, covering a wider swath, dotted the blue house's driveway like a child's discarded toys, and spilled over to the lawn.

Milo stood away from all that, on the sidewalk, wearing an exhausted, lint-colored sport coat, a white wash 'n' wear shirt, a sad burnt-orange thing aspiring to be a necktie, khaki cargo pants, and tan desert boots. The boots' soles were bright flamingo. Freshly soled. For the tenth time.

Next to him stood Detective Moses Reed, fair-haired, buzz-cut, and nearly as pink as Milo's shoe-bottoms, in a gray suit, navy shirt, navy tie. No matter how carefully Moe's clothes are tailored, his power lifter's build makes them look ready to burst at the seams. This morning, the tension had traveled to his eyes.

He's young but experienced. This had to be something.

I turned back to Milo. Ghostly pallid, but that's his default skin tone. His black hair was unruly in spots, his green eyes half lidded, his heavily jowled, pockmarked face immobile.

I said, "What's up?"

"Thanks for coming on short notice, Alex. Here's the deal: Three or so hours ago a moving van going north made impact with what the drivers thought was an animal."

He pointed to the first group of markers. "Turned out to be a human animal, young, male, and naked. Moses?"

Reed said, "Morning, Doc. My first thought was maybe a drunk student running around in the dark got hit by accident. Then a neighbor tipped us to this place, said people were coming in and out all the time, he figured it for a high-end brothel. His words. He had no evidence, just suspicion due to the variety of visitors, but when I tried to pin him down on a number, he admitted not that many. So I figured him for an old crank but went to check it out anyway, got no response at the front door, was headed to the back when I saw some blood in the driveway. One thing led to another and turns out there's a female victim inside, no doubt about that one being a homicide."

I said, "Any evidence of a sexual crime?"

Milo said, "Not so far. Why?"

"Naked guy in the street, could be her killer. Or an intended second victim who escaped but encountered bad luck?"

Milo said, "Hoping for the former but till we get the blood sorted out, no way to know. Ready to have a look?"

I never really am. "Sure, let's go."

Reed said, "Want me along, L.T.?"

"Not necessary, Moses. Manage the canvass."

Paper-suited and gloved up, I followed Milo through an open wooden gate. He pointed out the blood Moe had seen. Freckles, easy to miss, and by day's end likely faded to near invisibility.

We continued to the blue house's rear door, held open by one of those old-fashioned pneumatic devices you can kick to keep in place.

The service porch and kitchen were neat and well organized. More sprinkles of blood in the nearest corner. Larger, darker. What looked like low impact—something dripping from above, not the result of explosion.

Yet more blood on a tile floor in the utility space that segued to hardwood in the kitchen. Both had the potential to be decent surfaces for crisp shoe impressions.

Foot impressions, given a naked man.

Nothing showed here.

I said, "The blood stops?"

"And resumes. You'll see."

"What was the weapon?"

He pointed to an empty slot in a wooden knife holder. "For the female victim, big butcher thing, found near her, on its way to the lab. Techs went through the place and took tons of samples. If Naked Guy's prints turn up on the handle, one giant step for detective-kind."

I said, "Sounds like you could be well on your way. You called me in because . . ."

"If Naked does get confirmed as the bad guy, I'm still gonna need to put it together with both deaths explained. As in why he'd kill someone then run outside, smack into a moving van."

"I can think of all sorts of reasons. Panic, guilt, psychotic break. Chemical impairment."

"Exactly, Alex. I need someone who can think fast and sound authoritative while he's doing it. If the naked guy is my man, the question's gonna be murder-suicide or murder-accident."

"You want a psychological autopsy."

"I wasn't thinking formally but guess so." He smiled. "You've done them for the crypt. They pay okay, right?"

"Better than the department."

"Low bar, amigo. Okay with you if I call Basia, see if I can start some paperwork on that?"

"Sure."

He flexed his fingers. Antsy.

I said, "But if all you want is some theorizing, it won't be a big deal."

"Well," he said, smiling uneasily, "you never know. Too many weird things going on with this one."

"Like?"

"Nothing I can put a finger on, just a feeling. And, amigo, it's better when it gets weird."

"I'll take that as a compliment."

"Intended as such." He grinned. "Haven't seen you in a while."

He led me out of the kitchen and into the living room, beige and white and fastidious except for a rumpled duvet and a pillow atop the larger of two taupe sofas. A white door shut off entry to what I assumed was a staircase to the second story.

I said, "No forced entry, weapon of convenience, someone sleeping over. His clothes were also sent to the crypt?"

He frowned. "No clothes, that's part of the weirdness. Not anywhere here or, so far, outside. People aren't gonna let us into their castles but maybe we can glance at backyards. Or owners will and find a stash."

"The guy hid his the clothes and his I.D. somewhere then showed up naked?"

He shrugged. "Maybe the whole thing started as an adventurous booty call. Or if the grumpy neighbor's right, an adventurous in-call. Either way, he shows up starkers to spice it up, intends to come back later for his duds and I.D. The two of them start to party but it goes bad and he ends up on the couch."

"She lets him stay rather than kicking him out?"

The question vexed him. The way a persistent sore does.

"I know, I know—maybe he was tired, Alex, and she took pity. A date gone wrong could fit with that, too. She appeased him because they had a relationship. But instead of settling down on the sofa, he tossed and turned and worked himself up. What better way to cook up male rage than sexual rejection?"

I pointed to the white door. "Her bedroom's upstairs?"

"Right at the top of the stairs but no sign of romance or struggle there or anywhere on the second floor. That's why I'm figuring it started and ended on the first floor."

I said, "The party duds out, she asks him to leave, he bargains for the couch, she agrees and goes to sleep upstairs. Then for some reason, she comes back down here?"

"Maybe he was making noise. Hollering, pacing around, she has enough and comes down and now she is ready to kick him out."

"He's not hearing it, gets a knife from the kitchen and murders her? But not in the kitchen and not here, the blood's too skimpy."

"She's got defensive wounds, some of the kitchen could be from those if there was a confrontation. Or, it's his blood—knife slippage."

I closed my eyes, took a moment to imagine. "He chases her, stabs her to death, then runs outside and gets slammed by the van."

"You're the psychologist. You see it as impossible?"

When it comes to human behavior few things are impossible. But that scenario felt wrong. Contrived.

On the other hand, first impressions can be way off the mark. And Milo's got the highest solve rate in the department; his gut feelings deserve respect.

My silences can get him edgy. He kicked one heel with the other.

I said, "Not impossible. So where did it happen?" Though I already knew.

He opened the white door and we continued another few, terrible feet.

When women are murdered at home, it's most often in the bedroom, with the kitchen ranked second. This woman had been slaughtered in a narrow wood-floored corridor leading from the living room to what appeared to be an office. At the far end, a narrow staircase right-angled upstairs. Awkward design and placement. A tacked-on feature suggesting a later add-on.

My eyes had traveled to the staircase because my brain was delaying a look at the body.

No sense putting it off.

She was barefoot, with long, thick blond hair fanning around her head. Golden blond where the blood hadn't hennaed it. She wore a black silk bathrobe patterned with green and gold dragons and nothing else. The robe's belt lay at her sides, crinkled by hardened blood into what looked like sections of tapeworm. My first thought was someone had yanked the garment open to expose her sexually but as I took a closer look, I wondered.

Lust killers lack imagination and when manipulating their victims' clothing, they tend to follow scripts: stripping the body bare in order to degrade, ripping fabric to shreds in hormonal rage, or choreographing poses that grotesquely ape consensual passion.

The strip of bare skin of this victim, exposed by the robe falling away, was narrow and pristine.

Maybe just a garment loosening during a struggle.

Any struggle appeared minimal. Through plastic bags tied over the hands, I made out purple thatches of defensive wounds on both palms. But they looked scant and shallow.

Not a prolonged battle. A single, viciously effective wound had ended this woman's life: diagonal slash to the left side of the neck exposing veins and trachea.

This picture would stay with me for a while.

I pushed past that and forced myself to imagine the scene.

The look of surprised horror on her face as she tried to fend off an attack.

Failure. Pain. Collapse. Eternity.

Her face was canted away from where I stood. Taking several breaths, I kneeled and got a close look. Shot upward as if yanked by a rope, feeling the heat drain from my body.

Milo took hold of my arm. "You okay?"

I exhaled.

"Alex?"

"I know her."

CHAPTER

5

I'd met Cordi Gannett two years ago, in the mahogany-paneled chambers of a Superior Court judge in the main court building, downtown.

No, not met. *Encountered* is a better word.

The *in camera* session was an attempt to mediate a custody dispute between a pair of divorcing gym owners. My job had been to assess each of their abilities to raise their two-year-old daughter.

I've been doing custody evals for years and have established my rules.

Wary of being seen as a pay-to-play whore, I never work for either side, functioning instead as an impartial agent of the court. Sometimes it means everyone ends up happy with me, sometimes just the opposite. When I sign my reports I know I've been careful, fair, and as close to objective as any human can come.

Some custody cases involve feeling my way through blind alleys of emotional nuance and behavioral subtlety. Not so on the case that brought me into contact with Cordi Gannett.

The mother, a dancer/SoulCycle instructor, was intense and ambitious. Also loving and attentive to a daughter tending to shyness. The father, a former collegiate wrestler who taught weight training and a bit of mixed martial arts, was none of the above.

Added to that, he had a history of domestic abuse with three previous girlfriends, including a battery conviction that had earned him jail time.

The level of rancor hadn't risen that high with the only woman he'd married. So far.

When I observed him with his daughter, he had no clue what to do, spoke very little, seemed detached. When he tried to engage the child, she shied away from him.

When she was out of earshot, I commented on her social distancing and he shrugged it off. "She's too little to think."

Despite first impressions, I took my time as I always do, observing interactions in my office, at the family home, and in a nearby park. Rapport between father and daughter never developed and it didn't take long for him to begin canceling appointments.

I entered chambers with a clear notion of what I was going to say. Then the father's lawyer blindsided the mother's lawyer by announcing a surprise expert.

In the legal world, expertise is a formal status established in court. The process begins with direct examination of the purported sage by friendly counsel aimed at polishing image to a high gloss: ticking off every year of higher education, training, and experience; enumerating academic appointments, publications, teaching duties, professional awards.

When unfriendly counsel sniffs vulnerability, all of that is immediately challenged during cross-examination. When no chinks in the armor are spotted, the strategy shifts to damage control: try to cut the recitation short with a terse, "We stipulate."

The practice of family law—of law, in general—has nothing to do with truth and everything to do with brinkmanship and illusion. The less a judge or jury hears about a solid witness, the better.

For all that, during most *pre*-trial proceedings, including meetings *in camera,* no formal screening takes place. A fact that the father's attorney, a gruff-voiced bottom-feeder named Forrest Slope, had tried to exploit.

He introduced his savant with a flourish that raised the judge's eyebrows.

"This," he boomed, "is Dr. Cordelia Gannett!"

Moments later, in pranced a lithe blonde in her early thirties, wearing a tight black sheath dress, yellow stiletto-heeled shoes, and a centerfold smile directed at the judge. Then she turned the charm on me, tacking on a nanosecond pout.

Let's be friends? Puh-leeze?

The mother's lawyer was a hollow-cheeked, metallic-voiced SoulCycle fanatic named Lara Ettinger. Guess where she'd met her client.

She said, "Your Honor, expertise needs to be established."

"That's for court," said Forrest Slope, grinning. "This is a free exchange of ideas. Correct, Your Honor?"

The judge, on the bench for four months, looked befuddled.

I'd been trying to re-engage Cordelia Gannett. Since I'd ignored the pout, she'd studiously avoided me.

I whispered something to Ettinger.

Slope said, "*Ahem. Free* exchange, not covert maneuvers from *Mr.* Delaware, Your Honor."

Ettinger said, "*Dr.* Delaware. As a matter of fact, *Professor* Delaware."

Slope said, "Professor? Those who can't do, teach?"

Ettinger rose to her feet. "Your Honor, we had a predetermined agenda. Given Mr. Slope's last-minute attempt at disruption, I request a recess to confer with Professor Delaware."

"Professor," said Slope, twirling a finger.

"Your Honor, Mr. Slope is out of line and causing the situation to degenerate into ad hominem attacks. Clearly the actions of one who knows—"

Slope said, "What I know is that I'm well within my rights to advance—"

The judge quieted the room with what sounded like a moan. Wiping sweat from his upper lip, he said, "This does change things. How long a recess do you request, Ms. Ettinger?"

"An hour."

"It's nearing lunchtime, let's reconvene in two hours."

As we left, Dr. Cordelia Gannett finally turned to me. Smiling again but her eyes betrayed her. Not even close to happy.

When Ettinger and I reentered chambers two hours later, neither Slope nor Gannett was there and Ettinger, manically ebullient, made her move. "If it pleases Your Honor, I'd like to discuss some recently uncovered info—"

The door opened. Slope slumped in alone, chewing his cheek. "The least you could do was wait, Lara."

The judge waved him off. "What were you saying, Ms. Ettinger?"

Ettinger rubbed her palms together. "During the recess you so graciously granted, Your Honor, we did some background research on Mr. Slope's alleged *expert* and found her to be anything *but*. Her *alleged* doctoral degree is from an uncertified *correspondence* school, her *alleged* experience in the field of child clinical or pediatric *psychology* or any variant of such is *nonexistent* and in fact, last year, she was brought up on charges of *misrepresentation*—"

Slope's cheeks inflated. "Not relevant. Dr. Gannett knows my client well and has substantive information."

"She knows your client *quite* well," said Ettinger, "because she had an intimate *relationship* with him."

Like a horny pigeon, Slope puffed his chest and upped the volume of his squawk. "Exactly, Lara! *Intimate.* Derived from the Latin *intimatus,* meaning 'to make familiar.' That is our goal here—your goal, I'm sure, Your Honor. Making the *truth* familiar rather than leaving it as a hazy abstraction. I posit, Your Honor, that in matters of child welfare, familiarity is *highly* relevant and that Dr. Gannett is in a unique position to shed light on my client's interpersonal merits—"

Ettinger smirked. "*I* posit that familiarity can breed contempt, Your Honor. Which is precisely what Mr. Slope has shown this court and these proceedings by attempting to foist a charlatan on a profoundly serious—"

Slope gun-aimed a finger. "You. Are. Veering dangerously close to slander."

"Quite the contrary, Forrest. I'm speaking truth to the abuse of power."

The judge, looking shell-shocked, said, "Let's reconvene in a week."

The following day, the father relinquished his custody claim.

Milo said, "Because of Gannett?"

"I'm sure that was part of it," I said. "But he also got his ex to write him a check for half the gym's worth and he really didn't care about the kid in the first place."

"Sentimental fellow. So my victim was a big-time fraud."

"And a big-time risk-taker," I said. "Imagine trying that after being brought up by the state board for practicing without a license."

"How'd that resolve?"

"She pled no contest, promised not to repeat, was let off with a warning. A few months later she was on the Web selling herself as a relationship expert."

"No restrictions on that?"

"Nope."

He stuffed his hands in his pockets, thought for a few seconds. "I can see a gambler letting a naked guy enter in the middle of the night. How'd you figure out she was phony?"

"I didn't, it was luck. A few weeks before, I'd heard about her from a colleague. One of his patients had left to see her and it ticked him off so he researched her."

"He the one who reported her?"

"Him or someone else in a similar position," I said. "Anyway, once I told the mother's lawyer, she did a quick internet search out in the hall and got plenty of ammunition. Later, I was curious and did my own research. Gannett's pre-doctoral work history was unconventional, to say the least. Figure model, nude dancer, and there were suggestions she made a porn movie though I never found evidence of that. She got a mail-in degree, hooked up with a D-list actor, and began inserting herself into the almost-celebrity circuit."

"Sounds like perfect training for a relationship expert. Which actor?"

"Don't recall."

"Shame on you, son. This is L.A., where are your priorities?" Out came his hands, fingers restless, like typing without a keyboard. "So maybe the neighbor was onto something and she hadn't left the other stuff totally behind."

"Or," I said, "she chose the wrong relationship to coach."

Despite the lack of activity in the bedroom, I asked to see it, so we climbed the awkward staircase. The steps and the landing were carpeted and clean, as was Cordi Gannett's sleeping chamber, a modest, dim rectangle set up with a low queen bed in a bamboo box-frame. A quilted coffee-colored spread showed no sign of disturbance but for a turned-up corner. Red velvet slippers sat in front of a nightstand bearing nothing but a gooseneck lamp.

Meticulous woman but maybe not about the things that mattered?

I scanned the room. Residue of fingerprint dust appeared at various touch points.

Milo said, "We got a bunch, mostly one set, likely hers."

He was right. Nothing had happened up here.

We left the house and returned to the sidewalk.

"So," he said, "any way you can see fit to give me the name of the daddy whose kid didn't like him?"

I said, "Tyler Hoffgarden."

He blinked. "Just like that? No confidentiality issues?"

"Custody cases are public record."

"Once they squabble and put themselves out there, no protection?"

"Not unless you can get a suppression order."

"Who does that?"

"People with serious money," I said.

"Regular folk are fair game."

"As always," I said. "The main thing is the kids don't become fair game."

Noise from beyond the tape zone caught our attention.

Moe Reed, heading our way from up the block, had been waylaid by two women who'd come out of flanking houses on the east side of the street. One Colonial, one Mediterranean, each with a Range Rover in the driveway.

The women stood side by side, hands on hips, a mini-gauntlet. Both were in their thirties, slim, attractive, and well tended, wearing black cashmere tops that ended mid-thigh, leggings, and Technicolor running shoes.

A pair of blondes, one uniformly honey-gold, the other platinum alternating with black tips and intentionally irregular black roots.

Black tights for All Blonde, flesh-colored for her brindled friend. As if part of a dance routine, each of them freed a hand at the same instant and began wagging index fingers at Reed. Polished nails sparked in the sunlight, setting off tiny, luminous dots of color. Pretty faces scowled.

Unloading on Reed. The young detective tolerated it with Buddhic calm, was about to respond when Honey spotted Milo, pointed to him, and asked Reed something. Whatever he said caused her to turn her back on him and march toward us, her companion following close behind.

Milo said, "Time for public relations, hold on."

Loping toward the women, he met them at the tape line, did his own listening for a while though he appeared distracted. Finally, he said something that seemed to mollify them. They started to leave and I heard him say, "Just one more thing, please?"

Platinum-and-Black said, "What?"

Her volume must've made him conscious of his own. He dialed down, spoke for a fraction of a minute, listened for a whole lot longer.

An avuncular smile failed to pacify the women as they headed for their respective front doors.

Milo returned, shaking his head, and checking his phone before pocketing it.

I said, "*You're* the one in charge? Fine, *enough* with the disruption, open the street so we can take our kids to school and get our days *going*."

"You could hear all that?"

"Nope."

He stared at me. "That's pretty much word for word except for a couple of F-bombs." He laughed. "New generation of mothers, can't imagine mine cussing like that. How'd you nail it?"

"Call it a hunch. You agreed, huh?"

"No reason not to." He laughed. "Hell hath no fury like a mommy scorned."

6

Reed remained standing where the women had stopped him, talking on his phone. When he clicked off, Milo beckoned him over, murmuring, "Uh-oh, the kid's got that no-news-is-bad-news look."

When Reed got there, he said, "Zippo on the canvass?"

"Unfortunately, L.T. So far no clothes or wallet. We do have another block to go. If nothing shows up, should I expand it?"

"Yeah, go another three. Any problem getting access?"

"We're batting around . . . .700."

"Better than the majors," said Milo. "That include the indignant mommies?"

Reed laughed. "They're a pair, aren't they. Yeah, they okayed me talking through their doors. Then they must've called each other, decided they were ticked off. I did manage to ask them if they knew Dr. Gannett and the one with black patches in her hair blew me off and got back into opening up the street, her kid has a test, it's just not fair he should suffer. I said I'd ask you what the schedule is but when they found out you were the boss, they beelined."

Milo said, "Flattered. One of them also told me Gannett had been overly flirtatious with her husband but said it was no big deal. In any event, they're right about Gannett being a faker."

He related the in-chambers confrontation.

"Checkered past," said Reed. "That could complicate it. Anything else we should know about her, Doc?"

I shook my head.

"Anything else you want me to do, L.T.?"

"No, just keep searching for clothing and I.D. I'll let you know if that changes."

When Reed left, he said, "The kid's right, it could lead to complications. I've got a victim with a loose concept of the truth who flirts with other women's hubbies, invites naked guys into her home, and maybe continued to lead a double life as a wild child and human relations pooh-bah. Can you find out more about her? Like you said, she could've poached patients from other docs. How about contacting the shrink who told you about her and see what he or she knows?"

I glanced at the blue house. "What I saw in there didn't look like professional jealousy."

"Not to me, either, I'm just groping. But looking for anyone who had conflict with her could lead to something. Is it a problem, calling?"

"Nope."

"Great, thanks for taking the time. Give both of the beauties who put up with you a hug."

He's always inventive when he tells me to leave.

My drive home was smoothed by light traffic and polluted by bad pictures.

My house, designed by Robin, is white, crisp, generously windowed, and rests on stout round concrete pylons with a high entrance that maximizes view. I parked the Seville in front and vaulted the stairs to the wraparound entry terrace.

On the other side of the door was white, bright space, silent but for my echoing footsteps. Crossing the living room and the kitchen, I exited through the service door and descended to the garden where I stopped by the pond to feed the koi. When the fish had finished slurping in gratitude, I continued to the casita that houses Robin's studio.

She builds and repairs expensive stringed instruments, has an international reputation, and keeps getting busier. Today's agenda was triple-fold: emergency neck repair of a thrash-metal icon's acid-green Ibanez bass, continuing the painstaking restoration of an exquisite, century-old Martin, and fixing loose braces on a Nahhat oud made in Aleppo, Syria, in 1927, when that city was beautiful and civilized.

She was seated at her bench, petite and curvy, auburn curls kerchiefed by a red bandanna, wearing black overalls over a white T-shirt and square-lensed magnifying specs. One hand rose in a five-fingered welcome. The other tweezed a micro-tile of ivory inlay.

Flash of smile. "One sec, hon."

"Take your time."

A monumental blast of guttural noise shot forward from the rear of the studio.

Blanche, our little fawn French bulldog, was sprawled on the couch alternating between bassoon snores and piccolo dog-dream squeaks.

The rhythmic up-and-down of her body made me laugh. A salami respiring.

An eyelid lifted, revealing a soft brown iris.

"Hey, cutie."

Robin said, "I won't ask if that's her or me," and lowered the tile to the rosette rimming the guitar's sound hole.

Blanche yawned and deliberated her next move, finally wiggled down and landed on her feet. Shaking herself off and cocking her head, she sneezed twice, waddled to me, rubbed her head against my pant leg, and purred happily as I petted her.

Robin, still peering through the magnifier, checked the tile, removed the glasses, and got up. As she walked toward us, Blanche left me and ran toward her, panting as if reuniting with a long-lost relative.

"Nice try, girlfriend, but I know where your allegiance lies. And I'm going to give him a big smooch anyway, so deal."

We sat on the couch drinking coffee, Blanche wedged tightly between us. Snoring.

Robin said, "How does she do that? Just drop off?"

I said, "Clear conscience."

"For eighteen hours a day?" She leaned over and kissed the top of Blanche's head. "Sweet dreams, cutie—maybe she's got the right idea and consciousness is overrated. So what horrible thing happened this otherwise glorious morning, my darling?"

It's taken me a while to figure out how much to tell her. I've settled on enough not to insult her intelligence or make her feel excluded but not so much that her head also fills with the wrong stuff.

Walking that line, I summed up, including the naked man and the moving van but omitting the gore.

"Stabbed in the middle of the night in her own house?" She shuddered. "Every woman's nightmare. Who was she?"

"Do you recall a couple of years ago, I told you about someone trying to pass herself off as an expert in a custody case?"

"I do remember. You were pretty miffed. *That's* who it was?"

I nodded.

She said, "Crazy. Then again, you got called in, so why wouldn't it be?"

We sat for a while until, predictably, we both got restless. A short kiss was followed by a long one and a hand pat signaling Robin's need for solitude. She returned to her bench and I headed for the studio door, Blanche padding along after me.

Robin said, "See what I mean about allegiance? Now you're going to slip her a treat and solidify the favoritism."

I said, "Whatever it takes."

The man who'd told me about Cordi Gannett was a neuro-psychiatrist ten years my senior named Sheldon Strull.

Shel had an office on Camden Drive in Beverly Hills and a busy practice evaluating adults and children with seizure disorders and brain abnormalities. I used him for med consults and he sent me legal consults when the issues were outside his purview or when lawyers wanted more than one expert. He's well trained, outgoing, thoughtful, easy to work with.

He'd complained about Gannett at the tail end of a collegial lunch at a Greek restaurant on Canon Drive. Shel and I would both be testifying in an amusement park accident case that had injured a ten-year-old boy. The plaintiff's lawyer had asked that we coordinate our reports. We each refused, told him lockstepping at the outset was inappropriate but once the reports were done, we'd be willing to compare notes.

That time had come. Comparison had taken five minutes. Even without prep, we'd agreed on the basics. No big surprise, the injuries to body and soul were obvious and profound.

The rest of the time was spent talking about travel and hobbies—my guitar playing, his viola playing in a Baroque ensemble—and then, of course, Shel's grandkids.

When he finished extolling, he put a half-eaten dolma back on his plate and said, "Can I ask you about something else, Alex? Fair warning, I may start getting pissed off and don't want to ruin the atmosphere."

"Never seen you pissed off."

"There's always a first time."

"No prob, go for it."

He pinged the edge of his bread plate with a well-trimmed fingernail. "No offense, but I always thought psychologists had laws as strict as us about misrepresentation."

"We do."

"Well, it didn't stop some charlatan—is there a feminine version, we're talking a woman, a charlataness? Whatever, the regs didn't stop her from palming herself off as a psychologist and poaching a patient. The poaching part didn't bother me. You know how busy I am. But this particular patient—an adolescent, technically an adult, actually, she's eighteen. But not an adult, if you know what I mean."

I nodded.

He fooled with the stuffed grape leaf. Finished it. "The girl has an atypical seizure disorder plus multiple soft signs and requires a cocktail of meds that will likely change over time. Instead, she dropped out and started getting interpersonal therapy—whatever that is. *Is* it something?"

"Garbage-can term," I said.

"I figured. I tried talking to the mother and she seemed to agree with me but she wouldn't do anything about it, said the kid was adamant, thought I was out to O.D. her on drugs. It bothered me, not the part about me, my ego's just fine. The kid's not getting what she needs.

So I did something I wouldn't normally do and called the psychologist. Gave her a few days to call back and when she didn't, I looked her up. Your board doesn't list her. Is there somewhere else I should look?"

"She could have a marriage and family therapist license."

He shook his head. "Your board directed me there and they had no knowledge of her. Same for the social work board. I even tried the nursing board. Nothing. And she explicitly lists herself as a psychologist on the Web. Adults, teens, and kids. What do you think?"

"Sounds like she's a fake."

"The information age and people still do that?" said Shel.

"If they can get away with it."

"Guess so—to be honest, it happens to M.D.'s, too. Last year there was a guy in East L.A. practicing internal medicine. His training? Meatcutter in a bodega. Wonderful world, huh? So now I've got a stupid kid messing herself up because of a quack."

I said, "What's this person's name?"

"Cordelia Gannett. Ever hear of her?"

I shook my head.

He said, "Only thing on the Web is her site and it's not much, just her name, address, and some patient endorsements that I think look pretty tacky. Only other person by that name in cyberspace is a tropical tanning butter bikini model, obviously someone different."

"Unless Gannett leads an interesting life."

"Huh," he said. "You think?"

"I'd be curious."

"Huh," he repeated. "Now I am, too."

A week later, he called. "Guess what, Alex? You were right, we're talking the same bimbo. Bikini model claims she has a Ph.D. but doesn't have any kind of license. I told the stupid kid's mother. She wasn't happy but she still didn't commit to bringing the kid back—age of majority and all that. Which is fine with me, I've got enough cooperative patients, we both do, why waste time?"

Months later, I passed him in a courtroom corridor and told him about Gannett's *in camera* stunt.

He said, "She got brought up on charges and is *still* doing it? Unbelievable."

"Lame try," I said. "It didn't work."

"Didn't work out so well for the patient she stole, either. She ended up hospitalized with a serious seizure. Finally came back to me. Not the way I like to be right."

Per Shel's answering service, he was out of the office for a week. That sounded like one of his infrequent vacations. I requested a call-back but didn't frame it as an emergency.

Twenty minutes later, my service patched him in. His voice reverbed a bit, as if directed through a tunnel.

"Alex. What's up?"

"Remember Cordelia Gannett?"

"How could I forget?" he said. "What, now she's claiming to be a dentist and doing relationship therapy for gum disease?"

"She's not doing anything, Shel. She was murdered this morning."

Silence. "You're kidding me—obviously, you're not. Shit, what happened?"

"Unclear," I said. "The detective in charge—the one I told you about—"

"The guy who entices you into all the nasty stuff."

"Yup. I told him about my courtroom experience and what she'd done to you. He asked me to call you and find out if you ever dug up anything else on her."

"No, just the license scam." He laughed. "Hope that doesn't make me a suspect. Tell your friend I couldn't have done it because I'm in

Rome. Just had an amazing dinner in the Ghetto, they fry everything, kind of an Italian tempura."

"Have fun."

"Oh, I am. Sandra's here along with Bonnie and John and the grandkids. Kaylie's twelve and loves Renaissance art. She old enough to be my alibi witness?"

"No doubt."

"Seriously, Alex, this is crazy. You think it had something to do with Gannett's ethics? The lack of?"

I said, "Could be. Do you know of anyone else whose patients she monkeyed with?"

"No, but it doesn't seem beyond the realm of possibility, once you're amoral, you're amoral. You know me, Alex. Not exactly an excitable boy but what she did *really* annoyed me. Guess if she did that to the wrong person . . . hold on . . . Sandy's calling me over for something . . . restaurant's got a TV, Bocelli's on the tube, got to run."

I phoned the psych board. Lots of robotic voicemail followed by a bored-sounding, robotic human. Complaints against licensed psychologists were kept on record but unlicensed practitioners were handled by another office at the board of consumer affairs, he wasn't sure which one.

It took me a while to connect to the right person. Right, but not informative. Once cases were disposed of, they were disposed of.

I said, "To save trees?"

The woman on the other end said, "I have no idea."

Click.

I got on the Web, plugged in Cordelia Gannett's name, and watched the screen fill.

The first thing I looked for was another misrepresentation charge or a complaint by a doctor or a patient.

Zero. Just a hyperactive social network presence. Good place to dig.

But after I'd spent a long time scrolling through words and images, I was left with nothing usable.

Like any astute e-peddler, Dr. Cordi Gannett had used her laptop to market herself assertively. Scores of "friends" on Facebook. But a close look revealed they were folks like Sigmund Freud, Carl Jung, Albert Ellis, Madame Curie, the Dalai Lama, Paul McCartney, Frida Kahlo, Mother Teresa, and Meryl Streep. Interspersed in that august list were lesser-known actors and musicians.

No sense making a list for Milo; he'd be checking the same sites.

Gannett had also linked to what she called "words to live by, just for you."

Thirty-five two-sentence pronouncements; kind of a therapeutic haiku. I read a dozen.

Be kind. But don't let yourself be swallowed up by altruism.

Don't just think of yourself. But do value yourself.

Don't jump into anything prematurely. But don't pass up the wonderful opportunities that come your way.

Pick the right person to be intimate with. But don't forget less-than-intimate connections because social memory is like muscle memory; you need to practice.

The you-can't-pin-me-down banality of daily horoscopes.

No sense trying to interview Freud et al., so I returned to Gannett's homepage and searched for an actual communication from the sub-A-listers.

The only feedback she listed was a slew of anonymous endorsements.

Dr. Gannett helped me more than I could ever imagine. A living treasure. A.M.

Dr. Cordi is so kind and sweet plus she's brilliant. M.T.

I went to so many other shrinks and until Dr. Cordi I got no help. Call her. Now. B.T.

For all her cyber-exposure, Cordi Gannett had shielded her personal life from view.

I moved on to business and professional sites. The same endorsements verbatim, along with others in an identical gushing vein. Five-star ratings throughout. In the age of automated puffery that means less than zero.

I wondered if the temptation to resume faking her credentials had proved irresistible.

It hadn't. The titles she gave herself varied from site to site but she'd been careful to keep them ambiguous.

Relationship Counselor, Interpersonal Issues Specialist, Emotional Adjustment Consultant, and in one case, a bit of an ethical stretch with Psychologically Trained Conflict Arbitrator.

I switched to photo sites on the off chance some shots from her modeling days had found their way in. The images were of a type: "Dr. Gannett" behind a desk, aureate hair drawn back in a chignon, wearing a long-sleeved white blouse buttoned to the neck and big, square black-framed eyeglasses.

Beige room, books to her back. The office I'd seen just beyond her corpse. Several of the shots featured links to YouTube videos.

Twenty-five mini-movies ranged from one to three minutes. Most featured ads you could delete in five seconds. Enough time to get the message across from an organic cosmetics company, a manufacturer of cannabis-based sports liniment, a purveyor of handbags sewn from recycled denim, and—in a touch of big-time corporate sponsorships—two term life insurance companies trying to convince you they really *cared*.

The content of the videos was a rehash of Cordi Gannett's written advice. Below: the same endorsements.

My custody appointment was an hour away. I'd spent double that time at the screen, felt as if I'd been slogging through bread dough.

Too much of nothing can do that to you.

Just as I returned with a mug of coffee, Milo turned nothing into something.

8

The call from his private cell reached me during my first sip.

"What's up?"

"I caught you," he said. "Good. What's the name of the lawyer who tried bringing Gannett in as an expert?"

"Forrest Slope."

"Unbelievable."

"He's relevant?"

"Not in terms of breathing," he said. "Murdered a couple of years ago, open case. Do you remember when the thing in chambers took place?"

"Let me check . . . March."

"He got killed in November. Not here, down in Palm Desert. I found out because I was checking out your bad daddy, Hoffgarden, due to his relationship with Cordi and history of DV. Also, with his being a weight trainer, I figured a strong guy."

"Strong and big," I said. "Around six-three and two thirty, all muscle. Why's that a factor?"

"It's not for Cordi, but it could be for knocking out Naked then toting him outside figuring to ditch him somewhere. The van shows up, change of plans. Naked gets tossed straight at it, mission accomplished."

"Naked's off your radar as the killer."

"Far from it, he's right on the screen," he said. "But learning anything about him means waiting for the lab and I don't like doing nothing. The scene stinks of up close and personal. I've been through Gannett's place and there's no sign she had any current love interest, so maybe she and Hoffgarden were still involved on some level. An old flame burning out of control could do a lot of damage."

I said, "No love life fits what I've just seen on her social pages. All business."

"Really . . . so maybe she had a *deep* secret life."

"Or none at all and she really was all about commerce. In terms of someone removing Naked, why bother when her body was left in the house?"

"I was thinking a staging. Make it look like Naked killed her and ran out of the house crazed. Which is exactly what I assumed until the gray cells kicked in and I realized I needed to avoid tunnel vision. And the little I know about Hoffgarden gives me an itchy feeling."

"What's his connection to Slope?"

"Trainer–client. When I googled Hoffgarden his name popped up in a *Desert Sun* piece on Slope's murder. Apparently he moved to Palm Springs and opened a gym there, and Slope was one of his loyal customers. Hoffgarden was quoted along with a few other of Slope's acquaintances. You didn't think much of Slope, right."

"Not a big fan."

"Other folks were. Great guy, shirt off his back, the usual stuff you get with dead people no matter what they were really like. I phoned the detective who worked the case. It's technically open but cold. She figures it for a home invasion robbery that got ugly. Palm Desert's quiet crime-wise but Palm Springs has gang problems and there's also spill-over nastiness from Coachella."

I said, "Slope also moved to the desert?"

"Either that or he had a weekend place there. The basics are he didn't show up for golf with friends, ditto for a dinner later that day, so they went to check. Slope's car was there but he didn't answer the bell or his phone so they went out back, saw the sliding glass door to the back was unlocked, and called the cops. The house had been tossed and Slope was in bed, strangled with a ligature, probably a belt. There was an alarm system but it was switched off. Local D didn't find that nota-ble, like I said the area's safe and people get relaxed."

"Did the scene fit an invasion?"

"On the face of it," he said.

"You have your doubts?"

"Local D didn't seem like someone into working too hard, so with-out looking at the murder book I won't commit. The safe wasn't touched and there was cash in a bedroom drawer; the only thing missing was a bunch of expensive watches. None showed up at any pawnshop in the area. But if it was gangsters, they have other trading posts. Or some lowlifes are walking around sporting Rolexes and Patek Philippes."

I said, "Hoffgarden must've been happy with Slope's work on the divorce if he kept up a relationship with him."

"Yeah, but Hoffgarden's domestic history says relationships with him tend to go south. What keeps poking at me is both Slope and Gan-nett were killed in their homes in high-end neighborhoods and Hoff-garden knew both of them. I ran him through the databases, and prior to the domestics with his girlfriends he has an assault conviction and one for battery. Bar fights back when he was in college. There is a six-year period between college and his first DV but you know how it goes."

"People get away with stuff."

"The mulch in which crime germinates remains rich, amigo. In a perfect world, I could subpoena Hoffgarden's cellphone and see which towers it pinged at the time poor Cordi was getting stabbed but I'm several galaxies away from justification for a subpoena. Meanwhile, Naked still is a person of interest—calling him that sounds flip, wish I had a name."

"No match to his prints?"

"Prints haven't been run yet, he's still being processed." He laughed. "Another humanistic term from the world of law enforcement. So what else did you learn about Ms. Cordi on the Web?"

"She was a skillful self-promoter and seems to have avoided any other fraudulent claims."

"If what the neighbor saw means she *was* seeing clients at home, I haven't found any evidence of it. No patient files in the house and no office listing."

I said, "No files in the house doesn't mean anything. Licensed practitioners have to maintain records but there are no rules governing what she did."

"The wages of sin. Didn't think of that. However she was making money, there was plenty of it, Alex. Six hundred thou in an investment account at Morgan Stanley plus eighty in a checking account."

"That could be from ad royalties. She's got twenty-five videos running online and they're all sponsored."

"By who?"

I told him.

He said, "New-agey hip stuff plus old-school insurance."

"Old school could mean deeper pockets," I said. "Going corporate could've been her long-term goal."

He said, "Any weird comments on the videos?"

"The only posts are the endorsements she's got on her website. Verbatim."

"Controlling the info flow. Ms. Enterprising. How long do the videos run?"

"One to three minutes."

"You think ads on something that brief could bring in serious bucks?"

"People log on to see cats with Hitler mustaches."

"Good point. So I've got the possibility of a sketchy private practice full of clients I can't identify and/or a bunch of profitable cyber-jabber. There's a disconnected feel to this woman, Alex. Including no family relationships I can find. There was one listing on her phone for Maternal Entity, which doesn't sound too warm and cuddly. Comes back to an inoperative number."

"What are the rest of her contacts?"

"Business," he said. "Not shrink stuff, the basics. Landlord, plumber, electrician, Pavilions, Whole Foods, Trader Joe's, bunch of food delivery services, dry cleaner. One thing stood out: not a single restaurant. And there was plenty of food in the pantry and the fridge, so looks like she was a stay-at-home type. But you'd think just from a P.R. perspective she'd want to circulate, like back when she was hanging with showbiz types."

I said, "That could be the reason she opted for solitude."

"Been-there-done-that."

"And with that much income flow, why bother? Anything else on the phone?"

"Nah, just health stuff. Physical, not mental. Dentist, gynecologist, optometrist, so maybe I can learn something from one of them. In terms of the eye doctor, I found contact lenses in a container in her nightstand drawer and a pair of glasses on top. Big black frames."

"She wears those on her videos. I wasn't sure they were real."

"Putting on the scholarly image? Well, these were definitely real. Strong from what I could tell. You see where I'm going?"

I said, "Poor vision could've added to her vulnerability."

"Exactly."

"How deep were those defense wounds?"

He said, "Pretty shallow, as a matter of fact. Why?"

"Nothing we know about her says she was passive so more likely she was incapacitated quickly. With a neck slash it's much easier to exert force from behind. I'm thinking she was flipped around, immobilized, and cut. To me it has a premeditated feeling."

"Even with a weapon of opportunity?"

"Every house has kitchen knives."

"Good point," he said. "You're thinking assassination, not a crime of passion?"

"Not necessarily," I said. "Planned doesn't have to mean long-term plotting. And a sleepover doesn't have to be limited to two people."

"A threesome? Cordi, Naked, and another person . . . maybe Hoffgarden."

"Interesting setup."

"How your mind works. So what, a threesome that didn't work out?"

I said, "Maybe Naked got the couch but Number Three, whoever he was, got asked to leave. Cordi went upstairs to her bedroom thinking everything had been worked out. Then Three decided he wasn't going to be blown off like that and stayed *in* the house unbeknownst to the other two. Or right outside, keeping the back door unlocked. He stewed for a while, finally decided to act, took a kitchen knife from the block. First step, take care of his rival."

"The collision masked a stab wound?"

"Or blunt-force trauma if he decided to bash the guy over the head and deal with him later. A crush injury could've easily been masked. Once that was taken care of, he went for Cordi. But before he could get to her bedroom she came downstairs because she'd heard something.

She's drowsy and myopic and unprepared. Meets Three in the hallway, there's a brief confrontation, she holds her hands out, gets cut superficially, he overpowers her, slits her throat, and leaves her body there."

He said, "And takes Naked outside."

I said, "Maybe to confuse the scene."

"Sex, jealousy, money, stick with the classics. Okay, I'm gonna call whoever's doing the autopsy and see if they can separate any sort of earlier wound from the mess the van created. Thank you, Doctor, I can always count on you to lead me interesting places."

9

I looked up the *Desert Sun* article. Nothing beyond what Milo had abstracted. What I found interesting were the sources of the quotes about Forrest Slope.

"Personal trainer" Tyler Hoffgarden; a female barber named Lisette Montag, who described Slope as a client and friend and with whom he'd scheduled a dinner date; a married couple named Yokum who managed the landscaping at Slope's weekend house; three retirees, two accountants and a banker, who'd formed a regular golf foursome with the lawyer.

The duffers had been the ones to check out Slope's house because "Forrest was fanatical about making tee time."

What seemed to be relatively casual connections, every comment a variation on "he didn't deserve it."

No spouse or kin.

I searched for anything else on Slope's death, found only a funeral notice from a mortuary in Palm Springs. So he'd probably moved full-time to the desert.

Still no mention of family. An invitation to contribute thoughts about "the life and times of Forrest Slope" had elicited nothing.

Like Cordi Gannett, another social isolate?

All the lonely people.

That could lead to bad ends. Enough misfortune to populate a city of the dead.

Switching back to Gannett's social network pages, I took a closer look at her celebrity "friends." Probably puffery, but I copied down names, had gotten through a dozen before a familiar one came up.

A singer named Mare Nostrum. A few years ago Robin had patched up her guitar, and Nostrum had come by to pick it up when I happened to be in the studio. She'd shrugged off Robin's invitation to try out the instrument, looking uncomfortable at the suggestion. I figured the instrument was a prop.

Later, Robin had confirmed it. "Just spoke to someone who knows her, she can't play a note. And her voice is pro-tooled up the wazoo."

"Playing a role."

She said, "That's why they call it performance."

In real life, Nostrum had been slumped and emaciated, with a plain, round face and downcast eyes.

Her stage persona was a shrieking, galloping, spidery visage in Spandex wearing white-face makeup, kohl around the eyes, and spiky Technicolor wigs.

The day Robin had introduced us, I'd extended my hand. Still fixed on hardwood, Mare Nostrum had barely grazed my fingertips.

I smiled, said "Nice to meet you," and went to my office. A few minutes later, I heard the front door shut. Robin entered alone, shaking her head.

I said, "Shy."

"Petrified."

"Of me?"

"From what I can tell, of life. She could use someone like you."

"Why'd she name herself after the Mediterranean?"

"Did she?"

"Mare Nostrum," I said. " 'Our sea' in the words of the Romans."

She laughed. "The stuff you know. I have no idea. She's not even Italian."

Now, wondering if Robin had recent contact information, I headed back to the studio, made it as far as the kitchen where she sat at the table drinking orange juice.

I said, "Let's hear it for vitamin C."

"Let's hear it for sugar. Keep me company, handsome."

I sat next to her. "I was on my way to ask you if you're still in contact with Mare Nostrum."

"I'm not, hon. She hasn't been active in what . . . three, four years? Why?"

"She's listed as one of Cordi Gannett's friends."

"A real friend or a promo friend?"

"Don't know," I said. "She could also have been a client."

"Because of her issues?"

"She did seem sad and scared."

"What do you think she could tell you?"

"I don't really know," I said. "But Gannett seems to have had no current social life or family. Meaning no one for Milo to talk to, which is the ultimate case-killer. Be nice to find someone who knows anything about her. Not that Mare's the talkative type but you play the cards you're dealt."

She nodded, drank. "So no idea who did it."

"Nope, just theories." I told her about the naked man as either a suspect or a victim, the notion of a threesome gone bad.

She said, "In her house. What a terrible way to go." She finished the juice and stood. "Let's see if I can find my old address book and if Mare's number still works. *And* she's willing to talk to you."

"Deeply appreciated, sweetie. No problem if she says no. She did seem thrown by my presence."

"I remember that." She squeezed my arm. "Figured it was your overwhelming masculine aura."

I said, "My hat size is growing."

"Just the hat? I'm finished with work for the day. Ahem."

We got out of bed and dressed ourselves. Then I followed her back to the studio where she searched the carved walnut desk that she uses for storage. It's a dark, heavy, massive hunk of wood, not Robin's style. Fashioned for her lovingly by her father when she was fifteen. Reward for her mastering power tools.

"Not here . . . not here . . . where *is* it?"

Out came books, catalogs, copies of the Guild of American Luthiers magazine, other periodicals that she stacked neatly on the floor. The pile grew. "Darn, need to be more organized . . . not that anyone uses a book when you can store the universe in your phone . . . ah, *finally.*"

She held up a black leather spiral notebook embossed with the name and address of her dad's woodworking shop in San Luis Obispo. Flipping pages, she read off an 818 number that she tried.

Six rings. A drowsy "Hello?"

"Mare?"

"Yes."

"Hi, it's Robin Castagna."

A beat. "Who?"

"The guitar gal? I worked on your Gibson Melody Maker a few years ago."

"I sold it."

"Not out to buy it, Mare. I was wondering—"

"*Who* are you?"

"Robin. Castagna. You came to my shop off Beverly Glen."

"You had a dog," said Mare Nostrum. "A tan pug."

"French bulldog," said Robin. "That's Blanche."

"You still have the dog?"

"I do."

"Healthy?"

"Knock on wood."

"My dog died last year."

"Sorry to hear that."

"It's the rhythm of life, Janis was old. Is yours?"

"More like middle-aged."

"Take care of her."

"Will do, Mare."

"My cat also died."

"Sorry to hear that."

"She was twenty-two."

"That's a long life."

"She seemed okay," said Mare Nostrum. "Then she didn't. Cancer."

"Sorry to hear that—"

"Why did you call me?"

"I don't know if you recall but the day you came to pick up the Melody Maker my boyfriend was there."

Silence.

Robin said, "No problem if you don't remember—"

"I do," said Mare Nostrum. "Looked like an actor, you said he was a doctor."

"He's a psychologist. His name is Alex and he was wondering if he could have a few words with you."

"What about?"

"Someone who listed you as a friend on Facebook. Cordi Gannett."

"Another psychologist. They're friends? Competitors? Enemies?"

Robin looked at me.

I whispered, "Acquaintances."

She repeated the word.

Mare Nostrum said, "Sure."

"Sure—"

"I'll talk to him, why not?"

"Thanks, I'll put him on—"

"Not now," said Mare Nostrum. "The phone's basically the enemy. Strangers asking me political questions. Trying to sell me things I don't need. I like to look at people when they talk at me. I've gotten good at decoding."

"Got it," said Robin. "Can I put him on to arrange—"

"He can come here and talk. Not to my house, no one comes to my house. There's a park nearby, he can come there. Not now, it'll be dark soon, I don't go out in the dark. Tomorrow. After I eat breakfast. Ten o'clock."

Robin looked at me. I gave a thumbs-up.

"Sounds perfect, Mare. Where's the park?"

"North Hollywood. Kingsford Street. He's a doctor, he can figure it out."

"Thanks so much, Mare."

"I'm Mary, now. The other one was a fraud. My manager gave it to me. I didn't want it. I thought he was riffing on my nostrils."

Click.

I said, "I owe you."

Robin said, "There'll be opportunities to show your gratitude."

10

The following morning I learned what I could about the thirty-nine-month career of Mare Nostrum, née Mary Blank.

The name she'd been given at birth showed up in a *Billboard* piece on the singer's "retirement due to health and other personal issues." The quote came from her manager, a guy named Chuckie Rose. It had ended with a proclamation that "Mare Nostrum has left us and Mary Blank has arrived."

When asked if that meant an eventual return to the singer performing under her real name, Rose said, "Your guess is as good as mine." Knowing what I did now, I figured his client had ordered him to memorialize the change.

The rest of the article was a brief bio. With "a style that alternated between solemn and furious, the Iowa-born vocalist" had begun as a backup singer for a raspy-voiced British metalhead named Izzo Lacks, whose own solo career had floundered after walking out on a band called Thrombosis. Nostrum had toured with Lacks for a season, progressed to opening for slightly more successful thrashers in medium-sized venues, peaked as an arena headliner. Her highest chart had been 5, followed by 11, then 38. After that, the requisite downward slide.

The most recent appearance I could find was an unannounced drop-in at a club on Cahuenga two and a half years ago reported in the Calendar section of the L.A. *Times*. The "now sedate" Mary Blank had sung two Nina Simone songs "passably" before escaping into the wings.

After that, radio silence. Literally.

The park was in a marginal area of North Hollywood. I drove north on the Glen, crested the ridge at Mulholland that separates 310 from 818, drove east on Ventura Boulevard to Laurel Canyon, and followed a series of GPS prompts through a neighborhood of shabby apartments and tenacious single-story bungalows.

Kingsford Mini Park (so labeled by the department of recreation) was a sad smear of weedy grass surrounded by low pink block walls victimized by sloppy, indecipherable graffiti. A dozen parking slots, all empty.

An open gate led me to the sole bench in the space, wooden slats with concrete legs, built for durability not comfort. The doors to a public restroom were padlocked. More scrawl-filled block. Recreational equipment was limited to a pair of swings suspended by rusty chains over a bed of sand. One of the swings hung askew. Paper wrappers and crushed cans specked the sand. Glints of glass said proceed at your own risk.

They say the mayor wants to run for president. He's one of those simpering types, big on feeling everybody's pain. I had a pretty good idea what the parks were like in his neighborhood.

I checked the bench for foreign objects, sat and checked my phone for messages. One from a lawyer whose name I didn't recognize. He could wait. Ten o'clock passed, ten fifteen, twenty. I wondered if Mary Blank had changed her mind, decided to stick it out for another quarter hour.

At ten twenty-eight, she appeared, looking around, blinking. She spotted me easily because I was the only one there. I stood and waved, anyway. She remained still for a few more seconds then continued toward me.

She'd put on thirty or so pounds that rounded her nicely. Short brown hair had given way to shoulder-length pewter waves. She wore a cognac-colored velvet sweat suit and white New Balances. Clear skin, clear eyes, no adornment other than an incongruously flashy ruby ring on her left hand. Huge stone—five-or-so-carat marquis cut with enough clarity to sparkle in the hazy sunlight.

Sport something like that in a neighborhood like this, good reason not to venture out at night.

She sat next to me, facing forward. "You look the same."

"You look better."

She gave a start. "Now you're going to tell me you like fat chicks."

"Now I'm going to tell you you're not fat."

"Tell that to MTV. The screen adds fifteen pounds, I was always starving to not look like a porker. I got extra help. You know what I mean."

"Meth?"

"Not that evil," she said. "Prescription stimulants. Plenty of Dr. Robertses out there. So what do you want to know about her?"

"First off, I'm going to tell you why I want to know. She was murdered yesterday."

A couple more blinks. "And that's important to you because . . ."

"I sometimes consult to the cops."

"When's sometimes?"

"When they ask."

"Shrink on the scene," she said. "That could be a show. So what, it was psycho, the way she . . . the way it happened?"

"At this point, not much is known. Sorry, can't get into details."

"Don't want details. Don't want anything crazy in my life. Don't even know why I asked. Probably because I feel expected to make conversation."

"Makes sense."

"Does it?" An edge had come into her voice. She stared straight ahead. "That's the kind of thing people say when they don't mean it. As in shrink people. I've known a bunch. No one helped me. I had to help myself."

"Then I especially appreciate your seeing me."

"Because you're a shrink? Why wouldn't I see you? That would be prejudiced . . . Alan?"

"Alex."

"One thing I'm not is prejudiced, Alex. I've learned to judge each situation." Half smile. "You might turn out to be a jerk but at least I'll find out for myself."

I laughed.

She said, "Did you ever see my act?"

"On video."

"Meaning not till last night. Or this morning."

"Actually, years ago," I said. "The day I met you at Robin's she played me a tape."

"You wanted to find out who's this nerdy chick and how could she make it on stage."

"No, just curious. It's a character flaw."

She began to chuckle. Checked herself. "So what'd you think? Of my act."

"High-energy."

"That's about all I was, Alex. Loud like a fart after chili. Couldn't play an instrument, couldn't write, used to have a good voice but then I ruined it from screaming, got polyps, needed surgery, it never healed a hundred percent. The ENT said he'd fixed me, everyone else thought I sounded the same. My ears told me different. Things weren't going so great anyway so I quit. Didn't want to be a phony. Like her."

"Cordi Gannett."

"Cordi," she said. "That's about as real as the Nostrum bullshit my manager pushed on me. What was her real name? Carol?"

"As far as I know, Cordelia."

She looked disappointed. "That sounds . . . antique."

I said, "Maybe. Cordelia was one of King Lear's daughters."

"King Lear . . . Shakespeare, right? Maybe I was assigned that," she said. "Back in high school. Was she a hero or a villain?"

"More like a tragic figure," I said. "Her father's favorite but he ended up banishing her because she wouldn't profess her love for him."

"He sounds like a jerk," said Mary Blank. "Cordelia." She mouthed the name silently. "Well, this Cordelia was a bullshit artist. She showed up backstage after one of my gigs, hanging all over my drummer. He goes off to . . ." She pantomimed snorting. "Leaves her with me, she's all smiley. *Big* smile, *way* too big. She starts telling me she's a doctor of psychology, specializes in human relations or whatever. Some b.s. along those lines. I'm thinking why are you telling me? But I was brought up to be a polite girl in Ames, Iowa, so I say something like, 'Really?' and *that* gets her *into* it. Like I've cued her to pour out more bullshit. At that point, I blocked her out by imagining a tone in my head. B-flat. Used to do that all the time, people talking at me, I'm B-flatting them out. Even when I was sober. And her voice made it easier."

"How so?"

"Singy-songy," she said. "Syrupy."

"Coming on too strong."

"Fake. Singsong. Chanty, like a cult bitch. Trying to come on like she *really* cared about me even though we just met. Then she starts touching me. This weird little pat here."

Tamping a spot atop her hand.

"Then here." Her shoulder. "Then here." Her knee. "Like she's some sort of faith healer with the magic touch. *Then* she leans in real close like she wants to kiss me and says, 'Mare, if there's ever *anything* you need, don't *hesitate* to call. At *any* time. *Ever.*' I probably nodded because like I said, in Iowa you're polite. Big mistake. She chants more bullshit, then puts her business card in my hand. Like she's laying a gift on me."

Another chuckle formed low in her throat. This time she let it out.

"What I should've done is say get the fuck out of my dressing room. What I did say was something like, thanks, I'll keep that in mind. Then Zak—my idiot drummer—comes back and says, 'Okay, let's party.' And *she* says, 'Baby doll, we're discussing matters of importance.' Then I say, 'That's okay, got to pee, go party.' I went into the john and stayed there and thank God when I came out the two of them were gone and I could clear the B-flat from my head."

She folded her hands in her lap. "And that, Alan—Alex—is my experience with Cor*del*ia."

"Onetime deal," I said.

"No, actually I saw her once more. A party, don't ask me where or when, I was . . . chemical. That time, we didn't talk but she caught my eye and gave me that same I'm-going-to-help-you smile. A week later, I'm talking to my idiot manager and he says, 'Good for you, girl, you found someone to express yourself to.' I say what are you talking about? He says, this chick Zak fucked, she's a shrink, is all over Facebook saying you're BFFs. I go nuts and order him to get her to stop. He says sure, later he tells me the BFF part is gone but he couldn't stop her from listing me as a plain friend. But I shouldn't worry, no one takes that shit seriously. Now you're here asking me about her. So I'm still on her friends list."

"You are indeed."

"Internet's like an STD you can't cure." Pitching forward on the bench, she broke into untrammeled laughter.

Nice sound, at first. Then it lasted too long and turned unsettling.

When she finally stopped, I said, "Your instincts were good. She wasn't a psychologist."

"No? Then what?"

"She took a correspondence course, got busted for practicing without a license, and switched to calling herself a relationship expert."

"Little Ms. Bullshit," she said. "But like I said, Dr. Alex, I've found most of the *real* shrinks to be worthless. No offense." More laughter. "I guess that is kind of offensive."

I smiled.

Mary Blank rocked for a few seconds, then smiled. "You're not the touchy type, huh?"

A childhood spent escaping a violent drunk father can put some layers of numb on you.

I shook my head.

She said, "Yeah, good-looking guys don't need to be touchy, people touch you anyway. But that doesn't stop some of them from taking advantage."

We sat in silence for a few moments. She made no effort to leave.

I said, "Anything else you can tell me about her would be helpful."

"That's all I know, Joe. A murder, huh? If it was me, I'd look for someone she really annoyed because I sure found her a pain."

"Makes sense."

"Nice to know I can do that," she said. "Make sense. Sorry for that crack about shrinks, I'm sure you're a good one." She frowned. "Don't like myself when I get rude."

"Iowa," I said.

"You nailed it, Good Looking. Roots run deep."

I offered to drive her home.

She said, "No, thanks. I'm not far and I like walking. Say hi to your girlfriend, she's got golden hands."

I watched her plod away, hands stuffed in the pockets of her track-suit. Ring concealed.

Moments later, a young mother entered the park with a three-year-old boy. A glance at the broken swing, then me. She left.

I made my own exit, phoned Milo from the Seville.

He said, "I just got Cordi's mom's name from her birth records. Our gal was born as Carol Ann thirty-five years ago. County Hospital, mommy's Renata Gannett, no daddy listed."

I said, "County could mean tough times financially. How old was Renata?"

"Let me check . . . seventeen. Teenage unwed mother, good call, Alex. No silver spoon for our gal, I'm feeling a little warmer and fuzzier about her. Haven't come across any current listing for Mom so she could be deceased. The good news is prelim from the lab is due later today and, God bless, Basia's got the case. So what's up?"

I said, "I just talked to someone who met Gannett when she was claiming to be a psychologist."

I related the backstage encounter with Mare Nostrum and our chat moments ago.

He said, "Called her a cult bitch, huh? She got touchy-feely with a total stranger."

"To me it sounds as if she was trying to be hypnoidal."

"What's that, hypnosis-lite?"

"Basically," I said. "There's no formal induction or trance. You use eye contact and rhythmic speech to relax the patient and make them more amenable to suggestion."

"What about the touching?"

"Sometimes there's a reassuring pat on the back but jumping around from spot to spot isn't part of it."

"She overdid it," he said. "Manipulating eyes and speech is kosher?"

"If the patient's informed. There's nothing exotic about it, Big Guy. All sorts of relaxation techniques can be helpful in therapy. But subterfuge isn't. In Gannett's case, sounds like she was told Mare Nostrum was vulnerable and decided to make mind-game play for new business. She had no formal training so my guess is she read about hypnoidal approaches. But like anything else, it takes training."

"It wasn't effective with that subject but could've worked with others."

"It's possible."

"She took advantage of impressionable people."

"Vulnerable people," I said. "And if circumstances changed, that could backfire. Someone starting off compliant then feeling they'd been taken advantage of and growing resentful. I'm not saying that has anything to do with the murder, but anytime you manipulate people, you run a risk. What Mary Blank told me, combined with everything else we know about Gannett, paints a picture of someone ambitious, slick, and way over her head."

"That takes me back to Hoffgarden," he said. "Hadn't thought of him as vulnerable but did you pick that up?"

"Not in the least," I said. "The overall feel I got from him was detachment. But his arrest record's all anger-related so there's a whole bunch of sensitivity buried somewhere in his head."

"Potential for a serious backfire."

"Definitely."

"Interesting," he said. "And as of six months ago, he no longer lives in the desert. Guess where he moved?"

"L.A."

"*West* L.A., near Culver City. We're talking a twenty-minute drive to Cordi's place during rush hour, a lot less in the wee hours. Haven't found out why he closed down his gym but I'm guessing it wasn't a gold mine. And if he opened a place here, I haven't found it yet."

"Down on his luck?" I said. "That could kick up the sensitivity."

"Prodding the bear when he's hungry ain't a smart strategy," he said. "I definitely want to talk to him, already phoned him twice and got voicemail. Maybe I'll have Moe drive by his apartment. If Hoffgarden's gone and stays gone, he definitely gets pushed up the person-of-interest pole. You know what we detecting types think about rabbiting."

"Like those old movies. Don't leave town."

"The old movies," he said, "people listened."

Back in my office, I scrolled the message from the unfamiliar lawyer. Lewis Porer, a Mid-Wilshire number. I called and his receptionist put me on hold for too long. Porer's luck, I was fiddling with the computer and put up with it.

"Dr. Delaware? Lewis Evan Porer. Apparently, you've been assigned to evaluate one of my client's children. I'm here to fill you in."

I said, "What's the case?"

"The case in question is *Deeb versus McManus*. I'm representing—"

"Haven't received anything from the court on that one."

"You will," said Porer. "These are the essential—"

"Sorry," I said. "I deal directly with the court and hold off attorney contact until later in the evaluation." If ever.

Silence. "That's rather . . . different."

"It's the way I operate."

"Be that as it may, the way *I* operate is—"

"Don't want to cut you off, Mr. Porer, but this isn't the time for discussion. Once I hear from the court, I'll begin my evaluation. Thanks for calling."

"You are *cutting* me off?"

"As I said—"

"I heard what you said. What if I don't approve of your methodology and register a complaint with the judge?"

"Your prerogative."

"Family court is a porous institution. Things get around."

You'll nevah work in this town again, kid.

I said, "Be that as it may."

"Your attitude," said Lewis Evan Porer, "is inapt. Family law is all about communication and here I am attempting to communicate and getting rebuffed."

What you're attempting is an early jump on the opposition in order to bias my perception.

I said, "I'm sure your intentions are good but that's the way it's going to be."

"Is it?" he said. "We'll see."

Click.

◆

The computer fiddling I'd begun while waiting for Porer was an attempt to learn about Zak the drummer, a former love interest of Cordi Gannett.

Zak Z. Mountain, born Zachary Lee Mitchell.

Born forty-eight years ago in Lansing, Michigan, death two years ago from liver disease. No Wikipedia bio, just an obit on a site called Metal Memories. Mountain's five marriages had produced two children. The fickle nature of the music business plus drug and alcohol issues had led to retirement and a return to Lansing, where Mountain, now Mitchell, found a job painting cars in a body shop.

No mention of Gannett. Another transitory relationship. Had she ever experienced any other kind?

Wondering about that, I went for a brief run, came back, showered, put on a T-shirt and sweatpants, and checked in with my service.

Louise, one of the operators who's been around for a long time, said, "Hi, Dr. Delaware, I was just about to call you. Some lawyer insisted on leaving a long message, said it was urgent that you get it 'posthaste.' Shall I read it to you, posthaste?"

"Proceed at your own pace," I said.

She laughed.

"Let me guess, Louise. A guy named Porer."

"That's the one, Doctor. Puffed-up voice, like he's got a mouthful of whatever. He dictated to me like he was performing onstage, then had me read it back to him."

"Sorry for the hassle."

"Oh, it's okay, Dr. Delaware. Any bit of entertainment is welcome. Ready?"

"Shoot."

" 'Doctor, this is Lewis Evan Porer. I wanted to circle back to make sure we didn't get off on the wrong foot. Obviously, there were crossed wires. Obviously, you're the master of your own professional destiny and I'm more than pleased to accede to your wishes.'"

"Thanks, Louise."

"Never heard a lawyer eat crow like that, Dr. Delaware. All this time, you've never seemed the least bit frightening to me."

12

Milo had expected lab results later in the day but I didn't hear from him until ten the following morning. So his opening sentence was no surprise.

"The bad news is no prelim, yet. The staff's been in *ahem* training sessions. Not science, workplace communications skills. Didn't know you needed sensitivity to talk to petri dishes."

"Hey," I said, "microbes are people, too. What's the good news?"

"I found Cordi's mom in the marriage license files. She's been hitched twice, a short-term deal twenty-seven years ago and one that's lasted for seventeen years running. Her married name is Blanding and her current address is on North Camden Drive in Beverly Hills. I'm planning a drop-in, would appreciate your presence."

"When?"

"I'll work around you. If there's any time psychological wisdom can help, it's dealing with mothers of dead kids."

"It's an open day."

"Excellent. Pick you up in forty."

◆

I put on a white shirt, jeans, and a blue blazer, used the waiting time to learn what I could about Renata Blanding.

Pairing her name with *camden drive* gave me her exact address on the 700 block. A real estate site added specifics. Fifty-five-hundred-square-foot, single-occupancy dwelling on a quarter-acre lot. Built in 1927 and purchased fifteen years ago by the Gregory S. and Renata Blanding Family Trust.

Gregory S. Blanding turned out to be an ENT physician with an office in Century City. Specialties in throat conditions and septal re-alignment. No photos on any professional sites and no apparent work history for Renata, but the couple had been snapped at last year's Black and White Ball, a fundraiser for the Beverly Hills Police Department.

The two of them had posed flanking a city councilwoman, everyone with cocktails in hand. Gregory Blanding was tuxedoed, silver-haired, thickset, and bespectacled, with a warm smile. Renata wore a clinging, sleeveless yellow dress that set off long, center-parted black hair. Strong shoulders and a lean build suggested regular gym attendance. Also smiling, but with considerably less wattage than her husband.

I logged off and went outside to catch some sun before we clouded her day. Milo showed up early and we took off.

We'd barely exited my property and begun rolling down the bridle path that connects to the Glen when he said, "Any suggestions how to approach her?"

"Don't know her."

"You didn't look her up while you waited?"

I stared at him.

He said, "Hey, you're not the only one who can get clairvoyant."

I told him what I'd learned.

He said, "Snagged herself a doctor."

I said, "You'd know about that. And come to think of it, maybe your doctor knows her doctor."

"Hmm. Why not."

He phoned the man with whom he'd been living since I've known him. Richard Silverman is a trauma surgeon at Cedars-Sinai with a work schedule that rivals Milo's. They don't see much of each other but that seems to work out.

Milo managed to catch Rick between cases. "How's your day going?"

"It's going," said Rick. "Actually, it's going okay. What's up?"

"I'm in the car. Alex is here."

"So I shouldn't say anything inappropriate."

"Like that would happen," said Milo. "We're heading off to do a notification."

"Oy," said Rick. I've never seen him fazed by the blood, gore, and agony he sees every day. Emotional challenges are a different story.

"Oy, indeed, kiddo. I'm calling because my victim's stepdad is a medico. ENT named Gregory Blanding. Know him?"

Rick said, "He's in the tower on Century Park East, big group, they do a lot of ears but he's throat. He also attends here. Never worked with him but we were on a committee together. Standards of care. He came across as a nice guy. Has a good reputation medically. That's about it."

Milo smiled. "Thanks. Thoughts on dinner?"

"If you can wait until nine thirty, ten, I'm game for a sit-down. No wine, though. Up early tomorrow."

"Sounds like fun," said Milo.

"Better than doing nothing. Right, Alex?"

I said, "You bet."

Milo said, "I get famished, I'll eat earlier then renew the experience with you."

Rick said, "I figured."

After ending the call, Milo said, "Good reputation medically. Wonder what he thought of his stepdaughter faking it."

The house was a two-story pink stucco Mediterranean with a face as flat as a paper doll and undistinguished landscaping. A white Audi SUV sat in the driveway. Quiet block, no one out except a uniformed maid walking a rust-colored ball of yarn on legs, probably some kind of poodle mix.

Milo's knock elicited footsteps and sound behind the door. Brief movement on the other side of the peephole, then a woman's voice said, "Yes?"

"Police, ma'am." He held up his card.

"About what?"

"Are you Ms. Blanding?"

"Why do you ask?"

"If you are, we're here about your daughter, Cordelia Gannett."

The door opened on Renata Blanding, barefoot, now crowned by a hennaed pageboy and wearing a black Chanel T-shirt over gold jeggings.

"What's she gotten into now?"

Bare interest in pale-blue eyes. Her skin was lightly freckled and stretched tight over a handsome framework. The same muscular shoulders and spare build as in the fundraiser photo. Slightly oversized hands. Diamond hoop earrings dangled from close-set ears. A big, square solitaire diamond graced the left ring finger; on the matching right finger, a pink-and-white diamond band.

Milo said, "May we come in, Ms. Blanding?"

"Is that nece— I guess. Okay."

She stepped aside and closed the door after us. The house was neat, airy, brightened by a rear wall of French doors looking out to a yard dominated by a too-wide swimming pool. Three-step entry hall, three additional steps down to the living room. The room bore a faint smell of fruit—strawberries and citrus. Through the doorway to the kitchen, a blender sat on a counter. Someone fiddled there, unseen.

Renata Blanding folded her arms across her chest. "Now you're inside. What?"

Milo said, "It's best we sit down, ma'am."

Sculpted eyebrows climbed. "That bad? Last time I hung with the cops, it cost me big."

He pointed to a nearby sofa. Taupe ultra-suede, pale-blue pillows perfectly fluffed and arranged precisely.

An almost assertive neatness. Like mother like daughter?

Renata Blanding worked at remaining impassive but the blue eyes sparked and her jawline quivered.

"What?" she demanded.

Milo said, "Please, ma'am," and guided her to the couch. She sat on the rim, still cross-armed.

There's no way to do it but to do it.

Milo said, "I'm afraid, ma'am, that Cordelia is deceased."

"Impossible," said Renata Blanding. "Absolutely impossible."

Milo said nothing.

"Impossible," she repeated. "Fucking impossible."

She sat up higher, squeezed herself tighter. Stared at Milo with the pathetic defiance of a two-year-old. Then at me. Then back to Milo. *"Impossible."*

He said, "I'm so sorry, ma'am."

"No way."

Milo sighed.

Renata Blanding shook her head back and forth. Three more "impossibles" surrendered to an anguished "Oh my God!"

A dozen more of those. The oversized hands came loose and clawed air.

"Oh my God. Impossible. Oh my God."

She covered her face, had hunched forward just as a young woman appeared in the doorway to the kitchen. Tiny, Asian, wearing a black-and-white uniform.

Seeing her employer's posture made her mouth drop open. "Everything okay, Mrs. B?"

A muffled "Yes." Renata sat back up. At full volume: "*No,* Lynn, it's not okay. Finish up with the dishes."

Milo said, "Please bring Mrs. B some water."

"I don't *like* flat water," said Renata Blanding. "Don't care where it comes from, it always tastes *off.* I need aeration. Bring me a La Croix, Lynn. The yellow can. Pamplemousse. Remember what I told you? That means grapefruit. Not lime."

"Yes, Mrs.—"

"*Go!*"

Lynn ran off.

Renata Blanding said, "She's from Laos. She's usually very good. But things can throw her, sometimes I think I'm raising another daught . . ." Her face contorted in horror. "Another. There's no *another* anymore."

13

The maid brought aerated water in a squat crystal glass. Inside was a massive round ice cube.

"The big one," said Renata. "You remembered. Good, Lynn. Thank you. Sorry for snapping."

"It's okay, Mrs. B."

"Nothing today is okay, Lynn." Dismissive finger wave. "Finish the dishes then . . . just do what you want, Lynn. I need to talk to these men."

When the three of us were alone, Milo gave her the card he'd held to the peephole.

Renata said, "Homicide. You're telling me she was murdered."

Milo said, "Yes, ma'am."

"For the record," she said, "her name is Carol, not Cordelia . . ." Glance at the card. ". . . Lieutenant Sturgis. She grew up as Carrie. I birthed her and that's the nickname I chose to give her and I still think it's an awesome one and there was no reason to change it. She never did it legally, anyway. She's Carrie."

"Thanks for telling us, ma'am."

Renata Blanding's hands re-formed into avian claws. Attack mode but nothing to attack. She rested them in her lap, curling her fingers oddly. "Now you're telling me she was murdered."

"Unfortunately, ma'am."

"Where did it happen?"

"In her home."

"Where's that?"

Milo blinked. "A house she rented in Westwood."

"A house," she said. "Well, that's an upgrade. What part of West-wood?"

"Just east of campus."

"The good part of Westwood," said Renata Blanding. "That's a super upgrade. Last I heard, she was renting a pretty ratty two-bedroom in the Granada Hills. Using the second bedroom for her little movies."

Blue eyes widened. "Did they have something to do with it? Her movies? Putting herself out there, trying to be famous?"

"We don't know much of anything, yet."

"Yet," said Renata Blanding. "You're saying you're optimistic."

"We like to think positive."

"That's kind of weird, no? Seeing as you're all about negativity. Don't you feel . . . inconsistent?"

Milo smiled. "That's why we make an effort, ma'am. Do you know of any problems Carrie had due to her online postings?"

"Lieutenant," said Renata Blanding, as if explaining to a dull child, "Carrie and I haven't spoken in a while. I had no idea she'd gotten her-self a house, let alone in Westwood."

"How long have—"

"Two years," she said. "Even before that our contacts were few and far between. She doesn't like my family."

"Your extended family?"

"I have no extended family. This family, the one that lives here."

"Carrie didn't—"

"I'm not saying she outwardly rejected us. She just stopped having contact. No mystery, Lieutenant. We have a wonderful life and I'm sure Carrie resented that. Like changing her name. Why *do* that? The name I gave her was lovely. So why? The answer? It was a rejection. Of me. Of us."

Milo said, "Us, being . . ."

"The three of us," said Renata Blanding. "My husband, Dr. Gregory Blanding, and my wonderful, wonderful son Aaron. He's fifteen, skipped a grade. He loves Carrie." Three swift blinks. "They used to have fun together, then she cut off contact. He was devastated."

I said, "Must've been tough on all three of you."

"Greg was a rock," she said. "Never lost his cool. And let me tell you, there were times when . . . I don't want to talk about my daughter as if I didn't love her. I do. I did. She was gorgeous, could have . . . now you're telling me someone murdered her? Who would *do* that?"

The furled fingers began shaking. She opened and laced her hands together but within seconds the trembling had dipped to her torso, then her legs. She breathed in and out several times and forced her body still.

Another long whoosh of exhalation.

"Who would do that to someone so gorgeous? With so much potential, and Carrie had plenty of that. Potential. A monster is who. You need to find them, Lieutenant, and they need to be punished. I need justice. *They* need to suffer."

She gave a start. "Did *Carrie* suffer?"

Milo said, "It was quick, ma'am."

"It." Renata Blanding closed her eyes and moaned. "Like it's a thing, a reality of life. But it's not. Not for normal people. You come in here and . . . my world changes."

"So sorry, Ms. Blanding. If you don't want to do this now, we totally understand. But at some point, learning as much as we can about your daughter's life will be helpful."

"No, no, I'll do it right now, Lieutenant. My head is just—I need to *do* something. With my mind. My body . . . activity is nourishing. I always tell Aaron that, he just likes to sit and read . . . because he's brilliant. Carrie was pretty smart . . . where should I start?"

"The beginning's always a good place, ma'am."

She fooled with her hair. "I like all the ma'ams. You're doing it to respect me. I'm *feeling* respected. I like that feeling."

She drank, put the glass down, prodded the oversized ice cube with a turquoise nail. "The big ones diffuse more slowly, you get a subtler chill."

Milo and I waited.

Renata Blanding said, "The beginning. Okay. I'm going to spare nothing. Including myself. I got pregnant with her when I was a seventeen-year-old idiot living in Sacramento and doing everything I could to torment my adoptive parents. Not because they were adoptive, I'm sure I would've done the same if they were bio, that's the way I was back then. Stupid and insolent and stubborn. I mean it's not like birth control wasn't available, right? I know exactly when I got pregnant. At a party. What I don't know is from *who* I got pregnant."

She forced herself higher.

"Get the picture?"

"Yes, ma'am."

"You're saying that but you don't. It's one of those . . . you had to be there. Dope, alcohol. There was more than one of them and, frankly, I don't want to know. But don't go thinking I'm one of those people telling everyone they got victimized. Yes, I was drunk. No, I wasn't forced. It was a party."

She put the glass down hard.

"Stupid and stubborn," she said. "That's the long and short of me, back then. You're probably wondering, why is she so cool with telling us all this. The reason is because confronting reality on a regular basis is emotionally nourishing, that's what my ther— whatever, back on track. Carrie . . ."

A moment of hesitation, as if her daughter's essence remained coded.

She said, "Where was I . . . I got pregnant, my adoptive parents freaked out and threatened to force an abortion on me and no one was going to control my body so I ran away and hitched down to L.A. with a few truckers, then a guy who took me from Frazier Park near the Grapevine all the way to Hollywood. And yes he was one of those. Dirty old man, one thing on his mind. Not that he forced me, but he sure *wanted* me."

She crossed her legs, picked up the glass, and sipped. "When he found out I was pregnant he lost interest and *kicked* me out, I was homeless so I ended up at St. Vivian's downtown. It's a shelter, Catholic even though I'm not. The deal is they take you in if you pledge not to terminate. Which was what I already wanted, Carrie was wanted. Okay?"

We nodded.

"Just as long as you understand that," said Renata Blanding. "So I signed the pledge and went to Mass and pretended to care and the baby. Twenty-hour labor, right out of a torture chamber, afterward I was stitched up like a football. She was a cute baby. Cried a lot but good looking. I had no idea what I was doing. The shelter let girls stay there for the first year if they kept going to Mass, so I did. I got an evening job waiting tables at a Mexican place, met a guy, he became my first husband. *Not* one of those. Nice guy, Mexican, older, worked for the gas company, had his own house in Carson. We moved there, eight years later we got divorced. Friendly split. Frank was nice to Carrie but casual, know what I mean?"

I said, "No closeness."

Emphatic nod. "He never disciplined her but he also never treated her like one of his own. Because he had five of his own from his first two wives."

She laughed. "This is some soap opera, huh?"

We smiled.

"Glad you appreciate it," said Renata Blanding.

Acid smile.

"Always happy to entertain . . . anyway, after the divorce from Frank, with Carrie in school, I cocktail-waitressed at better places. Mostly hotels. Hyatts, Marriotts, that kind of thing. Then I kicked it up to luxury hotels downtown, the New Otani, served plenty of sake. Then someone told me about an opening at The Four Seasons on Doheny near Beverly Hills. That's where I met Greg, he was in the lounge having drinks with another doctor who wanted a job with Greg's group. That didn't go so well but Greg and I did. He's a total gentleman, brilliant, kind, stable. Never married before, kind of shy, which I find adorable. When we got married Carrie was eighteen and already out of the house for a year, living who-knows-where. Even then, she began distancing herself deliberately. We couldn't even find her to invite her to the wedding. A small but elegant affair *at* the Four Seasons."

Her fingertip rotated the ice cube. "So there you have it."

She'd talked a lot about herself, very little about her daughter.

Milo gave me the look.

I said, "At eighteen, Carrie had already drifted away."

Renata Blanding said, "There was no reason to. She lucked out with Greg as a stepdad. Frank was good luck, too, but Greg was a whole different level. I'm sure you guys have seen what it can be like with boyfriends and stepdads. Nothing like that for Carrie, I hooked up with two nice guys. No abuse, nothing inappropriate, never. But the difference between Greg and Frank is that Frank was casual, didn't make much of an effort. Greg really did. When Carrie finally showed up to visit, he couldn't have been nicer. Whenever she came by, which wasn't often, he worked at having a relationship with her. An adult relationship, he said, because she was a legal adult and deserved to be treated as one."

She sniffed. "If anything, he was the easy one. I wake up every morning grateful to have him and Aaron. They're my heart."

Touching the corresponding region of bosom.

"Carrie," I said, "wasn't interested in a relationship with Greg."

"Not with any of us. She'd blow in and out, acting breezy, like life was perfect and she didn't need us. Then, two years later, when I gave birth to my baby, when she did come by she was even frostier. Aaron was an adorable baby but she had no desire to pick him up or play with him."

She sprang up, walked to a far end of the room, and brought back two photos in standing frames.

Chubby bald baby; chubby, blond teenager. Identical, guileless smiles.

"My baby," she said. "He's a love."

I said, "Did Carrie's coolness come from jealousy?"

"Honestly?" she said. "I don't think so. Because to be jealous, you'd have to care, right? And she stopped caring about us. It was like the baby wasn't . . . relevant to her. Later, as Aaron got older and it was obvious how smart he was, she warmed up a bit. Brought him games, tried to sit down with him. I even let her babysit for him a couple of times and it went fine. Then she went off the radar again. Aaron loves her. He asked for her a couple of times and cried when I told him she wasn't interested in visiting."

Her hands began shaking again. "He's so sensitive. This will devastate him." She looked at her wrist. "Left my watch in the bedroom, what time is it?"

Milo said, "Eleven fifteen."

"Aaron gets home around three," she said. "God, I need to figure out a game plan. How to tell him . . . I'll call Greg. We'll put our heads together and devise a plan."

More deep breathing. She crossed her legs, placed her palms on her knees. "You probably think I'm a rotten mother."

"Of course not," said Milo.

"I really am not," said Renata Blanding. "One thing I've learned: People do what they want to do and you can't control it."

Again, shifting away from her murdered child. In someone else that might've been denial. In Renata Blanding's case, I suspected it ran deeper. Emotional circuits that had never fully connected.

I said, "What do you know of Carrie's adult life?"

"Do you know about her being a phony shrink?"

"We have heard—"

"*That* was embarrassing to Greg," she said. "Because he almost got set up."

She drank.

Milo said, "Set up how, ma'am?"

"She actually had the nerve to call him and ask him to refer patients. Said she could help with headaches and tension disorders. Greg didn't say yes or no right away. He thinks things through before he acts. He asked her for her résumé and she sent one that he found odd."

"Odd in what way?"

"Off," she said. "Not right. First of all, there was no formal training Greg could see and he didn't recognize the college where she'd supposedly earned a Ph.D. I told him it was impossible, her getting a Ph.D. She'd dropped out of high school, hadn't been to school since. I came close to my GED. She never even tried, though I begged her. I told her, 'Look at me, how we struggled. Those years when we had nothing. Because I was uneducated. You're a good-looking girl and a pretty smart one. Get educated, education paves the way.'"

I said, "The résumé got your husband suspicious."

"Not suspicious," she said. "Greg's not like that. He assumes the best not the worst about people. He got curious, looked up the place, and found out it was a scam—pay a fee, get a degree. It really upset him. That Carrie would do that to herself and that she'd try to get him involved. Can you imagine if he'd sent her a patient and she screwed them up and he got blamed? Or worse, sued for malpractice?"

Time for a question with an answer I already knew.

I said, "What did Carrie do between eighteen and when she claimed to be a therapist?"

Renata looked down. Fiddled with her hands. Her mouth twisted to the left. Her eyes climbed.

"I'd rather not talk about that. But I guess I need to."

Milo said, "Anything you can tell us would be helpful."

"Oh Lord . . . all right. Those years were what I call the lost years. Posing for bikini shots and probably worse. Not that I saw anything downright naked but it stands to reason, right? What's a bikini? Two strips of cloth. Someone pays you enough, you go further. And the people she was running with. Hollywood types—not stars. Makeup girls, those guys who move sets, extras, so-called actors auditioning— marginal Hollywood losers."

I said, "You met them?"

"Oh no," she said. "She was too smart for that. Too . . . crafty. She'd send photos from her phone. Look at how much fun I'm having with so-and-so and she just worked with Ben Affleck. Or whoever. Like I'd care. My husband saves people's hearing and speech, I was living on a different planet. Where things mattered. She'd send me that nonsense,

I'd delete immediately. It's when she sent a bikini shot to Aaron, he must've been ten, eleven, and it was a really skimpy bikini—a thong, you could see her— that's when we put an end to it."

"How'd you do that?"

"I sent her an email and told her to stop. Told her we didn't want to hear from her unless she had something of value to say. I know that sounds harsh but we couldn't have her corrupting Aaron."

"How did Carrie react?"

"She obeyed," said Renata Blanding. "We didn't hear from her for years."

"When did she resume contact?"

"When the other thing began. Pretending to be a doctor and wanting referrals from Greg. I never believed it in the first place. You don't go from eleventh grade to Ph.D. But I said, 'Great, good luck.' Then she tried to get Greg involved and that was over the line."

She poked the oversized cube some more. Rotated it several times. No sign the ice had melted.

"I know," she said, "that I sound cruel and uncaring, right out of a Disney movie, the witch, Cruella, whatever. That's *not* me. I loved my daughter. Did everything I could for her. She's the one who chose to leave."

Just as you did with your parents.

Milo and I nodded.

"When you leave," said Renata Blanding, "there are consequences."

I said, "Can you think of anyone who'd want to hurt her?"

Emphatic head shake. "To know that, guys, I'd have to know what her life was like, wouldn't I? A house in Westwood? I must say that's a surprise. I guess she was finally doing okay. Did she keep the place up?"

"Everything neat and in its place."

"Like here," she said. "Like me. At least we had that in common. Now if you'll excuse me, I need a lie-down."

◆

We walked to the door, Renata leading us, Lynn materializing from the kitchen and trailing at a distance.

Milo said, "In terms of Carrie's body—"

Another hand-wave. "Greg's a physician, he'll know what to do."

"I'll call Dr. Blanding and help him set it up."

"Sure," she said, touching her brow with a now open hand. "Good idea."

Turning her back on us, she hurried off. That was a cue for Lynn to scurry forward, open the door, and hold it.

Milo smiled down at her.

She looked away.

"Lynn, have you ever met Carrie?"

"Who?" she said.

"Not important," he said. "Have a nice day."

She watched, wide-eyed, as we walked to the unmarked. A glance-back from Milo caused her to shut the door.

In the car, I said, "Don't know about you but I've got a new sense of our victim."

"Empathy on the rise?"

"Sympathy on the rise. It can't have been easy growing up with someone like that."

"Mommy dearest," he said.

"All the notifications you've done," I said, "have you ever seen that level of hostility toward a deceased? On top of that, she kept steering the topic away from Cordi and back to her and her *amazing* family. Wanting us to know she finally got it right."

He said, "Guess that makes Cordi a throwaway. Yeah, my warm and fuzzy has definitely notched up."

I said, "The pancake approach to parenthood. Toss the first batch."

As he steered away from the curb, I said, "Clever the way you got access to the husband."

He smiled. "You noticed, huh? I figured if I asked her straight out, she'd get protective."

"When do you want to try to see him?"

"Now feels about right," he said. "It'll take ten minutes to get to Century City, just enough time for her to call him. Meaning I won't have to do *another* notification."

Gregory Blanding's receptionist was prepared. "Doctor said to tell you he'd meet you in the coffee shop down in the lobby."

"Thanks," said Milo. "When?"

"Text when you get there."

The black glass tower on Century Park East had once been a hospital. Now it housed the suites of several large medical groups, a couple of outpatient surgical facilities, and a rehabilitation center.

The building's coffee shop was a two-table affair wedged into a hundred square feet, much of the space given over to a take-out counter. Coffee, tea, soda, candy bars, pre-packaged pastries and sandwiches. The tabletops were aluminum disks the size of manhole covers. Unsurprisingly, no one was using them.

Milo surveyed the contents behind the glass. "Getting close to lunchtime but don't want to waste calories."

I'd never known him to keep count. "Makes sense."

"Also," he said, pulling out his phone, "don't want the eminent Dr. Blanding to spot crumbs on my shirt. Seeing as he's such a perfect human being."

He sent the text to Blanding's office, ordered black coffee for both of us, and brought the cups over. Recycled cardboard the color of old wheat. Paper pulp yeastiness flavored the coffee and I put it aside.

Milo said, "I second the motion," and did the same.

Two minutes later, Gregory Blanding entered wearing a long white coat over green scrubs and orange Crocs. Six-two and broad, with downcast eyes and a plodding gait. The weary lumber of a bull after stud season. Since the charity ball, he'd grown a full gray beard, added substance to his waistline, trimmed the scant hair atop his cranium to a downy buzz.

"Lieutenant Sturgis?"

"Doctor. This is Alex Delaware."

A pair of brisk, firm clasp-and-shakes. Blanding looked at the coffee, thought for an instant, and said, "Why not?"

He returned with his own dose of all-black, sat down and took a sip.

"You're not drinking yours? Wise move, it stinks, but for me it's medication. Had two tricky surgeries this morning, need the caffeine. Or maybe I shouldn't since my nerves are already jangling." He shook his head. "Poor Cordi. Horrible. I still can't believe it."

Milo said, "Your wife calls her Carrie."

Greg Blanding said, "It's the name Renni gave her. And when Renni's around, that's what I use. But soon after I met Cordi, she took me aside and asked me to call her Cordi so I respected her wishes."

"Sounds like you two got along."

"We did when we had contact," said Blanding. "Which wasn't often. As you've probably seen, Cordi and Renni had . . . issues. I chose to sidestep."

"Probably a smart move, Doctor."

Blanding looked at us balefully. "My brother has two stepkids and they hate his guts. At the outset I decided to avoid conflict."

I said, "Was that a challenge with Cordi?"

"Not really, no. She was already living away from home." He hazarded another sip, pursed his lips. "Cordi had problems, who doesn't? But at the core, she was a lovely girl. Bright, personable, lots of potential. I guess some things come down to luck."

"Hers wasn't good?"

"Did Renni tell you about her early days?"

"She did."

"So you understand. Neither Renni nor I grew up with money but ultimately, we've been fortunate. By the time I got to know Cordi she was eighteen and had been through a lot. Another reason not to get involved."

I said, "Because . . ."

"I figured she was pretty much formed. And it's not like she was asking me for my advice."

He drank more coffee. "This really is lousy . . . to be honest, what I'd like right now is some bourbon but you can't be poking around ear canals with an unsteady hand."

I said, "So you had no intention of molding her personality."

"None whatsoever. It's like the septum. That's a wall of bone and cartilage that separates the nostrils. In most adults it's deviated—bent out of shape. Some people are born that way, others get knocked in the nose. Generally it's not a big deal but when problems arise—breathing issues, sleep apnea—patients come in for a straightening. We do our best but we're up-front. The septum's a stubborn bit of gristle that keeps wanting to return to the way it was. Sometimes we get lucky. Other times?"

Blanding shrugged.

I said, "When it came to Cordi, you chose your battles."

"I choose not to battle at all," he said. "What would be the point? Not just with Cordi, I apply that to my own son. He's a good kid but he's not perfect. Super-smart, has finally developed a few friends we like. But when the mood hits him, he mouths off. What kid doesn't? What kid toes the line a hundred percent? When Aaron gets pissy I first try to reason with him, figure the more responsibility he takes the better. But if that doesn't work, I back off. The way I see it, if he chooses not to study for a test and bombs, that's on him. If he chooses not to go to Harvard, who the heck cares? But that's just me."

"Your wife has a different philosophy."

Blanding rotated his coffee cup with strong dexterous fingers. "Renni's highly invested in Aaron. And yes, in answer to your next question, as opposed to Cordi. Is that unfortunate? You bet. Did Renni actually get into details about those early days?"

Milo said, "Homeless, then in a shelter, waiting tables, trying to make ends meet."

Greg Blanding grew silent.

"Doctor?"

"So she didn't tell you about her illness."

Milo said, "Your wife's or Cordi's?"

"Do we need to get into it?" said Blanding.

"You brought it up, Doctor."

"So I did." Long sigh. "You're detectives, you could find out on your own—but please don't mention this to my wife. She's entitled to her privacy."

"Sure," said Milo.

"Renni has suffered from rheumatoid arthritis for years. So far, it's relatively well controlled. But when it acts up, life can be painful for her. I'm telling you this so you'll understand my wife."

"Understand what, Doctor?"

Greg Blanding's soft brown eyes rose to the ceiling. His lower teeth gnawed at his mustache. "Animals in the wild try not to show they're suffering. It makes them more vulnerable to attack. But when it comes to humans, whenever there's pain, there are mood issues. Renni tends to get angry rather than depressed. Which I think is a good thing— direct it outward, not inward. When she called me to tell me about Cordi she sounded angry so I'm assuming that's what you saw. I don't want you to think she's uncaring. Anything but. She raised Cordi all by herself and did a darn good job. She loved Cordi."

"Got it," said Milo.

"I hope so, Lieutenant. Renni was diagnosed with R.A. in her teens. Right after having Cordi. Like I said, it's well controlled but there have been some bone and lung issues. Fortunately, it hasn't affected her skin. That would be especially rough for her. When a woman gets used to hearing she's beautiful, she becomes invested in her looks."

I said, "Was that also true of Cordi?"

"From what Renni told me, Cordi had long banked on her appearance."

"The time she spent modeling."

"Modeling as well as hanging around the periphery of the movie business. When coke was big I repaired a lot of coke noses so I'm familiar with that world."

"Did you ever hear of specific issues related to that?"

"Meaning?"

"Did Cordi ever have a drug problem."

"Not to my knowledge," said Blanding. "She certainly never exhibited symptoms. I've always thought her big issue was self-esteem. She underrated her own intelligence. That's why I was glad to hear she'd switched gears to doing something with her brain rather than her looks. But then that went south. I know my wife told you about it."

I said, "Pretending to be a psychologist."

Heavy shoulders dropped. "How she could've imagined getting away with it is beyond me."

"Your wife also told us she tried to involve you."

"She wondered if I could refer patients to her," said Blanding. "No big deal, I was never at any sort of risk."

"Because you checked out Cordi's story."

"I'd do that with anyone approaching me to network. But yes, I was doubtful of Cordi's story. She was a high school dropout. Going from that to a doctorate made no sense."

I said, "You turned her down."

Blanding looked at the floor. "This is going to sound terrible but I simply didn't call her back. My default approach. I'd like to tell you it's rooted in the Hippocratic oath. Above all, do no harm. But I've always avoided confrontation."

Milo said, "Sounds pretty smart to me, Doctor."

"You're kind to say so, but now I wonder if I could've handled it better. Like having a sit-down and telling her she was capable of doing it properly. Buckling down and getting a real degree. Maybe not something as time consuming and daunting as a doctorate. But training to become a psychiatric aide or some sort of rehab counselor? Why not?"

I said, "How'd she react to your not reacting?"

Blanding smiled. "She didn't. Like father, like stepdaughter, I guess. Maybe that's why we got along. May I ask you guys a question?"

"Sure."

"After Cordi got caught, I know she rebranded herself as a relationship expert, which apparently doesn't require certification. I also know she was into the whole internet thing. Do you suspect any of that that led to . . . this?"

Milo said, "How so, Doctor?"

"Exposing herself to the world, as it were. I mean, what are the safeguards?"

"Are you aware of any specific problems she had because of her postings?"

"No, but I wouldn't be," said Blanding. "She'd really moved away from us. Psychologically as well as physically. I can't even tell you who her friends were. But there is something I thought you should know. It's probably nothing, but . . ."

"What's that, Doctor?"

"A couple of years back, Cordi was dating a man who was going through a custody battle. She decided to help him by testifying for him in court. Using her degree to suggest expertise. What's incredible to me is this was *after* she was caught practicing without a license. Why would she even consider that?"

"Pretty risky," said Milo.

"Risky and downright foolish," said Blanding. "And, again, she got caught. Don't know the details, just what she told me. 'I got nailed again, Greg.'"

"She talked to you about it."

"She talked to me because she had a problem. Apparently this guy got really upset with her. Felt she'd weakened his chances more than if she hadn't tried to help. She called my office and asked to meet. We sat right here." He smiled. "The coffee wasn't any better."

I said, "What did she want from you?"

"The usual," said Blanding, rubbing his thumb and forefinger together.

"Money."

"She asked for five thousand dollars to 'smooth things over' with this guy. It sounded bizarre so I asked if he was threatening her and she laughed it off and said, 'No, Greg, he's cool. I just feel I should do it.'"

Milo said, "Taking responsibility with your money."

Blanding smiled sadly. "I guess that sums up parenthood. She told me she considered it a peace offering and I shouldn't worry, she'd pay me back as soon as royalties came in from her videos—do you know about them?"

"We do, Doctor."

"Don't want to be cruel," said Blanding. "Least of all now, but to me they came across as the exposition of the obvious. But what do I know, apparently sponsors felt they're valuable. Because a couple of months later, she paid me back in full. I was pleasantly surprised, had already kissed off the money. I told her to keep it but she insisted."

Milo said, "Do you have a name for this person?"

"No, sir. I didn't want to know. But now I wish I did."

"You think he could be involved?"

"No, I don't think anything," said Blanding. "I don't know enough to hypothesize. I just thought I'd put it out there and you could do what you wanted with it."

"Thanks, Doctor."

I said, "Asking you for money was a regular thing."

Greg Blanding's thick body shifted. Loosely packed heft shimmered a bit. He faced us and the dark circles under his eyes became evident. Maybe all those surgeries. Maybe another type of fatigue.

He said, "It wasn't frequent, maybe once or twice a year. And with the exception of that one time, always before she created her internet presence. So I guess that was working out for her."

"Does your wife know you gave Cordi money?"

Head shake. "I handle the finances. The way it worked, she'd ask to have lunch, we'd go somewhere around here, I'd say how much, kid, and she'd smile and apologize and tell me and I'd arrange for some cash a few days later."

"How much are we talking about in total?"

"I couldn't really tell you," said Blanding. "Let me estimate . . . maybe a couple of thousand a year over . . . fifteen years? Thirty, give or take. I once joked to her that compared with Aaron's tuition, it was a bargain. She smiled but it was a sad smile and I knew I'd overstepped. She thought I was saying she was stupid. I didn't know how to patch that up so I said nothing. It was a while before she asked for money again, but she did."

I said, "You had a lot more contact with Cordi than your wife knew about."

"Oh, definitely," said Greg Blanding. "Does hiding it from Renni make me devious? I suppose, strictly speaking. But I'd like to think I was keeping the peace. Cordi was a girl who'd been saddled with some serious challenges and if I could help her without ruffling any feathers, why not?"

Milo said, "Keeping it copacetic."

Blanding frowned and stood. "I'm going to tell you something I've told no one else. I love my wife and I love my son. I *liked* Cordi a lot but I *didn't* love her. So maybe we're talking about guilt offerings."

A meaty lower lip trembled, beard hairs spiked and fell. "I've got patients to see. If I think of anything else, I'll let you know."

Tossing his coffee cup in a trash basket, he plodded away.

15

When Blanding had passed out of sight, Milo said, "Think he was screwing her?"

I said, "Get right to the point, huh?"

"Hey, we're seasoned professionals, no sense shilly-shallying. You didn't wonder about it?"

"His relationship with Cordi was different but no, I didn't pick up anything creepy. But that means nothing. I can be fooled."

"I thought your degree insulated you from that."

"If only."

"What really bugs me, Alex, is slipping her dough behind his wife's back. It's what you do with a mistress. What if it wasn't altruism?"

"Fee for services?"

"Older rich guy, good-looking younger woman? Cordi wasn't a minor when she met him. Blanding coulda rationalized an affair as not illegal. And strictly speaking, not incest."

I said, "If Blanding has something that explosive to hide why bring up the money in the first place?"

"Maybe he figured we'd find out. Maybe being a brainy guy, he figured it was best to play us by coming across open and honest and a gee-whiz nice guy. And physically, he's not exactly a featherweight. No problem overpowering a little guy on a couch or Cordi, especially with the element of surprise going for him. Easy to get the element of surprise if there was an affair: He coulda had a key to her place. On top of that, he's a surgeon and that throat slash was pretty precise, none of the false moves you usually see."

I closed my eyes and tried to imagine it. One of those scenarios that makes formal sense but doesn't feel right, though I couldn't say why.

Milo said, "Oracle of Delphi? Please converse."

I opened my eyes. "Nothing points against it."

He frowned. "Damning with faint praise. I know, it's just theory. But between Blanding's marriage and his reputation, there's a whole lot at stake. And for all we know he's been giving Cordi a lot more money than he just let on."

"She got greedy and upped the ante?"

"That, or she started taking herself seriously as a relationship hotshot and decided she'd been a victim. This is the me-too age. And we're talking about a woman who raked in big bucks by going public. Like Blanding put it, exposing herself to the world . . . which, now that I think about it, has a kinda sexual connotation, no?"

Received and registered, Dr. Freud.

He said, "I'm being too creative?"

"No such thing," I said. "And if you're right, we are talking about huge motivation to get rid of Cordi. An exposure video, a podcast, any type of exposure, would blow the Blandings' lives up."

"To smithereens. Plus Cordi mighta thought the exposure would help her professionally. A relationship guru who *understood.*"

"It's worth checking out. Meanwhile, there's still another large man to consider, who we just learned was upset with Cordi. And despite her denial, fear of Hoffgarden's anger could be the real reason she paid him off."

"Five grand," he said. "From what you saw, would Hoffgarden have been that pissed? It's not like she actually messed up his chances at custody. Which you said he didn't want in the first place."

I said, "True, but he did settle the day after Cordi's stunt failed. From what I saw, it was all about money for him. Maybe he'd expected more than just half the gym."

"Five grand would atone for that?"

"Like Cordi told Blanding, maybe a token to cool Hoffgarden's jets."

"Hoffgarden's ex signed her half over and got full custody."

"Yup."

"So Hoffgarden has a history of getting women to pay him off. Still, Alex, what's his motive to go after Cordi two years later?"

"Maybe he and Cordi resumed their relationship. Or he tried and she rejected him. He's got a definite history of violence and two people he associated with have been murdered. What if Hoffgarden didn't feel as warmly toward Slope as he told the paper?"

"He couldn'ta been mad at the way Slope handled the divorce. The two of them moved to the desert and he trained Slope in his gym."

"Maybe their moving at the same time wasn't a coincidence."

"Some sort of relationship."

"Not necessarily sexual. Something financial. Like you said, the case was tunneled as a gangbanger invasion with no alternatives explored in depth. Now that I think about it, would a gangster take the time to strangle someone in bed? A shot to the head would be a lot quicker and more efficient."

"Whatever Hoffgarden and Slope had going went bad."

I said, "And the same could go for Hoffgarden and Cordi. He's the kind of fellow you don't want to alienate."

He punched a preset on his phone. "Moses, that guy I talked to you about, Hoffgarden? It's time to check him out more closely. His address is on my desk, to the left of my monitor . . . Culver City? Thought it was West L.A. Either or, it's a hop-skip. You have time to go over there? . . . Excellent. If you find him at home, see if he'll talk to you about Cordi. Not as a suspect, don't get his hackles up, we're contacting all of her friends. If he's not there, try to talk to neighbors, a landlord, anyone you can find. See if it looks like he rabbited, here's why."

He repeated Blanding's account of the 5K payoff. "Yeah, it's bizarre, the whole damn case is, I'll fill you in about the family when we get together. Meanwhile, you're the right guy to approach Hoffgarden because you can probably outlift him . . . hey, no false modesty, kid. Long as I have you, anything from Basia, yet? Okay, I'll handle the crypt, you do Mr. Universe."

We rode a crowded elevator down to the parking lot and retrieved the unmarked in the *No Parking at Any Time* slot he'd scored by over-tipping the attendant.

The man licked his lips when he saw us. "I been warned twice by security."

Milo added a five.

"Thank you, sir."

"Consider it a guilt offering."

We sat in an uphill queue of vehicles exiting the lot, finally made it to Century Park East where he turned right, heading north. Away from the station.

I said, "Where to?"

"Taking you home. Thanks for your time."

He drove through Century City. At a long light at Santa Monica Boulevard, I said, "Cordi's doing well financially."

"Like I said, nearly seven hundred K worth of well. And . . . ?"

"What reason would she have to ask for a five K loan to pay Hoff-garden off? I know she told Blanding she was waiting for a royalty check but do her records show her living from payment to payment?"

"Hmm . . . no, the opposite, actually. The balance in her investment account was stable and rising."

"What about her checking account?"

"Same thing, Alex. Small outlays for bills but she took in more than she laid out."

I said, "A good money manager. What if reaching out to Blanding wasn't about money? It was symbolic. Her way of feeling connected to him."

"Daddy issues?" he said. "Rich stepdaddy, dip into the till?"

"She was a prime candidate for daddy issues. No birth father of record, no paternal presence at all during her early years followed by a stepdad who kept his distance emotionally. Then along comes Blanding, when she's an adult. He likes her but doesn't love her and she was smart enough to sense that. She could've also figured out that for all his nice-guy persona, he'd be an easy hit. By his own admission he's an emotional coward unwilling to engage. So giving her money could've served his needs, as well."

"Getting off easy by doling out cash? Okay, could be. You see it as relating to her murder?"

I said, "Just thinking out loud."

The light changed. He crossed Santa Monica, turned left to Comstock, continued north grinning. "Hey, I can get symbolic, too. Ready for some Dr. Milo?"

"Go for it."

"Maybe when Blanding told us he didn't love her, that was code for 'I didn't have sex with her.'"

I said, "He really twangs your antenna affair-wise."

"Too-good-to-be-*true* twangs my antenna," he said. "On top of that, I'm trying to stay in practice."

"How so?"

"Thinking the worst of everybody."

He drove to Wilshire, hit another red. "By the way, the crypt did manage to roll prints from the poor guy on the sofa. No match anywhere, which is why I forgot to mention it."

I said, "Maybe Missing Persons can tell you something."

He said, "Called the West L.A. D but nothing fits. When I have time to go through all those faces, I'll go online."

"When are Alicia and Sean coming back?"

"Who the hell knows? I'm not into helicopter parenting."

At the green, he lurched forward.

In one of those moods, when nothing but negativity would do. As long as that was the case . . .

I said, "Cordi's phone listings were all business. The neighbor reports people coming in and out so she had to make appointments. Where's the record of all those contacts?"

Silence. "Maybe she booked on her computer—if no one messed with it, the lab will tell me."

"Or there's another phone."

"Or that." He gripped the wheel, big hands tight, mottled like lunch meat. "Jesus, why didn't I get curious about that? I'm slipping, amigo?"

"No one can think of everything."

He looked at me. "What's that, supportive therapy?"

I smiled.

He said, "Jesus, your brain's like a sponge. Yet another reason to have you ride shotgun."

◆

He drove west on Wilshire, through the immaculate canyon created by high-rises lining both sides of the boulevard.

As he approached Beverly Glen, I said, "We could talk to that neighbor again and try to get more details about the visitors. How they showed up, maybe physical descriptions. You could show him photos of Hoffgarden and Blanding."

"Reinterview Scrooge." He phoned Reed again, got the neighbor's name.

"Rainer Gibbs, might as well. When do you wanna do it?"

"I'm free right now if you are."

He said, "Westwood Ho," leaned on the throttle, and sped past the Glen.

16

Rainer Gibbs, wearing a robin's-egg-blue Columbia U. sweat-shirt, baggy pleated gray dress slacks, and black wingtips, opened his front door and let out waves of organ music playing at thunderous volume.

Bach's Toccata and Fugue in D Minor. Work of genius unfortu-nately rendered comical by use as a backdrop for too many old horror movies.

For all its virtues, not exactly easy listening on a sunny day.

Gibbs stared at us and scowled.

Milo showed his card.

Gibbs pursed his lips and said something that was drowned out by the music. I wondered if he was partially deaf, cranking up the volume to that level the cause of hearing loss or an effect or both.

He cocked his head the way puzzled dogs do, revealing a beige but-ton in his right ear.

Milo said, "Sir?"

Gibbs's lips moved silently as he gave the card another examination. Stomping inside his house, flat-footed and stiff, head extended like that of a curious turtle, he stabbed a button on a tape deck, returned to the doorway poking at his right ear.

"Lieutenant, huh? Already talked to that kid with the crew cut. Did he forget to tell you?"

Milo said, "He didn't, sir. I was wondering if we could talk again."

"About what?" said Gibbs.

Allergic to pleasantries. Put him in a room with Milo on a bad detective day and the planet might shift on its axis.

"May we come in, sir?"

"Hmmph." Turning his back on us again, Gibbs stepped inside, trudged across a cramped, domed entry space and into a front room dimmed by heavy drapes and low-watt bulbs. Leaving the door open in place of an invitation. Milo closed it after me and we stepped in.

Gibbs had settled himself in a black vinyl recliner. The rest of the living room furniture was overstuffed floral chintz and delicate carved tables in that bland finish that libels pecan trees.

Doilies on chair arms. A woman's touch once upon a time? A bottle of Bud, three empties, a bowl of nachos, and a well-squeezed tube of cheese suggested it had been a while.

Gibbs tapped his wrist, as if a watch sat there.

Milo said, "You told Detective Reed that Ms. Gannett had frequent visitors."

"That her name? What I told him was I suspected she had a brothel going on."

"Why's that, Mr. Gibbs?"

"Because they showed up after dark." Gibbs bared his teeth in an unpleasant smile. "Maybe I should be a detective."

"Happy to put in a word with Human Resources."

"Don't patronize me, young man. I've got kids older than you."

"No offense intended, sir," said Milo. "Can you give an estimate of how many visitors she'd have, say in a week?"

"No, I cannot," said Gibbs. "That would require me to have wasted my time spying and taking a count. I'm a busy man. Taking care of my investments is time consuming in and of itself."

"What I'm trying to get at, sir, is was there a steady stream of visitors, say on a daily basis? Or occasional visits."

"You're still asking me to quantify and my answer's the same."

"No problem, sorry for bothering you."

Milo closed his pad. Easy cue for Gibbs to get rid of us. He picked up the beer bottle, looked at us defiantly, and took a long, deep swig.

"Nectar of the gods, don't let one of those yuppies tell you good old American brew is lacking."

Two more swallows before the bottle joined the other empties. "Don't go thinking I'm some sort of lush. I had a kidney stone five years ago and the doctor said beer was good for it."

Milo smiled, "I'll remember that, sir."

"You've had a kidney stone?"

"Thankfully, no."

"Get your calcium too high it could happen," said Gibbs. "Wouldn't wish it on my worst enemy." Another evil grin. "Strike that. I would wish it on the bastard who thought he could take my wife from me. Then cancer took her first, joke was on them."

He rose with difficulty, padded out to an unseen kitchen, rattled around a bit, and returned with another bottle. "I'd offer you some but I know the rules."

"Appreciate the thought, sir."

Gibbs looked at me. "He always such a kiss-up?"

I smiled.

Gibbs said, "Like you'd say so. You probably taught him to be a kiss-up. Okay, you want a number? I'll pick one out of the air—one or two a week give or take."

Milo said, "Always after dark."

"If you were sneaking off for some mercenary whoopee would you want to be seen?"

But you managed to see.

Milo produced the screenshot he'd taken of Gregory Blanding's DMV photo. "Was this individual one of the visitors?"

Gibbs snorted. "Visitors."

He got up again, pulled open a drawer on one of the dainty tables, and returned to his recliner holding a pair of reading glasses.

"Give me that." He took the phone and studied the photo. "Can't say yes and can't say no."

Milo reached for the phone. Gibbs hesitated for a moment before returning it. For all his curmudgeonly loner stance, glad to break routine and reluctant to let go of the merest novelty.

Milo repeated the process with Tyler Hoffgarden's headshot.

Rainer Gibbs said, "Yup, he was here. More than once."

"Even though it was dark—"

"Are you doubting me, young man?"

"No, sir, just trying to clarify—"

"Him I remember," said Gibbs, "because he was huge. Must've been six . . . five?"

"Six-four," said Milo.

"Add shoes and it's exactly what I said, six-five." Gibbs crossed skinny, sun-spotted forearms across a pigeon chest.

"So you saw him more than once, sir."

"Didn't I just say that? Again with the quantifying? By that I meant two, maybe three times. I noticed his size and the fact that his car was puny, one of those little boxes. Ludicrous, like one of those circus shows, a bunch of clowns crowd into a box on wheels."

"When's the last time you saw him, sir?"

"Now I'm expected to be your calendar? Not recently, if that's what you're after. Weeks ago. Maybe months. It's not as if I was sitting here taking notes. I just remember this palooka because he was oversized and his car was undersized."

"Okay, thanks," said Milo. "Anything else you want to tell us?"

"Not a thing," said Gibbs, remaining in place. "So tell me, this job of yours, you find it satisfying? All the reprehensible types you come across day after day?"

"There is that, Mr. Gibbs, but we also get to bring justice to victims' families."

"But not to the victims, when you're gone, you're gone." Snapping a finger.

"That's true, sir."

Rainer Gibbs said, "I could never do your job. Too damn unfinished."

Milo smiled and stood and I did the same.

Rainer Gibbs looked up at us. "Is it something I said?"

"No, sir—"

"That was a joke, young man. You could both use some humor in your lives. See yourselves out and shut the door firmly."

By the time we reached the doorway, the fresh bottle was at his lips.

As we approached the unmarked, Milo paused to look down the block at the murder house, then back at Gibbs's place.

"Crusty old bird. Compared with him I'm sweetness and light."

I said, "Well . . ."

He cracked up and loped toward the car.

I said, "What does Hoffgarden drive?"

"Ten-year-old Mini Cooper."

"So Gibbs definitely saw him."

He nodded, started up the engine. Turned pensive. "I suppose she coulda been running a very expensive brothel but no evidence of that and my bet is it came out of Gibbs's horny old head. So let's give Cordi the benefit. She had a social caller once in a while. Or maybe she was doing her emotional coaching thing."

I said, "Making the bulk of her money online but seeing a few private clients."

"Exactly," he said. "Though with Couch Man being naked, it doesn't sound like any therapy I know of."

"Whatever the specifics, Hoffgarden got in and surprised the two of them."

He nodded. "Guy keeps turning up in all the wrong places. I need to talk to him but the case is bound to go public and I don't want to spook him into burrowing deep. That's why I told Moe to soft-pedal it."

I said, "One other thing: Gibbs is no lover of women. That crack about his wife's cancer being a joke was pretty damn cruel even if she did cheat on him."

"Yeah, he's a vindictive old coot but do you see him as physically capable of doing what we saw?"

"Probably not."

"Hedging your judgment?"

"I try to avoid always and never."

"You do that always?"

I laughed.

He said, "Fine, we'll keep all options open. Now in answer to a previous question."

He phoned the duty sergeant at the station, asked when Alicia and Sean were due back, said thanks and hung up.

"Tomorrow, as it turns out. If I get to conscript them, I'll have them do a recanvass of the neighborhood, see if anything unsavory about ol' Rainer comes up. And maybe miracle of miracles, Naked's stuff will show up under a tree."

He drove a couple of blocks, surprised me by turning onto a parallel street, pulling to the curb, and punching a preset on his phone.

"Hey, Moses. Gibbs, your grumpy old man, just I.D.'d Hoffgarden as one of Cordi's visitors. He hasn't seen him recently but that doesn't mean Hoffgarden couldn'ta come over late without being noticed. Any progress locating him?"

"Unfortunately not yet, L.T. I was just over at his place. Six units with a live-in manager and she didn't seem too in touch about anything, including the tenants."

"Impaired, apathetic, or resisting?"

"None of the above," said Reed. "She's nineteen years old and doesn't speak English well. Her parents own the building. They live in Taiwan, sent her over here to go to pharmacy school, she's waiting for some visa stuff to come through. She was easy to deal with once I got used to her accent. Took me right to the sub-lot and pointed out Hoffgarden's parking spot. Empty. She denied he ever caused problems, but then again she said no one did, so I'm not sure that means anything."

He laughed. "Or maybe she lucked out and has a great bunch of tenants. How long the Mini's been gone, she had no idea. I'm not sure she ever noticed it in the first place. She did let me ride up to Hoffgarden's floor and knocked on a couple of doors hoping some neighbor would know something. No one home. There was mail visible through the slot in Hoffgarden's box in the lobby but from what I could tell it looked like bulk junk and the manager doesn't have her own key. Want me to put out a BOLO on the Mini?"

"Not yet," said Milo. "That could come back and bite us. At some point this case is gonna get exposure because of Cordi's internet presence. Maybe on a big scale. All we need is for Hoffgarden to get pulled over, get alerted he's a person of interest, and burrow deep. See if you can find out what he's doing to support himself in L.A. You're the perfect man for the job, start by calling gyms, see if anyone hired him. If that doesn't pan out, I can call one of my federal pals and try to get a peek at his tax returns. If he's freelancing on a cash basis and there aren't any, I'll scour his social media."

"Sounds like a plan, L.T."

"Man plans, God laughs."

Reed said, "I like that. Going to use it when the opportunity comes up."

We traveled back to Wilshire and Milo turned left. "Now I am gonna take you home."

A block later, his cell played Beethoven. *Für Elise.* True easy listening.

"Sturgis."

Basia Lopatinski's bright, Slavic-tinged voice came on. "Hello, guys—I'm guessing Alex is there but if he's not, hello to only you."

I said, "Good guess, Basia."

"Probability judgment. I have some results on your double, Milo."

"Love to hear them."

"There's a lot to go through. Can you manage a trip here?"

"For you, Basia, I'd walk."

"Well," she said, "then it's good you have a car. I'm free tomorrow until noon but I'm working late tonight, so if you want to come before, say, eleven p.m. I'll be available. You can bring Alex, too."

Milo said, "Is that a suggestion or an order?"

"A recommendation. It's a psychologically interesting *mieszanina.*"

"What's that?"

"Polish for what you'd call a hodgepodge. If you prefer something romantic, mélange. See you when I see you. Bye."

Milo clicked off and ran his hands over his face, like washing without water. "If it was me alone, I'd turn around, traffic be damned. But she recommends you be there."

I said, "I'll call Robin and let her know."

17

The freeways were cruelly jammed so Milo took a seventy-eight-minute slog to East L.A. on side streets. Twenty more minutes were added by a stop at a food truck at Olympic and Alvarado where he scored a monumental burrito big enough to require a building permit.

Demolition took place in stages, during red lights.

When we arrived, my nose had saturated with the aroma of refried beans and shredded pork. He parked in the open lot behind the coroner's, checked his face in the rearview, wiped salsa from around his lips, and said, "Here we go. Mélange."

The L.A. County Medical Examiner's office, known to those who work there as the crypt, sits on North Mission Road at the bottom edge of the USC Medical School–County Hospital complex. I'd taught a few courses at the med school but until I met Milo, I'd never ventured to the U-shaped stucco building. The color is that grayish beige that identifies generations of L.A. government structures. There's solidity to the design, a curious blankness that fails to mask its function.

Two stories are visible aboveground but plenty goes on below. Square-edged columns separate the short arms of the U. Both are accessed through gleaming glass doors. The right-hand door lets you into what you'd imagine: refrigerated closets where bodies are stacked like firewood; spillover corpses lying on gurneys in the hall; brightly lit rooms filled with stainless steel where bodies are taken apart and interpreted; the offices of those who cut and probe and squint into microscopes.

To the left is administrative space: clerical offices and a check-in counter where next of kin fill out forms, wait to collect belongings, and arrange for body transport. A lot of weeping goes on in the left-hand space. For some reason, little black flies like to congregate just outside the left-hand doors, as if summoned to remind visitors what to expect.

As we headed for the clinical wing, I saw a young, grim-faced couple get out of an SUV and trudge toward the left. The woman clutched papers. Both she and the man looked shell-shocked. Maybe here to see about a parent. Or a child.

I've accompanied parents seeing about the remains of their children. Give me gurneys and autopsies and even decomp, any day of the week.

Basia Lopatinski, M.D., Ph.D., was in her office, a small, windowless space not far from the dissection rooms.

She's somewhere in her forties, five-two and slender with soft brown eyes, feathered blond hair, full lips, and a wide smile that nearly bisects a triangular face when she turns up the wattage. Today she wore a gray cashmere dress kicked up by a gold silk scarf artfully knotted.

Trained in Warsaw, she'd had to endure a probationary period before being hired on. Last year she'd been promoted to deputy coroner, the county exhibiting a burst of atypical wisdom.

She's single, rides horses for recreation, and that's about all I know about her, personally. Work-wise, she's brilliant, inevitably cheerful and tireless, never hides behind jargon.

She hugged both of us and settled behind a desk piled neatly with files. "Good to see you guys."

"Same here," said Milo. "You scared me with that 'interesting' bit."

Basia let the grin spread. "As the psychopaths like to say, it is what it is."

Lifting the thickest file, she hefted but didn't open.

"First, your female victim, Ms. Gannett. No big surprises there, well nourished and in good health before the murder. Death from blood loss caused by a single incised wound to the left side of the neck. Likely a right-handed assailant coming from behind. The carotid and jugular were both severed and when I retracted the skin flaps, some spine was immediately visible."

"Deep cut," said Milo.

"Deep and inflicted with considerable force," said Basia. "That could imply rage but the lack of overkill makes me wonder. Alex?"

I said, "Maybe focused rage. Stew on it, devise a plan, put it into action."

Basia considered that. "So you're okay with premeditation despite use of an opportunistic weapon?"

Milo flourished a hand at me.

I said, "Every kitchen has knives."

"Hmm . . . interesting. The opportunistic attacks I've seen have tended to be frenzied and far less organized so yes, you're making sense. In any event, whatever struggle took place was minimal, her defensive wounds were comparatively shallow. Now on to your male victim, still unidentified."

Milo said, "Damn. His prints still haven't matched anything?"

"Unfortunately, no." Basia flipped the file open, read for several moments, and closed it.

"Apparently he's got no criminal history or a job that required him to get printed. At this point, he's John Doe Number Twenty-Three. But don't despair, the interesting part is what his body tells us."

Milo scooched forward, pad and pen at the ready.

Basia said, "The first thing I noticed was how atypical his wounds were for someone interacting with a motor vehicle, especially such a large one."

"No damage except the head."

"Exactly. When people confront an oncoming force of that magnitude, the tendency is for the body to fly upward and travel along the hood toward the windshield. That causes significant injury to the entire front of the body—knees, ankles, wrists, ribs, face. This gentleman had none of that, just, as you said, damage to his face, with a slight bias toward the right side. In addition to that, the photos I saw indicate relatively minimal damage to the van's bumper, suggesting a single carom-like bounce. As if he'd been propelled toward the van."

Milo said, "Pushed in front of it."

"That was my initial assumption. Then as I continued to examine the body, something else interesting arose. In addition to the frontal damage, there's a single crushing blow at the back of his skull, along the lower edge of the occipital bone. Just above the foramen magnum, where the spine enters the skull. With the major damage being frontal, I found that placement puzzling. How could he incur such serious frontal damage then bounce back and get in dorsally? Theoretically, I suppose it could be due to a fall backward after impact with the back of the head bouncing on the sidewalk. But there's no scraping at all to the rest of his dorsal skull. The other theoretical possibility is he spun in some weird way and incurred damage to both front and back. But neither feels right to me, especially the spinning scenario."

Milo scrawled rapidly. Basia waited until his pen paused.

"Another point of interest: The wounds look markedly different. The facial damage is raw and ragged and fits the shape of the section of the bumper that's bloodstained. The rear wound is a single patch of broken skin surrounded by significant swelling out of which blood had leaked."

"Leaked not spurted?"

"Exactly," she said. "There's all sorts of important stuff running through the foramen magnum. Arteries, membranes, ligaments, a major nerve. When I dissected I found no damage to any of that but there was major edema in and around the brain stem. That's lower brain, it controls respiration."

"A blow could be fatal," said Milo.

"Easily. And quickly. At that point I began wondering if he was dead before he hit the van. Then the blood work from the kitchen and the driveway came in and that clinched it. Most of it was his, and the relatively sparse amount plus the low-impact dripping is consistent with a single, blunt-force impact that shut off his vital functions without causing extensive gushing. So the obvious question is, how did a dead person encounter the van?"

"Like you said, shoved into it," said Milo.

Basia nodded. "Carried outside and flung. Possibly to obscure the fatal head wound."

"Any idea what he was bashed with and where?"

"Where is easy," she said. "Some blood trickle appeared close to the couch where he was sleeping and continued across the living room and into the kitchen."

Milo said, "I didn't see anything on the couch or the living room."

"Not on the couch, near it. Consistent with being on his stomach asleep and hanging slightly over the edge. The reason you didn't see it was because it was faint—pinpoints. They grew progressively larger as the body was carried. But still, no major blood. Detective Reed is to be commended for noticing the spatter in the driveway."

"One good blow but not a bloody attack."

"But fatal nonetheless," said Basia. "If you wanted to pick one spot to bash lethally, it would be right there."

"Got it."

Basia said, "You're not surprised by any of this?"

"His not being the bad guy is one of the contingencies we considered."

"Then good for you, it surprised me. You get a man versus van, you figure man versus van."

She sighed. "Yet another humbling lesson in the evils of assumption. In terms of the weapon, the only thing I can tell you is it did its job without shattering the occiput. There is a certain finesse to that."

I said, "So nothing like a baseball bat."

"No way, Alex. A bat would've shattered the skull like an eggshell. Something smaller and lighter but dense."

"Maybe one of those retractable batons."

"Sure. Or a piece of pipe. Though we found no metallic residue so the hard plastic of a baton is a possibility."

Milo said, "Or a good old-fashioned leather sap."

Basia said, "I saw a few of those in Warsaw, not yet, here."

"Last one I saw was at the academy museum," he said, tenting his fingers. "Guy's snoozing, one good whack, lights out, he's hauled out to the street and is made to go airborne."

"You do have a way with words. In terms of no blood on the couch, it's also possible bleeding didn't begin until he was up on his feet and gravity took over. It really is a small wound for something that lethal. The cause of death was compression, not blood loss."

I said, "Most of the blood in the kitchen and on the driveway was his but not all."

Basia faux-pouted. "There goes my drama."

She thumbed pages in the file. "The blood typing is where you really got lucky. Ms. Gannett is A positive and the male victim is O positive so drawing a distinction between them is simple. The pool around her body is hers alone. While most of the trickle in the driveway is his, a small quantity of hers is mixed in."

I said, "It traveled on the soles of the killer's shoes."

"Most likely. We know it isn't the killer's blood—one of those slippage things you get in cuttings—because we found a third sample of blood in the kitchen and now you *really* get lucky. Also O positive so easy enough to assume it was the male victim's. But you know me, neurotic. Lacking DNA data and with the certainty of a third person present, I ran some subtests and found that the second O-positive sample had different HLA characteristics than that of the male victim. We double-checked the knife to make sure we hadn't missed slippage blood and confirmed there was none. So your bad guy likely brushed against something in the house before hauling the male victim outside. I've already sent the techs back to check, instructed them to concentrate on the kitchen. Hold on."

She punched a preset on her desk phone. "Hello, Roosevelt? This is Dr. Lopatinski . . . already? Wow, that's great. Take tons of photos and send them to me as soon as you can. Thank you, thank you, thank you."

She laid the phone in its cradle, flashed the full-on face-splitting smile. "They just found the point of contact. Not in the kitchen, on the way *out* of the kitchen. An edge of the metal insulation strip around the door is cracked and the edges are burred—tiny metal thorns and on several of them was O-positive blood and I'll lay odds the HLA will confirm that all or most of it is your perpetrator's."

Milo said, "Not neurotic. Brilliant."

"You're too kind, Lieutenant."

I said, "The male victim is a small guy but factoring in deadweight and distance, we're talking about considerable effort to transport him a hundred or so feet. You're moving quickly in the dark, it's easy to brush up against something."

Without consulting the file, Basia said, "He's five-five, a hundred thirty-one pounds. Toting him would be about the same as carrying a medium-sized woman."

Milo said, "Bride over the threshold. If they still do that."

The three of us, unmarried. No one with a ready answer.

I said, "Adrenaline would help but so would superior strength."

Milo said, "Hoffgarden."

Basia said, "Who?"

He explained briefly.

She said, "A weight lifter? Piece of cake. He could toss it at the van like a used tissue."

Milo said, "In terms of I.D., any way to get a facial reconstruction?"

"Sorry, no. The facial bones were pulverized by the collision and many were detached. Some actually fell out of the wounds when I was working—little splinters and chips. I sent radiographs to the three artists I use and all of them agreed there was too much damage to create anything useful. There are people out there who'd claim they could reconstruct but I wouldn't trust them or what they produced."

"Anything from the organs and the toxicology?"

"Ms. Gannett had what looks to be partially digested chicken salad in her stomach plus a small amount of pale alcoholic liquid, probably white wine. Her blood alcohol came in at .03, which is basically nothing. Your male victim had some sort of vegetable concoction in his gut and the same beverage but a lot more of it. His B.A. was .16. At his weight, I'd guess at least three glasses, though people differ in their ability to metabolize. No drugs in either of them."

I said, "They drank together but had separate dinners?"

"Or," said Basia, "they sent out for different take-out meals and ate together. Did you find any evidence of that?"

Milo said, "Not that I saw. Hold on."

He phoned Reed, got a quick answer. "Nada."

Basia said, "So you could be right, Alex. They ate before they got together, he came over, they drank. But that seems to be all they did. No recent sexual activity for either of them."

I said, "Platonic sleepover."

Milo said, "How long to get DNA on the two male samples?"

Basia said, "Last time I checked, ETA was twelve to twenty weeks."

"I thought they'd gotten more efficient."

"There's a cold-case serial from Merced County taking up a lot of lab time."

Milo said, "Yeah, I heard about it, bodies in the forest, no leads. They make any progress?"

"From what I hear, not yet," she said.

"And here I am, just a piker with two fresh bodies."

"I'll put the request in today and ask for priority."

"Deeply appreciated. What's the print situation?"

"Still waiting on the lab for latents lifted at the house. We rolled your male victim here. I know he didn't match because I cajoled someone I know at DOJ to do a quick AFIS."

"Maybe that same Samaritan's cajolable on the DNA."

Basia laughed. "Push, push, push. You remind me of my father and my professors in Warsaw. If you weren't Irish, I'd wonder if we were related. So, this is a curious one, no? Two victims, two weapons, three if you count improvising with the van. Any psychological insights, Alex?"

I said, "Nothing close to insight, just what-ifs."

Both of them sat back.

I said, "Cordi Gannett was likely the primary target of a well-planned execution. The killer sneaked into the house after dark, took a knife from her kitchen, and advanced toward the bedroom where he expected to find her. On the way, he came upon John Doe, sleeping on the couch, dispatched him quickly with some sort of blunt weapon well aimed."

Milo said, "He's got the knife in hand, why not just cut the guy?"

"Maybe there was something symbolic about using a blade and he was saving it for Cordi. Or he figured a quick, hard blow to the head would be quieter and less likely to cause a struggle."

Basia said, "Impatient because he's lusting for the main kill."

Milo said, "Talk about a way with words. But yeah, makes sense."

I said, "He planned to kill Cordi in her bedroom but she surprised him by coming downstairs so he dispatched her in the hallway. The orderliness of the scene tells us he spent time in the house cleaning up and making sure he didn't leave footprints or other evidence. That could've given him time to think about John Doe and deciding to use him as a distraction."

"Staging it as a psycho murder-suicide," said Milo. "John Doe being naked would've helped the crazed-killer image. He totes the poor guy outside. Along with John's clothing and I.D, which he stashes somewhere we still haven't found."

Basia said, "I can see staging it as an unclad, mentally deranged person stalking the neighborhood and finally deciding to destroy himself. But with that single wound to the back of the head, suicide would be out of the question so he had to use the van."

I said, "Or he planned to take the body somewhere and stage differently. Then the van showed up and he saw it as an opportunity."

Milo said, "Stage differently, how?"

"Shoot him and pose it like suicide."

"Why not do that in the house?"

I said, "The noise made it too risky. Especially in the early-morning hours, everyone sleeping in a quiet neighborhood."

He said, "The van was a lucky break. Cut short how far he needed to take the body."

"And obliterated the clubbing."

Milo grinned at Basia. "Unfortunately for him, someone was paying attention."

She blushed and thumbed the edges of the file. "Now I have a question for you, Alex. The intention to kill her in the bedroom, are we talking a sexual crime? There were no signs of assault."

I said, "The act of stabbing can be sexual but impossible to say."

Milo said, "We've seen a few of those moon-howlers, the knife's a—what do you call it, Alex?"

"Surrogate weapon," I said. "On the other hand, the bedroom could simply have been the place he expected to find her."

She smiled. "He's the psychologist and he avoids psychologizing."

"Tell me about it," said Milo. "I sweat to get every drop of wisdom. Anyway, however we put it together, we've got someone who likely knew Cordi, was familiar with her house and strong enough to subdue her and to shot-put a little guy like John Doe straight at a moving vehicle. And that fits someone we know."

Basia said, "Mr. Hoffgarden with his anger issues."

"He's six-four, works out for a living. And maybe has another homicide under his belt."

He told her about Forrest Slope.

She said, "Wow."

"The good news is he's got an arrest record. Get me DNA from that second O donor and once I find the guy I'll either have grounds for a sample warrant or I'll go the discarded coffee cup route."

"Maybe the organic juice cup route," said Basia. "Seeing as he's a fitness type."

18

As we stood to leave Basia's office, Milo said, "When you have a chance, a copy of your findings would be great."

She opened a desk drawer and drew out a manila envelope. "I had a chance."

"Thanks a mil. And when you can—"

"Talk to the DOJ, I will pester them." She walked around her desk and patted his shoulder. "I'll walk you out. Fresh air's always welcome."

She stood gazing at the parking lot and past it, at the looming bulk of the county complex. Was still there as we slipped out of view.

Milo said, "Amazing human being. One day some private outfit will probably offer her mega-bucks and I'll have to settle for a mere mortal. So what do you think?"

I said, "I think it firms up what we already suspected. John Doe unlucky and got used as a prop."

He nodded. "This is a very bad person we're talking about. Smart, too, at least in the calculating criminal sense. You've spent time with Hoffgarden. Is he bright?"

"He didn't come across particularly clever or dull but I didn't give him an IQ test."

"You do that with the parents?"

"I was kidding. We actually didn't talk much because he was detached from his daughter and bored with the evaluation process."

"Wanting the gym, not custody," he said. "Using his own *kid* as a prop. Interesting, no?"

I nodded.

"Something else," he said. "You always say people go for the familiar even if it's destructive. So a guy with lousy daddy skills might've appealed to someone like Cordi, no? Then maybe she smartened up and rejected him and he didn't like it."

"Could be."

He said, "Not a rousing vote of confidence. Am I off base?"

"Not at all," I said. "Just digesting. Given my history with Hoffgarden, I can't be there when you interview him but I'd sure like to observe once you've got him in a room."

"When, not if."

"There's your vote of confidence."

"Hmmph. Meanwhile, I've still got an unknown victim and you heard what Basia said about facial reconstruction. Any suggestions?"

"When we considered John Doe as a suspect we framed his sleeping on the couch as possible evidence of a spat. Now we know nothing sexual happened so maybe he was just a friend without benefits."

"Platonic sleepover." He laughed. "Sounds like the name of an indie band. The media blitz is bound to come. Best case, someone who knew them both will come forward."

He drove a bit more, checked Waze at the next red light. All the freeways pointing westward were snarled heavier than when we'd arrived.

"City of Angels," he said. "Okay, let's try for the best room in hell."

◆

I commandeered Waze and we began a homeward trek through sad, gray miles of warehouses, fast-food joints, knock-up apartments, and geriatric frame houses in varying states of decay.

A tedious mile later, approaching another red on an access road lined with dumpsters, he sailed through and continued way above the speed limit.

I said, "Scofflaw."

"Executive privilege. Any sign of the thought police?"

"What do they look like?"

"Tight-lipped, tight-eyed, tight-assed gnomes clutching reg books and rubber stamps. Not in view?"

"Not unless they're hiding in the trash."

"You never know," he said. "Okay. Time for more theory. As a member of a sexual minority, I'm self-designating as being permitted to suggest that a platonic relationship between a male and a good-looking female might have significance."

I said, "John Doe was gay?"

"It's worth considering, no? And to make matters even more boorishly insensitive, I'm now going to wonder out loud about a stereotypic gay occupation."

"Homicide detective?"

He fought laughter, lost, sputtered, took a moment to recover.

"The department *has* made progress and I haven't gotten hate mail in my locker for a long time," he said. "But I was thinking more on the lines of hairdresser, maybe one of those fashion stylists. Because Cordi's goal was to become a mega-bucks online celeb. Plus she had modeling experience. So I can see her using someone to help her look her best."

I said, "Good point and so far, other than dating Hoffgarden two years ago, we haven't found any romantic connections. So maybe she was avoiding intimacy in order to concentrate on her career. If so, a gay man would've been a great candidate for friendship."

I pulled out my phone. "Here's her website . . . at the bottom of the homepage there are two small-print credits. The company that set up the site and someone named Caspian D who she thanks for 'helping me to achieve my personal best.'"

I keyworded *caspian d hairdresser* and pulled up five hits on a "master stylist" named Caspian Delage. All were tributes from people identified by their initials. Gushing posts praised Delage's "wizardry." One rater tagged him a "hair god."

I searched for Delage's website, found only a couple of pages of Instagram photos. Nearly all were headshots of good-looking young women sporting an impressive variety of hairstyles. But two in the center, slightly larger, featured a young man in a black T-shirt with a pale roundish face and a wry smile. His own hair had been shaped high and swirly on top, like a brunette cockscomb.

I enlarged one of the images and showed it to Milo.

His jaw set. "Narrow shoulders . . . right age . . . definite possibility. What's his address?"

"None listed," I said. "Hours by appointment, contact via email or a phone number. Nine-three-two exchange, probably a cell."

I tried the number and switched to speaker. Two rings, then a pleasant boyish voice.

Hi, this is Caspian. I'm out beautifying the world. Love to hear about your aesthetic conundrums and tricho-anxiety so leave a message and I'll most certainly get back to you. Ex-Oh-Ex-Oh-Ex.

Milo said, "Trick anxiety?"

"Tricho." I spelled it. "Related to hair."

"Guy knows Latin?"

Greek derivation but no sense belaboring it. I said, "Maybe he had a classical education."

He said, "Speaking of education, barbers and stylists need a license. Basia just told us there were no prints on file."

I checked the state regulations for cosmetologists. "Plenty of other requirements but being printed isn't listed as one of them. One good thing: If he is licensed, there'll be an address for him."

"If? He could be winging it? Like Cordi?"

"Lots of laws in California," I said. "It can lead to improvisation."

Dumpster Drive gave way to a residential neighborhood overshadowed by a dizzying series of looping freeway ramps seemingly at battle with one another. Treeless streets were lined with shoebox multi-units. Landscaping was an alien concept.

Not a human in sight. City of the dead.

Milo pulled to the curb, worked his phone, gave a thumbs-up.

"Looks like ol' Caspian didn't always improvise. He got licensed five years ago but let it expire three years ago. Last place of employment was The Go-For-It Salon on Sunset . . . just east of San Vicente. Right on the way home once we enter purgatory."

Five miles north to Sunset took thirty-five minutes. Go-For-It Unisex sat on the north side of Sunset between a smoke shop and a laser-removal/spray-tan outfit. Time to mellow out and achieve your personal, honey-baked best.

Milo pulled into a red zone. "Stay here and guard the car against the meter Nazis."

I said, "Happy to try but what's my leverage?"

"Dazzle them with psychology. That doesn't work, drive away before they get out their little handheld, then circle around for as long as you need to and pick me up."

A civilian driving a police vehicle was utterly illegal. This was the second time in a year he'd had me do it.

I said, "Sure."

He hopped out of the unmarked, strode to the salon, was inside for less than a minute before emerging shaking his head.

Just as he made it to the driver's door, a gangly West Hollywood meter cop rolled up in a golf cart and stepped out looking hungry.

Milo saluted, gave the wolf grin, said "Thanks for your service," and flashed his badge at the guy's gaping mouth as we traded places.

"Sir," said the parking enforcer. Pimply with a gaping mouth. He looked to be around fourteen.

"I know, amigo, it's a red zone. As in blood. As in we're investigating multiple murder. Appreciate your cooperation."

Gunning the engine, he pulled into the westbound traffic stream, cursing silently.

I said, "Delage no longer works there."

"No one has any idea who the hell he is. All the barbers are free-lancers, longest any of them has been there is a seasoned veteran hand of eleven months. She said the place was sold two months after she arrived to a group based in San Diego that has a bunch of other facilities. One thing, though, there's a little cooler next to the register. Free beer while you wait."

"Thinking of trying it out?"

"The thought occurred. Anyway, no brick-and-mortar workplace fits with Delage going to clients' houses. The night of the murder, there were no signs he'd cut Cordi's hair so it's definitely looking like a social visit. So maybe just like you said, her new BFF, she was the target, he was unlucky. Let's pray for the whole mess to go public soon and kick something up. I'll get you home."

At a light near the Roxy, he said, "There's still the databases to run Delage through. Your computer's faster than mine. Mind if I bop in for a sec, see if I can learn anything about The Hair God?"

I said, "*Mi casa es su* research facility."

And *su* cafeteria. I phoned Robin.

She said, "Hi, handsome. When are you coming home?"

"On the way."

"Great. I felt uncharacteristically domestic so I'm going to fix us a nice dinner."

"Looking forward to it," I said. "Milo wants to do some work in my office."

"Got it," she said. "Take out an extra steak. Or two."

There's nothing like a dog to make you feel appreciated.

When I get home and Blanche is in the main house, she runs up to greet me as if we've been separated for eons. When she didn't show herself, I figured she was out in Robin's studio. Then I smelled kitchen aromas and got it: Devotion has its limits.

The table was set, complete with pitcher of ice water and a bottle of Rioja.

"Hi, guys." Robin stood over the range, managing two skillets as she pan-seared massive slabs of beef.

Blanche sat at her feet, beatific expression on her flat face. Messiah's arrival was imminent.

Milo's eyes took on a similar glow as they shifted to the steaks. Counting.

Robin turned and smiled and winked.

He said, "You shouldn't have."

"I'll call you when it's ready, do what you need to do."

He kissed her cheek. I kissed her lips.

Blanche ignored both of us and kept her nose on the prize.

◆

During the eight minutes it took to set up dinner, Milo had conducted enough research to learn that no database recognized the existence of Caspian Delage.

He entered the kitchen, announcing and grumbling. But discontent melted at the sight of rib eyes, pasta salad, Romaine tossed with olive oil, salt, and pepper.

Before his butt had hit the chair, Robin had forked the largest steak onto his plate.

He settled heavily. "This thing is massive. No room left for veggies. I love you madly."

She brought him a second plate. "Just in case chlorophyll beckons."

Blanche knows where to go for handouts and stuck by my ankles as I sneaked her bits of meat. She accepted the offerings with a soft mouth, licked my fingertips after swallowing, swooned and pressed her head against my shin.

Robin said, "I know what's going on down there."

I said, "Whatever it takes to get some love. Want me to stop?"

"No, she's had two nice walks and was a patient little girl while I worked, so she deserves some upgrading. Just keep it reasonable, darling."

She turned to Milo. "Caspian Delage sounded phony to me the moment I heard it. Like something plucked from a movie. Or random words."

He said, "The Caspian's a sea, don't know about Delage."

"A French car manufactured a while back," she said. "Up to the fifties I think."

Milo wiped his mouth with a napkin. "Didn't know you were a motorhead."

"I'm not," she said. "One of my clients drove one. This was years ago, Brian Bonnaro."

Milo looked at me. I shrugged.

Robin said, "Hair-band star for about five minutes. He went into real estate, bought himself all kinds of toys, including a bunch of vintage cars. I remember the Delage because I'd never heard of it. He offered to give me a ride."

"Ah," said Milo.

"Nothing to ah about, Big Guy, I declined. He was staggering at the time. All the time. That plus the way he'd tortured his guitar told me his motor coordination was shot. But it was a pretty thing, a blue convertible. So maybe your hairdresser also had an interest in fine motoring."

Milo said, "If we're talking mega-bucks, maybe a theoretical interest."

I said, "Or he just liked the sound of Delage."

Robin said, "French does have that elegant connotation. Well, maybe you can find a name change application for him."

Milo said, "Already tried. No one bothers anymore, you don't have to. And this guy, even if he had to, probably wouldn't. He's been working without a license for years."

"The shadow economy," she said.

"Alex puts it down to too many rules."

"That and people get lazy. There's another steak once you finish that one."

"Thanks, but even I have discretion."

He'd gotten three massive bites down when his phone beeped a text. "'Scuse." He got up and walked back to my office.

When he was out of earshot, Robin said, "In the middle of a meal? Must be important."

During Milo's absence I thought about Cordi Gannett and Caspian Delage reinventing themselves. L.A.'s the place for that, a company town where illusion's the commodity and the best pretenders become the elite. The city sprawls westward manically until it confronts the Pacific. Last chance for a new persona before you hit the edge of the continent.

So many people intent on burying the past. All those abandoned identities moldering in psychological graves.

The real city of the dead.

Robin said, "What's on your mind, baby?"

"Great meal."

She let it pass and filled my glass. Sometimes a great relationship depends on not challenging falsehood.

I smiled and held her hand and took a long, slow swallow of Spanish wine.

Milo returned to the kitchen, looking straighter and taller.

"Sorry for the interruption. I put an alert on to let me know when anything about Cordi shows up and it buzzed. Nothing in the newspapers or the networks but the e-citizenry is weighing in."

I said, "Anything of value?"

"Mostly the usual fast-and-loose." He ticked his fingers. "Cordi was a psychologist, a psychiatrist, a sociologist, a professor of human relations. One genius confidently offered that she'd once taught at Yale. Obviously, *he* hadn't. But tucked in with all the bullshit was one post that sounded as if the person actually knew Cordi and, God bless her, she left her real name. Turns out, she's a makeup artist Cordi used for some of her videos and, double halo, she answered her phone. Poor thing was pretty shaken up about Cordi and she got really worked up when I described about Delage, she knew him, had to take a cry break before getting back to me."

"She knew him, as well?"

"Through working on Cordi. She has no idea what his real name is, though she thought it might be Charles something. I asked her to meet me and she said sure and gave me her address. Tomorrow morning at ten. I also asked her—her name's Shari Benedetto—to post about Delage and see if anyone knew him and she said she would."

"Model citizen," I said.

"Without them, I'd be toast."

20

Shari Benedetto seemed to be one of those trusting souls parents worry about.

She'd accepted Milo's story without asking questions and agreed to meet at her apartment on Fountain Avenue in West Hollywood.

Lovely old Spanish building just east of La Cienega, mercifully preserved and beautifully maintained. Easy entry from the street, no security of any sort.

Two stories of units formed a C around a courtyard edged by ferns and sagos and palms and centered by a blue-tiled fountain that spat glassy bits of spray into the morning sun.

Shari Benedetto's unit was in the central arm of the C, on the second floor, accessed by wide, stone steps. A bronze-framed peephole formed an eye in the carved, varnished door but no movement behind it before the door opened on a beautiful woman around thirty.

Not bothering to check.

"Lieutenant?"

"Ms. Benedetto. Thanks for seeing us."

"Of course."

Shari Benedetto had long, gleaming, black, side-parted hair that enhanced an olive, heart-shaped face. A baggy, gray cashmere sweater hung to the knees of black leggings. Her feet were bare. A gold ring banded the big toe on her left foot. Other than that, no adornment.

Her eyes were wide-set and nearly as dark as her hair and fringed by long, curving lashes. Pretty eyes but a bit blurred by fatigue. If she was wearing any makeup besides mascara, I couldn't tell. In her line of work, maybe the mark of professionalism.

As if making a sudden decision, she shot her hand out toward Milo's. They shook briefly then she looked at me.

"Alex."

"Hello, Alex." Soft fingers touched mine and retracted. She ushered us in.

A tiny front space was set up with minimalist furniture and abstract art prints biased toward gray and black. A single doorway to the right made me think of the place where Cordi Gannett had died.

The front area was an ode to multitasking: sitting, dining, and whatever cooking you could pull off in an open kitchenette the size of a broom closet. Clear counters and the absence of food smells said no recent attempts.

The almost-home of someone prone to frequent absences.

The sitting part was assigned to a six-foot, white leather couch with red metal legs, the obvious place for us, and a black leather sling-back chair where Shari Benedetto settled gracefully and faced us, legs crossed yoga-style. Her palms lowered to her knees and her eyelids fluttered. But she kept her eyes open and curious.

The couch was as soft as concrete. Milo did a fine job of looking comfortable. "Thanks for meeting with us, ma'am."

She mouthed, "Ma'am." Amused by the word, as are lots of young women. "Of course. I'd offer you something but I've been traveling and there's nothing in the house."

"Out on a shoot?"

She nodded. "A pilot filmed in Vancouver. I got to see a trained grizzly bear do some pretty amazing stunts."

As Milo took out his pad, a sleek black cat with onyx eyes glided in from the doorway. Crossing the room with confidence, it jumped up effortlessly and sank into Shari Benedetto's lap.

Feline in silent repose, but studying us with an expression that evoked a genetic link to panthers and leopards.

Milo said, "Nice cat."

"To me," said Shari Benedetto. "Boris has been known to get aggressive with other people."

I wondered if the presence of an attack cat explained her trust level. Hopefully not; I knew of pit bulls and rottweilers who'd faced off against guns or knives and ended up as vital as stuffed animals.

Milo said, "Guess we'll have to be on our best behavior."

Shari Benedetto smiled weakly and let out two puffs of exhalation.

"Mindfulness," she said. "Cordi's actually the one who told me about it."

"May I ask if you were her—"

"Client? No. We just used to talk while I was prepping her for some of her videos."

"Some but not all?"

"Just some," she said. "I travel a lot. If I was in town, I'd help her. That's actually where I met Caspian. He was doing her hair. And by the way, his real name is Charlie Baxter."

Milo's pen danced. "Really. How'd you find out?"

"By posting like you said. No one knew except one of my friends, also a makeup artist, who worked with him on an MTV shoot years ago. He told her his real name was Charlie Baxter and that he hated it and decided to go exotic."

Milo scrawled some more. "Thanks, that's super-helpful. Would she be willing to talk to us?"

"Mariah's in Singapore working on a film and was definite about that being all she knew. We both agreed that we liked Caspian but neither of us was close to him."

"Is there anything you can tell us about him? Or Cordi."

"From the little I saw, he was sweet, very soft-spoken." She sniffed back tears. "So terrible, a sweet guy like him . . . no, there really isn't anything beyond that, Lieutenant. Basically, the three of us would chitchat when he was doing her hair and I was waiting around to touch her up. I did work with him on a couple of other jobs but not by plan and only a couple. Both were private parties. A woman from Encino who wanted to be one of the Real Housewives had me tart her up." She stuck out her tongue. "Another woman from Brentwood wanted to surprise her husband on their anniversary with a tattoo and a makeover."

I said, "You travel a lot."

"All the time. Mostly in Canada because it's cheaper to shoot there, but also in New Mexico and Utah and South Dakota."

I said, "You do a lot of westerns?"

She smiled. "Good guess. Yeah, they're coming back. Bears and wolves and actors trying to be cowboys. Most of my time is spent making people look like they never used sunscreen but still stayed gorgeous."

"Do you know if Caspian took jobs out of town?"

"Couldn't tell you," she said. "He was easy to talk to but never revealed much about himself. In our business that helps. People want it to be all about them."

Milo said, "Like being a therapist."

"We probably hear more juicy stuff than most therapists."

Back when I was in grad school, a professor had proposed giving bartenders and barbers a few courses in active listening and client-centered therapy. No progress on the project that I'd ever heard, but he had a good point.

I said, "So Caspian was easy to talk to but private."

"He was easygoing, period. Which was part of his being great with hair. He didn't try to push his ego on people. He took the time to find out about them so he could learn what they were after and give it to them."

That synced with the varying hairdos on the Instagram pages.

I thought of gentle, agreeable Caspian Delage, sinking into wine-enhanced sleep and never waking up.

Brain stem destroyed, then hurled like garbage at a lumbering beast of a vehicle.

Shari Benedetto sniffed back tears. "They didn't deserve it. Who would do this, guys?"

Milo said, "Wish we could answer that. But your help identifying Caspian gets us closer."

"Good," she said. "I felt so hopeless. Hearing about it. Can you tell me where it happened? No one seems to know."

"In Cordi's house."

A hand shot to her mouth. "Oh my God, that's my worst nightmare. Every time I come home after being away, it's like approaching a strange place. So first I go and collect Boris from Mrs. Lipschitz, my neighbor down below. She's around ninety and has lost eight cats to cancer or gout or whatever and Boris must sense her neediness because he's super obedient with her."

She stroked black fur. "*Aren't* you, little *man?*"

The cat purred, shut its eyes, sank lower.

"Goo-*boy,* you *rest.* So I get Boris and check with Mrs. Lipschitz if anything weird has happened. One time there was a suspected burglar, so I called West Hollywood Sheriff's to see if there was anything I should know and they said they caught someone who was probably him. After Mrs. Lipschitz, I check my camera feed on my phone, then I make sure the alarm's still set and I untrigger it on my phone. *Then* I step in."

Milo said, "Impressive." He scanned the room.

Shari Benedetto smiled. "Looking for the cameras? The first one's right in the peephole. Then there are two magnets on the fridge and in two of the lamps. In my bedroom, I've got six more plus a motion detector. The alarm code's on my phone but there's also a keypad in my bedroom closet and both have a two-digit panic number."

"Beyond impressive."

"My dad's idea, he insisted. He's a Broward County sheriff in Florida. Didn't want me to leave until I put together what he approved of as an adequate security plan. When I got off the phone with you, I called him and he checked you out. If you'd have been hinky, I'd have called the cops."

Her fingers danced just above Boris's spine. "What kind of security did Cordi have?"

"Nothing like yours."

"It happening in her house, does that mean probably someone she knew?"

Milo said, "We're nowhere near theorizing."

She nodded. "That's what my dad says. Assume means make an ass of you and me."

Something her security setup had illustrated brilliantly.

She uncrossed her legs, stretched them in front, retracted, placed her feet on the floor and her hands back in her lap.

No more fatigue in her eyes. Talking about frightening things can do that.

I said, "Caspian didn't talk about himself much. Did Cordi?"

"Oh yeah, all the time. But not about being afraid of anyone. I have to say, to me she always came across pretty frickin' fearless." She looked away. "Guess that wasn't the best approach."

I said, "Fearless as in risk-taking?"

"I can't tell you anything specific, it's just a feeling I had. Like she wanted to conquer the world and would do what it takes."

"What about her dating life?"

"I never heard about one. She never got personal, it was all about her career, how excited she was about her videos, why she wanted a specific look. Like, check me out today, I'm a professor type. That kind of thing."

"She had serious professional goals."

"Oh, definitely. She thought she'd found the perfect way with her videos. But that's risky, isn't it? Put yourself out there and talk about emotional issues to a world of strangers? It's bound to attract at least some crazies."

I nodded. "Did she ever mention anyone bothering her?"

"No, she was always up. Full of positive energy."

"How about guys in the past? Someone she'd cut off."

"Hmm," she said. "She did hint around about when she was younger she'd made mistakes. Tied it in with her mom, who she said had a total thing for wrong guys."

"What else did she say about her mom?"

"It was pretty clear they had issues," she said. "I mean it's not like her mom came up as a frequent topic. But when Cordi did mention her it was to point out the wrong thing to do. It's something she was planning to do in a video."

"Talk about her mom."

"Yes, but she said she wasn't ready."

"Afraid of causing conflict with her mom?"

"I guess."

"Did she mention any other family members?"

Shari Benedetto thought. "Not to me. And when her mom did come up it was basically pre-shoot talk. Caspian's blow-drying her and she's like 'My mom had low self-esteem so she gravitated'—that was a favorite word of Cordi's, gravitated, gravitational pull—'she gravitated toward losers. And that's what I'm going to discuss today.'"

I said, "She used her mother as source material but didn't mention her."

"Exactly."

"And she told you when she was younger, she'd made some of the same mistakes."

Emphatic nod. "That was a topic on one of the videos I worked on. How to get away from old patterns. Cordi was a very wise person."

Milo said, "No hint someone from her past had reappeared."

Shari Benedetto's dark eyes widened. "That would be scary, wouldn't it? Like one of those slasher movies?" Her voice caught. "This isn't a movie. This is frickin' real."

CHAPTER

21

We sat with Shari Benedetto awhile longer, rephrasing questions we'd already asked in a way that wouldn't seem repetitive or manipulative.

Boris the cat began viewing us with increased suspicion but the woman he loved remained pleasant, bright, and eager to help. When we left, Milo thanked her and used his best smile but the moment the door closed behind us, he was downcast.

When we were back in the car, he said, "Nice kid but she told us zilch. Unless you think the tension between Cordi and mom coulda led to something."

"Big stretch, doubtful," I said. "One thing, though. When you looked at her phone directory it was all businesses and that fits with what we just heard. She didn't have an extensive social life, was obsessed with success. Caspian went from doing her hair to being close enough to sleep over. Maybe he's on her contacts list as Hair or something similar. That means you'll be able to pinpoint when the two of them spoke. More important, there could be other mixed listings."

"The friendly plumber gets too friendly and things go bad."

"She wasn't one for boundaries."

He chewed his cheek and phoned Moe Reed.

The young D said, "Just about to call you, L.T. Alicia and Sean are both back, I filled them in. So far they haven't picked up any 211s or other minor stuff and they're gung-ho to help."

"Perfect timing, Moses." He gave Reed Caspian Delage's possible real name. "Start digging on that, if you confirm, let me know A-sap. Also, Alex raised an interesting point about Cordi's phone. It might tell us more than we thought so get it from the evidence room and have a look." He explained my theory.

Reed said, "Interesting point, I'll give it a go."

"For all we know Hoffgarden's also in there under Health or Exercise or whatever. And speaking of Cordi's phone, any progress from her carrier on the complete records?"

"Not yet," said Reed.

"Then there's another assignment for whoever can take it. Also, give Hoffgarden's landlady a follow-up call on the off chance she's seen him since you were there. Nothing turns up on him by tomorrow, we'll go with the BOLO on his car."

"Landlady might be tough over the phone," said Reed. "Like I said, her English isn't great."

"Rely on charm."

Milo took La Cienega north to Sunset and drove through the Strip, passing the shop where Caspian Delage née Charles Baxter had once worked a chair.

Just before we reached Doheny Drive and where clubs, restaurants, and office buildings transitioned to stately ficus trees and gated estates lining Beverly Hills' share of Sunset, Reed called in and reported no sighting of Tyler Hoffgarden at home or anywhere else.

He's not one for long recitations but he kept talking, maybe to blunt any kill-the-messenger response from the boss. "I'm starting with the Baxter thing, Alicia's phoning the contacts, Sean's dealing with the carrier. I figured his patience level would sync well with being on hold."

"Psychology," said Milo. "Our favorite social science. And y'know what, get that BOLO rolling now."

At Sunset and Beverly Glen, his phone played Puccini's "O Mio Babbino Caro." More gorgeous music reduced to electronic beeps. It hurt my soul. One day I'd say something.

He said, "Who? You're kidding . . . okay, keep him there, I'll be there A-sap."

He clicked off. "As if it couldn't get any weirder."

I said, "Hoffgarden showed up?"

"Nope but Cordi's little brother did. Fifteen years old, walks up to the desk and asks for whoever's handling his sister's murder. If he witnessed anything, I'm allowed to talk to him without parental consent. I don't see it going over too well with Renata but if he did see something, I'm not turning him away. You mind a change in plans? As in being there?"

Detective II Alicia Bogomil and a blond boy waited near the locked door to Milo's office. If the thought was a woman would be softer with a minor, false assumption. Alicia's tough-minded, action-oriented, and doesn't suffer fools. I don't know if she rides horses, but with a rangy build, sharp eyes, a tight jawline, and weathering skin stretched across a handsome face, she brings to mind a veteran cowgirl.

One change since I'd last seen her. She clipped her long brown hair to ear length and tinted the edges pale blue. Maybe Al Freeman, her new boyfriend, liked it that way, maybe she just wanted a change. She wore a short gray bomber jacket tailored to accommodate her handgun, a black blouse, fitted black jeans, and black suede Chelsea boots. Tucked behind one ear was a pen. She studied her notepad, showed no interest in the boy.

He didn't seem to mind, working his phone with two busy thumbs.

Alicia saw us and said something to him. He looked up from his mini-screen, pocketed the phone, and watched us approach.

"Loo, this is Aaron. Aaron, Lieutenant Sturgis, he's in charge."

Aaron Blanding made eye contact with both of us in turn and nodded. Six feet tall or close, he was slope-shouldered, milky pale, lightly zitted, had his father's soft, bulky build.

Waxy blond hair long on top awned a tightly clipped side fade that jugged his ears. Huge dark-blue eyes and moist lips that failed to completely cover his incisors suggested a newborn calf. A bile-green polo shirt bore a single food stain above the navel; something tomato-based. Brown cargo pants sagged over graying white Vans. Give him a few decades and he might be a master of Milo-chic.

Milo said, "Hey, Aaron. Do your folks know you're here?"

"Of course not." The boy's metallic-edged voice began at alto, dropped to baritone, then cracked and ended up as something you couldn't characterize.

"Why of course?"

"They'd try to stop me so why would I tell them? Don't worry, Lieutenant Sturgis. I checked and you're allowed to talk to me without their consent because I'm here of my own volition."

Milo suppressed a smile. "You got yourself a legal opinion?"

"Wikipedia," said Aaron Blanding. "I find it for the most part accurate."

Milo unlocked the office door and swung it wide. "As you can see, there's no room for three of us in here, so how about we talk in one of the interview rooms."

The boy's eyes widened. "One of those dark places where you inter-rogate suspects?"

"Interview and interrogate," said Milo.

"What's the difference?"

"How we feel about the person we're talking to. And FYI, Aaron, no one uses dark rooms. That's movie bullsh— movie fantasy for visual drama."

"Oh." Grave expression, as if listening to a weighty lecture.

Milo said, "So you're okay with that?"

"Sure. I'm kind of looking forward to it."

"Then c'mon. Thanks, Detective Bogomil."

Alicia saluted and hurried off toward the stairs.

The three of us took the same route, Aaron Blanding walking be-tween Milo and me, bright-eyed and looking around like a spectator in an exotic zoo. Milo unlocked the second door we came to, switched on the lights, and began rearranging the layout from table in the corner meant to isolate and intimidate to three chairs arranged in an open triangle that said *We're all friends.*

"Sit wherever you like, Aaron. Can I get you something to drink?"

"No, thanks, Lieutenant Sturgis." Blue eyes studied fluorescent ceiling panels. "I see what you mean about light. Does it help?"

"Help with what?"

"Getting perpetrators to crack."

"Hmm," said Milo. "I guess if they come in already tired it might nudge them a little."

"So you didn't plan it that way."

"Personally? No. This is basically government one oh one."

Studious nod. "I should've known better. About the dark rooms. You're right, in the movies it's always dark with a spotlight shining down, but on the true-crime shows it's like this . . . one thing I've noticed is that guilty people often try to fall asleep before they're questioned. Why's that?"

Milo looked at me.

I said, "They're putting themselves in another place to avoid stress."

"A dissociative reaction," said Aaron. "That's a psychological term."

Milo said, "You know a lot about all kinds of things."

"Not really, sir. I know a little about as many things as I can find out. My dad calls it a mile wide and an inch deep, says it would make me a perfect politician but please don't go that route."

"Let me guess: He wants you to be a doctor."

"A physician," said Aaron. "But I don't like blood so I'm looking seriously at psychology."

Milo grinned. "Then guess what, my friend, you came to the right place. This is Dr. Delaware, our consulting psychologist."

The boy turned to me, wide-eyed. "Really? That's *exactly* what I'd like to do. Do you find it stimulating and fascinating?" He blushed. "Stupid question, why would you be here if you didn't?"

I smiled. "It can be intellectually challenging." *When it's not boring or terrifying.*

"Do you profile?"

"Not strictly speaking."

"What do you mean?"

"Official profiles stem from the information at hand. Let's say a profile is developed based on interviews with a group of incarcerated murderers. Which is exactly how the FBI started. They may not be representative of all murderers. On top of that, criminals lie. Most important, as new information comes in, patterns can shift. Not adjusting for that is called sampling error, Aaron. So anything too structured gives false confidence and raises the risk of a high error rate. Profiles get a lot of coverage. Kind of like dark rooms in movies. But they rarely solve crimes."

"So what does?"

"Hard work, open eyes and minds, and often a whole lot of luck."

"Hmm," he said. "Okay, that makes sense. So what *do* you do?"

"I start every case from scratch, avoid tunnel vision, observe carefully, and do a lot of thinking."

"Got it," said Aaron Blanding. He scratched his head. "But was I right about dissociation?"

"Hundred percent. Good call."

"Cool."

Milo said, "How about we sit down."

CHAPTER

22

The seating triangle allowed everyone to look at two people. Milo had constructed it perfectly, with equal distance among the chairs.

Aaron Blanding nudged his chair slightly closer to mine. Kept sneaking looks at me.

Psychologus americanus. The animal in the exotic zoo.

Milo said, "So, Aaron, what can we do for you?"

The boy shifted back to him. "I decided to come here because I thought I could offer some insight into the dynamics of my family. Unless you've already solved my sister's murder and don't need that."

Now both of them were looking at me.

I said, "The more we know, the better. What can you tell us, Aaron?"

"For starts, I want to say that though I'm coming across relatively chill it doesn't mean my sister's death didn't affect me emotionally. It did. It does. When I heard, I cried and I'm not ashamed to admit that. But then I woke up this morning and I felt I should get myself together and try to help. My mother had already said I could stay out of school so I told her I was walking to the Beverly Hills library to do some reading. Instead, I took the bus here."

"Appreciate the effort," said Milo. He crossed his legs.

"Okay . . ." Dark-blue eyes floated around for a while. "Okay," he repeated. "For most of my life, there wasn't much relationship between Cordi and me because there's so many years between us and she wasn't around much. Also, my mom wouldn't talk about her and if I brought her up, she'd try to change the subject."

He waved his hand dismissively. "But my dad answered my questions. He's not her dad, just her stepdad, that's probably why he's . . . less intense about Cordi. Later, when Cordi and I finally started to talk, what she basically told me was what Dad told me so I know he was honest."

I said, "When did that start?"

"About a year and a half ago," said Aaron Blanding. "I just got tired of having this half sib and not knowing her so I reached out and she was super-appreciative. In fact, she cried and said it meant a lot to her, she'd thought I didn't want to know her. I said I absolutely did so we started talking."

"By phone?"

"At first, phone and text. Then around a year ago, we started getting together at various Starbucks. Near my house, if I didn't have transportation, near hers if I did. We did it like every three, four weeks. I'd cut school because school is basically crap and learning about my sister was way more important." His voice caught. "I wish it could've lasted."

His lips knotted as his face lowered. He covered it with his hands, exposing grubby nails and ink-specked fingers. Forcing back tears led to more grimacing. A fifteen-year-old confronting a reality most people never faced.

It took a while for the hands to drop and after they did, he stood shakily and headed for the door. But instead of leaving the room, he circled once and sat back down.

"Sorry. That was cheesy."

Milo said, "More like a normal reaction, Aaron."

"Really?" A look to me for confirmation.

I nodded. "You've experienced a terrible loss and it's courageous of you to come forward."

"No, I don't think I'm very courageous . . . more like I keep thinking about my own feelings and it kind of rises up in my stomach."

"Exactly," I said. "Normal. You need to look out for yourself, Aaron."

"Maybe . . ." Deep sigh, drop of shoulders.

I said, "So around a year ago you and Cordi started hanging out at Starbucks."

"Or Jamba Juice. It was instructive."

"How so?"

"I got to understand Cordi," he said. "And myself, Dr. Delaware. The fact that Cordi and I shared some chromosomes but our childhoods were totally different."

Hesitant smile. "She once told me, 'Baby bro, we might as well have grown up on different planets.' Not in a jealous way. She thought it was kind of funny. I told her that made me feel guilty but she said don't be a wuss, guilt is crap, it can only hold you back. Then she said everyone has challenges, no matter how they grow up. Hers was making something of herself despite her childhood and what did I think mine was. I said not getting dependent and lazy because Mom tries to spoil me rotten. Not that it's Mom's fault, it's up to me to deal with it. At some point I will."

I said, "Two different planets."

"Probably more like two different galaxies, Dr. Delaware. My sister had no idea who her biological dad was and when she was growing up Mom was attracted to bad guys and had all sorts of issues."

"Financial issues?"

"Financial, psychological." He scooted forward, tight-faced. "Mom's all Beverly Hills now, with her tennis and her mani-pedis. But back then, she used drugs and was pretty wild. Obviously, I'd never bring that up with her, she'd go insane. But it helped me to know."

"To understand your mom."

"To understand why she needs to control everything. Cordi told me about guys beating Mom up. Not treating Cordi well, either."

Milo said, "In what way?"

"I don't know," said Aaron Blanding. "She just said none of them were nice to her and that she never had a real father figure. Then she laughed and said she probably wouldn't know a father figure if she met one but she'd never wallow in weakness. That's the way she was. Fierce."

His right knee began shaking. "She once told me the reason I was so much smarter than her was probably because Mom was on something when she was pregnant with her. Then she made a stupid face like this."

He crossed his eyes and stuck out his tongue. "Obviously, I didn't think that was true and I told her, Cordi, you are highly intelligent, you just missed out on education through no fault of your own. I, on the other hand, totally lucked out, I don't get gold stars, okay? There's a fund set up for me, I'll never have to deal with student loans. I'll probably have to go to some snotty Ivy League place. So I'm determined to give back. When I'm finally free, I *will* give back."

"By becoming a psychologist."

"Probably," he said. "Also by not becoming a spoiled snowflake asshole."

Determined, less calf than guard dog.

I said, "You've got good insights, Aaron."

"For my age?"

"For any age."

"I don't know," he said. "I spend a lot of time thinking and some-times I think it's just a waste of time. Now I mostly think about Cordi . . . about never seeing her. It just really *hurts.*"

He clutched his belly. His head took another dip. This time when he looked up, his cheeks were moist. "It's fucking unfair. I barely got to know her."

"It is unfair," I said. "We're so sorry."

"I mean," he said, "something like that happens and Mom won't talk about it? Not a single fucking word? She keeps saying it'll upset me too much, like I'm a fucking fetus."

I said, "Dad told you."

"Yup. He told me whatever he knew. Which wasn't much. I asked him where the fuck it happened and he said at Cordi's house. And then I thought, fuck, I've never even been to my sister's house. Then I thought, Cordi said it was a good neighborhood, one day she'd have me over . . . that could be relevant, right? A good neighborhood? I mean, it's not like gangs are roaming around, right?"

Milo said, "We don't know much yet, Aaron, but sure, it could mean something."

"But not necessarily?" said Aaron Blanding. "I get it, you're careful. But doesn't it raise the probability that whoever . . . that it was someone Cordi knew?"

"That's a possibility, Aaron."

"Do you have any potential suspects?"

"Nope, wish we did, Aaron. Is there anyone you can point us to?"

"Not a specific person," said the boy. "But I was thinking, maybe someone she dated back when she was dating?"

"When was she dating?"

"She told me she stopped like two years ago. That her life focus was on growing as a person without dependency and building her career."

Milo said, "As an internet star."

"That sounds superficial," said Aaron Blanding. "Like she was just one of those stupid influencers. Cordi was more than that. She didn't have education but she understood people."

He turned to me. "She could've been a psychologist if she'd had a chance. We talked about that. She admitted she'd missed out and was adapting to it in her own way. I told her she should go for it, she was still young but she said it was impossible, she hadn't even gone to college, would have to start at the beginning and be old when she was done. Then she said she probably wasn't smart enough. I said sure you are, if that's what you want, go for it. Then she kissed my cheek and hugged me and said look who's being the emotional advisor. Then she said she had to go. That was the last time we hung out."

Milo said, "When was that, Aaron?"

"Like two months ago. After that, we spoke on the phone a couple of times but just to say hi, she always sounded busy. I didn't mind, I'm sure she was mega-busy and I was happy about that. She promised to call me when things quieted down. I'm sure she would've."

"So the last time you spoke was . . ."

"Like . . . maybe a month ago. She was in the middle of a shoot, still took the time to answer when she saw it was me."

He looked at the ceiling again, then down at the floor before the blue eyes took a wide lateral swing toward the door. "I'm sure she meant it. Can I have some water?"

"On the way." Milo got up and strode to the door.

Aaron said, "So you do this, too. Am I being analyzed?"

"Nope, just listened to," I said. "I meant what I said about courage."

"I don't think it's a big deal, Dr. Delaware. She was my sister."

Milo returned with a bottle. Aaron said, "Thanks," twisted the cap off, and swigged half of the water. A few drops spattered his shirt.

Milo said, "Is it okay to go back to Cordi's social life for just a second?"

"Sure. But I don't know anything, Lieutenant."

"She told you she'd had no dating life for a couple of years."

"Yes, sir."

"How about before that? Did she ever talk about a relationship that got unpleasant?"

"Not really," said Aaron.

"Not really but maybe she hinted?"

"She said Mom had gone through a lot of frogs before she met Dad and that she'd done the same but her prince hadn't appeared. That's what convinced her not to depend on a man for her happiness."

"There was no one she was scared of."

"I never saw her scared of anything. She was much stronger than me because she had to be. Like annealing steel. You heat it then cool it—basically you stress it and it gets harder."

"Aha."

Aaron Blanding said, "I learned it in physics, no big deal."

Milo said, "Now I'm going to tell you something your dad didn't tell you. Cordi wasn't the only person who died. There was a second victim."

Aaron gaped. "You're saying she did have a boyfriend, it was some kind of . . . passion deal?"

"No, this person was just a friend. Her hairdresser, actually."

"Caspian? Caspian was *also* . . . oh, fuck-shit. It was . . . like a massacre? Was there anyone else?"

"Thankfully no, Aaron. So you knew Caspian."

"I met him once. At Starbucks in Westwood. Cordi brought him along because she had a photo shoot in an hour and he was doing her hair and neither of them had eaten. Cordi still wasn't going to eat because she wanted to look thin for the shoot, she said the camera put on like ten pounds. But she wanted to make sure Caspian got some nutrition, was joking that if she didn't feed him he'd mess up her hair. She got him a whole wheat roll and some . . . avocado spread, I think. Something spread. He ate it all up, so obviously my sister was right."

"What was your impression of Caspian?"

"Nice," he said. "Respectful."

"Respectful of Cordi?"

"Of Cordi and me. Of our meetings. He told me they were a great thing, it was great to have a sibling to talk to. By respectful I mean that when he got his roll, he went off to another table so we could have our time. That doesn't always happen. An adult treating someone my age like a person. It's like he didn't make a difference between Cordi and me because of our ages. Now you're telling me . . . *fuck* that to hell. *Fuck*."

A fist pounded a palm. "I can't believe this. Oh, man, this sucks, it's . . . it's . . . it fucking *sucks*."

Milo said, "That's for sure, Aaron. And what's making the investigation even more difficult is we don't even have Caspian's real name yet."

"You don't?" Amazed. "That I can tell you. Charlie Bankster. He said it sounded too much like gangster so he changed it. Joking about it. The whole time was like that, Cordi joking, Caspian joking." A breath. "I laughed a lot, which was . . . then Caspian went to eat and Cordi and I hung out."

Sad smile. "I didn't joke. A sense of humor is something I'm working on."

◆

He finished the water, refused Milo's offer of a second.

"How about some grub, Aaron? I'm sure I can scare up some pastries or a bag of chips."

"No, thanks, Lieutenant. My stomach's turning inside out." Placing a hand in the middle of his abdomen to demonstrate.

"Got it. Anything else you want to tell us?"

"I wish," said the boy. "I wish I knew something . . . oh man, Cordi and Caspian. The time I was with both of them was nice. And now I'm the only one still alive."

We walked him downstairs and out to the street. No more curiosity about his surroundings. He looked smaller, younger.

"Need a lift home?" said Milo.

"No, I'll catch the bus. Obviously, I should keep this meeting secret, right?"

"From your parents?"

"Mostly from Mom. She'll go nuts and probably want to take my temperature or something."

"Well," said Milo, "I can't order you to go covert but sounds like a good idea."

"Covert." Aaron Blanding dredged up a smile. "Like a secret agent. Bye, Dr. Delaware. If I have questions about psychology, could I ask you?"

"Sure." I gave him my office email.

"Great. Thanks. Excellent."

We watched him walk north on Butler, a softly built adolescent with an ungainly, waddling walk.

Milo said, "Some kid. Renata was right, he is brilliant."

"Brilliant with a stainless-steel moral core," I said. "Also helpful: Charlie Bankster."

"Better get the troops off Baxter and onto Bankster. Unusual name, gift from the gods."

We took our usual places in his closet-sized office: Milo sinking into his wheelie chair as I wedged myself into a corner, barely able to flex a limb.

He called Reed and informed him of the name change, extracted a wooden-tipped cigar from his desk, jammed it into his mouth. Strong, white teeth embarked on the destruction of the wood.

He said, "Maybe the kid was helpful on a whole other level."

"Insights into the family?"

"This is gonna sound out there, Alex, but given what we just heard, maybe I should be looking at an evil-mom deal. When we talked to Renata, it was obvious there was no love lost, but the kid just made it sound a helluva lot worse. Renata trying to *erase* Cordi because Cordi upset the idea of her perfect little family. What if, on top of that, she found out Cordi and Aaron were meeting, worried Cordi was influencing the kid? Or divulging Renata's past. Talk about a serious sense of threat."

I said, "Cold-blooded murder of a daughter to keep up her self-image? That's pretty strong even for a bad mother. And no way she'd have the strength to take care of Caspian."

"So she hired someone . . . I know, way out there. But you know that some of the nastiest stuff gets cooked up on the family stove. This is a lady with a bad past who's moved on to tennis and mani-pedis. Last thing she'd want to be reminded of is the bad old days. Toss in her chronic pain, maybe some mood swings due to arthritis or meds? She's in no shape to do the deed herself but maybe her past came in useful."

"She knew people."

"Bad guys, like Cordi told Aaron. I mean it's not *im*possible."

When it comes to people, nothing is. But it didn't feel right.

I said, "Her phone records could be educational."

"If I could get them." He frowned. Had wanted more from me. As I was thinking of something to say, his desk phone jangled. No music abuse coming through the department's wires; small blessings.

He picked up, listened, grabbed a pen. "Okay, go." Scrawling rapidly, he hung up and shot a fist in the air.

But despite the gesture, no glee on his face, just an odd distracted look.

"That was Moses, he got Charlie Bankster's address, turns out to be close to here."

He stood and tossed the unlit cigar with its splintered tip.

The lack of cheer puzzled me. I said, "Sounds like good news."

"If the roomie's there and has something substantial to say. If not, it's another dead end plus a goddamn notification."

23

Two names on the mailbox: Kramm/Delage.

One of sixty or so boxes in the unlocked, whey-colored lobby of an eighties-built nine-story building on Barrington Avenue three blocks south of Wilshire.

That decade was renowned for the abandonment of architectural style in favor of cramming as many renters as possible into sad, jerry-built warrens. Zoning laws have since been passed but they still vanish when you know who to phone at City Hall.

A few years ago, a sex trafficking gang had operated out of a tower just like this one. Women from Eastern Europe lured to sunny L.A. by a group of former Lebanese army officers with promises of modeling gigs, only to be stripped of their passports, confined, and rented out by the hour.

A woman had died. Someone had talked. Headline arrest, everyone deported. No one with a working brain believed it had made a difference.

I thought about that as Milo pushed the Kramm/Delage button.

A female voice said, "Yes?"

"Ms. Kramm?"

"Yes?"

"This is Lieutenant Sturgis of LAPD. Could we please come up and talk to you about Caspian Delage?"

"Caspian? Something happened to him?"

"Could we come up to discuss it, ma'am?"

"Um," she said. "That doesn't sound good . . . let me come down to the lobby, make sure you are who you say you are."

Milo said, "Great, thanks."

To me: "Smart move, if I was a scammer I'd probably split."

Six minutes later, the elevator door slid open and a red-haired woman wearing a pink silk kimono patterned with white peonies over black leotards and red ballet slippers walked toward us.

Mid-thirties, pretty in an elfin way. Keeping her distance as she assessed us.

Milo flashed the badge. "Ms. Kramm?"

"Mona . . . I guess that looks pretty official."

He smiled and stayed put. "Couldn't be more official."

Mona Kramm held back for several seconds. Then, like a wary animal tempted by food, she stepped forward tentatively. When she was close enough, she read the badge. "Pretty fancy. Okay, let's go up."

The elevator groaned arthritically and took a while to reach the fourth floor. No one spoke.

Milo and I were keeping silent because bad news is best handled in a private place. Mona Kramm, tapping her foot and playing with her hair, maybe for the same reason. But also because she was in a confined space with two male strangers, however official.

During the ride, she bent her knee, placed her sole against her shin, and stood perfectly balanced. When the elevator belched, shuddered, and stopped, she unfolded slowly as the door made spitting noises and ground open.

Mona Kramm said, "Piece of junk. I usually take the stairs but didn't know if you guys were into that."

The three of us stepped into an off-white corridor faced with plywood doors painted black. At Unit 407, Milo and I stood back as Mona Kramm removed a key ring from her wrist and unlocked.

The apartment was what you see in L.A. when people settle for whatever they can get. Small, dark, close-feeling, all the charm of a hospital room.

Besides the expected doorway to bedrooms and lav, the rest of the layout was what's peddled as open-plan but really means *let's save money by knocking up as few walls as possible.*

Maybe two hundred square feet. Another arbitrary living area, eating limited to three stools at the counter of a kitchenette that made Shari Benedetto's efficiency look like something out of a design magazine. The counters were some kind of turquoise plastic that made no pretense at being natural. But food prep went on here, nearly every inch crowded with pots, pans, utensils, a microwave, an industrial-strength juicer, assorted boxes and cans.

A single window on the far wall revealed the guano-specked stucco of a neighboring building. The furniture was tired, the sole nod to personal three posters of modern dance concerts. New York, Paris, London.

That plus the ballet shoes, the leotards, and the flexibility spelled out Mona Kramm's passion. This place said so far, love had turned out unrequited.

She sat yoga-style, like Shari Benedetto. Unlike Benedetto, she remained tense as we faced her on a nubby gray couch redolent of ramen.

Milo said, "You're a dancer?"

"In theory," she said. "In reality, I teach little kids at a studio in Brentwood." She smiled. "It's not bad. They're rich but not messed up, yet."

A dancer and a stylist sharing this drab place. Two people who'd set their sights on creativity and beauty but lived without much of either.

Milo said, "There's no good way to say this but—"

"He's dead."

"I'm afraid so."

As if a sluice had been opened, Mona Kramm went from taut to traumatized.

"Oh God, no!" She made a retching sound and pitched forward.

Milo had one of his clean hankies ready. But she ignored it and wiped her eyes on a kimono sleeve. "How? Why Caspian?"

"Wish we knew," said Milo. "What I can tell you is that Caspian was one of two people murdered a few nights ago."

"Cordi Gannett," she said. "Her, too?"

Stomach sounds rose from a flat belly. She groaned and slapped a hand over her gut.

"How did you know?"

"Because Caspian was sleeping over at her place a few nights ago. Cordi was also killed? This is . . . I don't know what it is. What do you call it? A double?"

Milo said, "Two people dead."

"Omigod. I can't believe this."

Milo said, "Did you know Cordi?"

"No, but I knew *of* her," said Mona Kramm. "Caspian—his real name is Charlie, by the way—Caspian talked about her a lot. He thought she was brilliant. No, I never met her but from what he told me I worried she might get him into trouble."

"How so?"

"My feeling is that he started to get too attached to her and when that happens things can get weird, right?"

"They can," said Milo.

"Hero worship," said Mona Kramm. "I've never seen it go anywhere good."

I said, "Caspian worshipped Cordi."

"It didn't start out that way but it came to that. Poor Caspian. He was so sweet. Gentle, quiet, considerate. Plus neat and clean and try finding all that in one person. When he answered my Craigslist ad I had a terrific first impression and it only improved. He was the *best* roommate you could ask for. Now he's . . . this is unreal."

"How long have the two of you lived together?"

"Two years," said Mona Kramm. "Cordi." She shook her head.

I said, "Caspian got attached to Cordi in a way that made you worry."

"I never worried about something like this, no, no, nothing like *this*. Jesus . . . I just thought she was . . . I don't want to disrespect a dead person."

Milo said, "Anything you can tell us is helpful."

She freed her legs, stretched, returned to the yoga fold. "It started off as work for Caspian. Doing her hair and makeup. This was like . . . a year and a half ago. But then he started talking about her more and more and I could tell he was getting . . . hooked."

"What did he say about her?"

"What a brilliant shrink she was. How deep her insights were, she had a talent for tuning in to people's souls. He's like you have to watch her videos, Mona, she really gets it. I'm not into that stuff but just to be nice I watched a couple."

She stuck out her tongue.

I said, "Not impressed."

"I thought she was slick and superficial. But I told Caspian they were great. Why make him feel bad? I didn't have the heart to say what I *really* thought."

I said, "Which was . . ."

"Basically, she was either doling out common sense—be attracted to people who are good for you—or telling people what they wanted to hear. Kind of like what those fake psychics do? When I saw the videos, I was still in therapy with a real therapist and she looked Cordi up, watched, and agreed. Later she told me she'd found out Cordi had been busted for impersonating a shrink. So I'm thinking whoa. I guess I should've told Caspian but I didn't imagine it would—something would happen to him. He was so needy, I figured he'd found a friend and that was better than nothing."

I said, "Caspian didn't have friends."

"Just me, for what that was worth," said Mona Kramm. "And we never really did anything together, we were just compatible roomies."

"What was their friendship like?"

"I don't know," said Mona Kramm. "I never actually saw them together so maybe I'm being too judgmental. But I can tell you this: In the beginning she paid Caspian his full fee but then he began styling her at a discount. He claimed it was his idea, but who knows? Either way, Caspian wasn't exactly rich, even with his other gigs. She had to know that. To me that sounds exploitative."

"Caspian struggled financially."

She waved a hand. "I guess it's pretty obvious looking at this dump that neither of us is doing the privilege thing. I hoped it would work out for Caspian eventually. He was super-talented and not temperamental, had been in town for five years but only working for himself for the last two. It takes time to build up but business did seem to be growing. Still, he was a long way from having any savings and he sure could've used every penny he got from her."

Milo said, "Do you know where he was originally from?"

"Ohio," she said. "Columbus. He didn't talk much about that. I got the feeling his childhood wasn't great."

"So he came here."

"And did the struggling thing." Mona Kramm's lips slitted and her eyes flashed. First time I noticed their color. Olive green with rusty rims. The pupils, dilated by cold light.

"This is a vicious town," she said. "I'm not bitching. I could've chosen to be a social worker or a respiratory therapist like my sisters. You make choices, you live with them. But Cordi had to know Caspian needed every dollar he earned so why would she allow him to work cheap even if he offered?"

I said, "Did you see any other signs she took advantage of him?"

"When she wanted him for a shoot, she'd call at all hours. Beckoning. Like a queen summoning a servant. Need you in five hours. When he could, he'd reschedule to accommodate her."

"His favorite client."

She frowned.

I said, "Was sleeping over at her place a regular thing?"

"To my knowledge, he'd done it only once before. Came back gushing about what an elegant time they had. Sushi, sake, listening to spa music."

"Flutes and whale sounds."

She laughed, checked it, as if realizing glee was uncalled for. "Exactly. Doesn't that sound kind of pseudo-shrinky?"

I nodded. "Did he say anything about the sleepover a few nights ago?"

"Just that he'd be bunking down at Dr. G's crib. Like it was a privilege. He was excited. Giggling. A kid about to go on an adventure."

"He called her a doctor."

"Exactly. And she wasn't," said Mona Kramm. "But what was the point of arguing? I'm all about harmony. Caspian and I had achieved it and I wanted to keep it that way. I figured if I challenged him, he might freak."

"You figured he'd be that sensitive about Cordi?"

"I did, sir. It's like religion. People choose their form of worship and they punish infidels."

Milo said, "The Church of Cordi."

She stared at him. "That's great. That's really great, I'm going to remember it. Can I get you guys something to drink?"

"No, thanks, Mona. So what else can you tell us about Caspian?"

"Like I said, his real name was Charlie. Charles Bankster. I found out because one day he left his wallet open on the kitchen counter and his Social Security card and driver's license were on top, in these little compartments covered by plastic. I asked him about it and he said he'd grown up as Charlie but decided when he came to L.A. to go for something with *panache*."

She shook her head. "Caspian Delage, that's a mouthful, huh? But like I said, no comment from me. Roommates as good as Caspian don't come often. Plus, I really did like him. He was *really* likable. I can't imagine anyone wanting to harm him. It *had* to be something to do with her."

Looking at us, expecting an answer.

Milo said, "Too early to know, Mona, but you could be right."

"Of course I'm right. She was a user and a phony and someone probably got pissed at her. I mean think about it. You post about yourself, tons of strangers get to watch you. Study you. Judge you. I mean some of them are bound to be psychos, right? It's like a bad dating app times a bajillion."

Milo smiled. "I'm going to remember *that*."

Victim's warrants are the general rule before entering the residence of a person who's died violently. But Milo questioned Mona Kramm about the particulars of her arrangement with Caspian Delage and learned she was the sole lessee of the apartment, Delage an off-the-books co-tenant.

"And yes," she said, "it's against the rules to sublet but the way this dump is managed, no one pays attention and I don't imagine you guys care about that kind of thing."

"Not in the least, Mona. How about we take a look at Caspian's room?"

"Sure, but please don't judge me."

"About what?"

"His space. I didn't design this dump."

The doorway opened to a skimpy, dark hall. Tiny, meticulous bedroom to the left—maybe nine by nine, dominated by a queen bed covered with a filmy salmon-colored throw, the walls crowded with more danc-ing prints.

On the opposite side of the corridor was a spotless fiberglass bath-room. Translucent window, flesh-colored towels, brightly colored lo-tions on the shelf of a shower nook.

Milo said, "Okay if I look in the medicine cabinet?"

"Nothing to hide, go for it," said Mona Kramm. "Since you're a detective you can probably figure out who uses the tampons and who uses the electric shaver."

He laughed, did a quick search, exited a moment later. "No pre-scription meds."

"We're both healthy," she said. Her face fell. "Were."

Sharing the right side with the lav was an even smaller bedroom, not much larger than Milo's office, with a high, narrow window admit-ting a struggling spray of murky light.

No bed, just a futon on the floor. Three wire-mesh boxes were filled with precisely folded clothing. One was topped by a slab of plywood that served as a nightstand. Four pairs of shoes were lined up at the bottom of a particleboard closet. Inside, hanging garments and a couple of shelves.

"See what I mean?" said Mona Kramm. "But that's the way they built it."

As I thought about cells for captive women, Milo got busy, checking garment pockets, finding nothing. A reach to the rear of the closet's top shelf produced a bag of marijuana and a bottle of pills prescribed to Amalia Beniste.

Mona Kramm's eyeblink said she knew about the weed. A puzzled look said she'd never seen the pills.

Milo turned to me. "Frovatriptan?"

I said, "Migraine medication."

"Oh," said Mona Kramm. "That makes sense, sometimes he complained of headaches, could really eat ibuprofen—you saw the big bottle. His, not mine."

"Any idea who Amalia Beniste is?"

"Never heard of her. Probably someone being nice and sharing."

She pulled a phone out of a kimono pocket, did some thumbwork. "Here she is, works in wardrobe at Warner Bros."

She showed us the Instagram page of a chipmunk-cheeked, purple-haired, steel-pierced woman in her twenties trying to pull off a gang sign but coming across goofy.

Milo copied in his pad. "Thanks."

"You guys still use paper?"

"And buggy whips."

Mona Kramm smiled. "Maybe Caspian met her on a job, got a bad headache and she felt sorry for him."

"Makes sense."

"You're going to talk to her, too?"

"Any reason we shouldn't?"

"Not really," said Mona Kramm. "I just figured it's not about Caspian, it's about *her*."

The rest of the room search turned up nothing; Caspian Delage had led a life curiously devoid of details. And of pajamas. Or sweats. Anything resembling sleepwear.

I said so.

Mona Kramm said, "Oh, that. Caspian said he had sensitive skin, always slept in the nude. I had no problem with it. I mean . . ."

"No sexual tension between you."

"Well, yeah, he was— does that matter? I mean . . . c'mon, is it really necessary to always be judging? Does that have to be part of your job?"

Milo smiled. "We dig stuff up, other people judge."

"If you say so," she said, sounding doubtful.

My thoughts were elsewhere. *No sexual tension here or with Cordi Gannett.*

Two victims, neither of whom appeared to have any sort of romantic relationship.

Had that been the basis for their bond? Or, as Mona Kramm suspected, was it just another hero-worship thing?

Either way, for Caspian Delage a sleepover at his idol's house had been a big deal.

Light banter, food and wine, slipping into peaceful, platonic, naked sleep.

I hoped his final dreams had been blissful.

Mona Kramm said, "Are we through?"

Milo said, "We are, thanks. Where can we find Caspian's car?"

"He doesn't have one, used Uber and Lyft. So do I."

"The traffic."

"And the cost," she said. "Caspian said L.A. driving scared him. But I still think the main reason was the money."

"Speaking of which, any idea where he keeps his money?"

"I'm not sure he had any to keep other than some cash in his wallet for expenses."

"What kind of expenses?"

"Like I just said, transportation. Plus food plus his forty percent of rent and utilities. He was never late and since I did have a good first impression I decided to give him a break on the utilities. Flat thirty bucks a month and trust me, that's a deal. I also cut the rent I was asking because his room is even dinkier than mine. But still, all that probably ate up everything he earned."

"Can I ask what the rent is?" he said.

"Eighteen hundred a month—yeah, I know. Again, don't judge me. I already hear enough from my parents and my sisters."

On the elevator ride down, Milo hummed "Eleanor Rigby."

I said, "I've had more than one patient scared by that song."

"All the lonely people?"

"That, minor key, the graveyard stuff, and the fatalism."

"Still, it's a jaunty tune, no?"

"Makes it worse."

"Beatle-phobia," he said. "What do you do to cure them?"

"Tell them to listen to something else."

"What's that, tough love?"

"Keeping things simple. Caspian not having a car made me realize I didn't see one at Cordi's."

"Nothing registered," he said. "No doubt Uber et cetera for her, too. What do you think about Caspian's lifestyle. Kinda Trappist, no?"

I said, "Like she said, it's a vicious town."

"She does have a point. And I think she was right, it does tell us something about Cordi. Poor guy's scratching by, she gets him to discount his fee? She's a complex girl, our victim, should've come equipped with a decoder."

I said, "Idolized by her brother and Caspian but not too popular with anyone else we've talked to."

"Including her own mother. You see any similarities between Aaron and Caspian?"

"Males with whom sex wouldn't be an issue for her. Fits with her abandoning relationships and concentrating on becoming famous."

"That's what I'm thinking. So Ms. Kramm coulda just nailed the motive. You've heard of those involuntary celibates, hate themselves, hate women, sometimes they snap. What if one of those watched her online, got enamored, convinced himself romance was on the horizon. He managed to make personal contact, she either ignored him or rejected him. Either way, he couldn't handle it and boom."

I said, "You wouldn't need celibacy, just unfulfilled fantasy. Classic celebrity stalker situation."

"Even though she wasn't much of a celebrity yet."

"You don't have to be famous anymore, just out there."

"Yeah . . . I'd love to check out the correspondence her videos pulled but she set it up so it got cleaned out every month. And nothing we've seen recently was suspicious."

A block later, he said, "What if the scenario featured the short-tempered Mr. Hoffgarden? Who she actually did sleep with once upon a time. She breaks it off, he goes nuts. *There's* your stalker deal. You've spent time with him, what do you think?"

"Can't eliminate him."

"That's it? Nothing he did tipped you off?"

"The brief time I spent with him focused on his parenting skills."

"Which were nil."

We drove a bit.

I said, "Caspian sleeping in the nude clarifies one thing. He wasn't stripped by the bad guy. He was a neat person, so his clothes were probably folded near the sofa and the bad guy took them and the I.D. to delay identification. Or, if Caspian was mistaken for a lover, carrying him naked into the street and making sure he was found that way would be an additional way to demean him."

"Red-hot lover sleeping on the couch?"

"Sleeping naked could still have connoted sex," I said. "Finding Caspian was likely a surprise, the killer might not have been thinking logically. Another reason could've been to take trophies. That would explain why you haven't found the clothing discarded."

"Loco-man slavering over his stash."

His cell began chirping something Baroque. Mercifully, he answered by the third note.

Alicia Bogomil said, "Learned a few things about Mr. Delage, Loo. Sad story."

"Let's hear it, kid. I took my antidepressants this morning."

She laughed. Gave the details.

When she finished, Milo said, "Maybe I need a higher dosage."

24

Longevity wasn't a thing for the Banksters of Columbus, Ohio, and Alicia had the paperwork to prove it.

She met us outside Milo's office and handed him a sheaf.

"He's not in our system, Loo, but if you want, I can try digging around some more."

"Good job, kiddo. Go for it."

As she hurried off, Milo and I studied what she'd presented. Starting with death records from Social Security.

Zorena Bankster, the mother of Charles Bankster aka Caspian Delage, had passed away seven years ago, age forty-eight, from liver cancer. Two years later, her husband, Joseph Bankster, Sr., had succumbed to emphysema, age fifty-two.

Only one other relative could be located, an older brother, Joseph, Jr. Currently thirty-six years old and living in L.A.

If you could call it that.

The remainder of the paperwork revealed a disability history of nearly two decades for Caspian's only sibling. Profound head injuries caused by a single-vehicle motorcycle accident on a highway outside of

Dayton, the formerly healthy, eighteen-year-old Joseph, Jr., surviving in seriously diminished condition.

Following the death of both parents, Caspian had moved himself and his brother to L.A. and found an apartment near Skid Row for himself and a care facility downtown for the quadriplegic, minimally conscious Joseph. Just over two years ago, the brothers had shifted westward, Caspian subletting the flat on Barrington, Joseph transferred to a rest home in nearby Palms.

Round-the-clock maintenance at Palms Tudor Care Center cost six figures a year, with most of that covered by government payments.

Most, but not all; a nearly fifteen-thousand annual overage remained. Caspian Delage had assumed that obligation.

The real reason he'd lived like a monk.

I said, "Mona has no idea what Caspian was dealing with but given his closeness to Cordi, I wonder if she did."

Milo said, "And still took a discount? Yeah, that ain't morality."

We examined the money trail, including another futile search for credit or debit accounts, followed up with a visit to Palms Tudor Care Center.

That led to confirmation of what we'd read: fifteen grand paid faithfully for two years, per the facility's administrative director, a round, cheerful man named Hector Aguirre packed into a white polo shirt with a TCC logo and mustard-colored slacks.

The drive from Delage's apartment to Palms Boulevard just south of National had taken thirteen minutes. Convenient when you rented rides and wanted to be near your helpless sib.

Milo said, "So Mr. Bankster was a good client."

Hector Aguirre said, "Well, Joey's the actual client, but sure, Charlie's been fine."

He beamed nervously at us across an empty almost-wood conference table. On the way, we'd passed several people slumping in wheel-chairs, heard the beeps of I.V. monitors, anguished throat clearing and wet coughs, passed attendants coming and going at a steady but unhurried pace.

The facility was done up in that strange mix of colors—orange and pinkish tan—that you see in medium-sized airports and places like Palms Tudor.

Milo said, "He paid on time."

Hector Aguirre looked at his watch. "Like clockwork. 'Course, we facilitated by billing only three times a year."

Milo and I looked at each other. How that helped was unclear.

Aguirre saw the boast had fallen flat and tried to recover. "The main thing, we trimmed off the top because what the heck, you have to be human."

Trying to sell it smoothly.

Milo said, "How much did you take off?"

"Five hundred dollars."

"Per . . ."

"Year."

"Ah."

"We're under no obligation but why not?" said Aguirre. "He seemed a nice fellow, Charlie. Delicate, you know?" Smiling and waiting for a reaction that didn't come.

"Good guy," he said. "Can't believe someone would do that to him."

"Is there any other family you're aware of?"

"Nope. I'm sure of that because Charlie told me he was it."

"How often did Charlie visit his brother?"

"From what I saw, once a week?" said Aguirre. "Can't tell you if he came in when I wasn't here. We don't keep visitor records, we're an open facility."

"Are you aware of Charlie ever having any conflict with anyone?"

"Here?"

"Yessir."

"No way. Nice guy, cool with the staff. We don't have conflict."

Milo said, "What about with another client?"

"Sir," said Hector Aguirre, "our clients are incapacitated."

"How about with the relative of another client?"

"Nope, never," said Aguirre. "And yeah, I can be sure. I'm not going to lie, we don't get that many visitors."

"People stash their relatives and forget about them?"

Aguirre winced. "Man, you come right out and say what you think. I'm not going to lie and tell you that doesn't happen. Dumping. It does, it's not good but it does. But also I like to think families get relaxed because they trust us to service their loved ones."

That sounded like something a mortician might say. This place felt like eternity's waiting room.

Aguirre said, "Do I like the clients not being visited more? For the ones who can tell the difference, sure I don't like it. Is it reality? What can I say? I'm not going to lie and tell you *no* one comes but on a given day it could be no one or one or two or three. Except on birthdays. Then they show up. We bake cakes. Tasty cakes, the families like them. Clients who can eat solids like them. We do balloons, those acetates . . ."

As if realizing he was bombing onstage, he trailed off.

Milo said, "Did Charlie ever visit Joey with anyone else?"

"Couple of times, there was a girl," said Aguirre. "I remember her because she was . . . hope I'm allowed to do this but seeing as you're guys."

Grinning, he outlined an hourglass.

Milo said, "Hot."

"Oh yeah. Lots of shape, lots of blond. I figured her for a friend of Charlie's. A pal, if you catch my drift."

"Not a love interest."

"Love interest," said Aguirre, as if learning a new term. "Well, you know. He, Charlie, was obviously of the gay persuasion."

"Did he ever show up with a boyfriend?"

"Nope, just her, the blonde. And like I said, just a couple of times. Literally. Two . . . at least that I saw and I usually see everything from seven a.m. to nine p.m."

Milo said, "Long shift."

"Goes with the job. They make it worth my while."

"The owners."

"You bet," said Aguirre. "Great bunch of people, they're a family based in Seattle. I know what people think but you'd be surprised."

"What do people think?"

"Owners of places like this are vultures. People who think that should try doing it themselves."

Suddenly pugnacious. An argument he'd been compelled to offer often.

Milo said, "So just the blonde."

Aguirre slipped his smile back on like a comfortable shoe. "Yup, only her and trust me, she's someone you'd notice."

Milo showed him Cordi Gannett's internet photo.

Aguirre's pupils dilated. "That's her, all right. Who is she?"

"A friend," said Milo.

"Just like I said," said Aguirre. "You do this job long enough, you get a feel for people."

I said, "So what's going to happen to Joey with Charlie no longer paying the overage?"

Aguirre shrugged. "We'll work it out. One way or the other."

We left the conference room and headed for the entry with Aguirre just ahead of us.

Milo said, "Could we have a look at Joey?"

"You already have," said Aguirre. He pointed to one of the wheelchairs lined up near the front door.

A shrunken form of indeterminate age was strapped in at mid-chest and waist-level. Withered legs were propped straight out on slide-out rests and similarly belted. Sunken cheeks, gray stubble, toothless mouth, and the collapsed jawline caused by a toothless mouth. Static eyes were mere suggestions within dark hollows. An oxygen mask dangled from the back of the chair.

Milo said, "Joey?"

Hector Aguirre said, "He's blind and deaf so you probably don't want to waste your time."

We left Tudor Palms and Milo checked out the neighbors. Foreign car mechanic to the north, tire dealer to the south. The air on the sidewalk was thick with auto fumes but my lungs felt liberated getting out of there.

I said, "That was cheerful."

Milo said, "Dante would be proud. I ever get like that, pal, shoot me with my service revolver and set it up like a suicide. By now, you know how."

"What's in it for me?"

He laughed. "Reciprocity? Maybe push you over a cliff in the Seville?"

"Let me think about it."

We got in the car, he swung a U-ey on Palms Boulevard and sped north.

I said, "Cordi knew Caspian was footing a big bill for Joseph but she still took a discount."

He shook his head. "Like I said, complex. Which, in my business, is a filthy word."

◆

Milo's office computer revealed that Amalia Beniste, the source of Caspian Delage's headache meds, had no criminal record and that while her hair color changed frequently, her "major passion" never wavered.

Self-labeled as a member of "the migraine community" the twenty-four-year-old advocated for all headache medicines shifting to over-the-counter status and expressed a clear intent to "give anyone and everyone anything and everything I have in my vascular-hell repertoire. NO ONE SHOULD SUFFER NEEDLESSLY. NO FUCKING ONE!!!! HEAR THAT FUCKING FDA?"

Milo said, "Sounds like she could give herself a headache. But unlike Cordi, she actually gave the poor guy something, can't see any reason to show up at the studio and terrify her."

He checked with Reed. Still no sighting of Tyler Hoffgarden, no results from the BOLO on Hoffgarden's Mini.

He hung up. "Another day of Mr. Muscle flewing the coop, how's that for evidence of guilt? Do me a favor and call Hoffgarden's ex, on the off chance she's seen him."

"Not a good idea," I said.

"Why not? Divorces are public records, you're not breaking any rules."

"Gray area."

"Meaning?"

"Drawing a patient into a homicide investigation. Sorry."

"Fine." He pulled out his pad. "What's her name?"

"Like you said, public record."

He stared at me. "You're kidding."

I shrugged.

"Unbelievable—do you ever break rules?"

"I've driven your unmarked twice."

"What? How do you get two?"

"The Swoboda case. You wanted to do some phone research and then some napping so you asked me—"

"That? We're talking what, half a minute?"

More like thirty.

I said, "That I'd be happy to do again."

"What's the difference?"

"Patients are vulnerable. You're not."

"Shows how much you know."

His face had reddened at the corners. "So when do you come up for beatification?"

"Nothing from Rome yet, but a guy can hope."

"Fine, no big deal, I'll look her up. And yeah, yeah, if I meet with her you won't be coming with, got it. Is there anything you can tell me about her before I talk to her?"

"Nice woman."

"Another one who hooked up with a bum. Okay, tell me why that happens, oh sage of Beverly Glen."

I said, "If I knew, I'd write a book."

"People who don't know write plenty of books."

"Exactly."

Grunting, he wheeled back to his monitor, typed and squinted, got up and left the office, flinging the door wide. Ten minutes later he returned with coffee. One cup. Facing his computer again, he resumed working.

I said, "Guess I'll be going."

"Yup."

He stayed fixed on the screen as I left. I covered half the distance to the stairwell before hearing, "Alex!"

He was loping toward me. Someone else might've seen a bull elephant charging and dashed for cover. I waited.

He caught up and clapped my shoulder and said, "Sorry for being pissy, it's sleep deprivation along with what Bobby Zimmerman says: too much of nothing."

I said, "Don't worry about it."

"I always worry, couldn't do the damn job otherwise. Anyway, I think I found her, the former Mrs. Hoffgarden. Courtney, thirty-six, lives in North Hollywood, works as a dental hygienist in Encino."

He waited for confirmation.

I said, "Ace detective."

25

The following morning at ten, he phoned and said, "Just met with Courtney Hoffgarden, now back to Courtney Giraldo. Confirmed as a very nice woman, says she was a fool to stick with Tyler as long as she did. She's engaged to a dental student, some resident who circulated through the office."

"Congrats."

"And the kid's doing fine."

"Great."

"And just to show you I'm the one should be beatified, I'm not gonna hold back on what else I learned from her."

"Thank you, Cardinal," I said. "If you could see me you'd know I'm kneeling."

"Faith is not to be scoffed at, young Alex. Anyway, she confirmed that Tyler's a scary guy. Never got physical with her but came close, there was always what she called a dread. Like waiting for a tightly coiled spring to snap. Unfortunately, she's had no contact with him for a year, no idea where he might be. I asked her about the relationship between him and Forrest Slope and she said they'd become buddies, acted like frat boys during the custody thing. She called Slope a sleaze, had no idea he'd been killed and I didn't tell her. Bottom line: There's no obvious link between Hoffgarden and Slope's murder but you never know."

I said, "Friendships can go bad. Did she know about Cordi?"

"Just that Tyler had dated her after they separated and that he tried to use her as an expert but it fizzled. Telling her about the murder took all the color from her face but she had nothing to add. Though she did say that despite her feelings toward Tyler, she couldn't believe he'd ever do something like that."

"Why not?"

"She just didn't see it," he said. "Oh yeah, one other thing. She told me about the custody thing working out because she had this great psychologist who continued to work with her kid afterward, helped both of them adjust."

"Nice to hear."

"What's with you?" he said. "The emotional oven got set to Low?"

"I like to keep the worlds separate."

"What we do and your normal shrink stuff—oxymoron though that may be?"

I laughed.

He said, "Emotion, finally—hold on, Alicia just walked in, has a look on her face."

Muffled conversation for a few moments, then he came back on.

"What's that thing you explained to young Aaron? Making assumptions before enough info comes in?"

"Sampling error."

"Just happened. Mona Kramm didn't know it but Caspian's got another sib. Younger sister who lives in Albuquerque. She uses her married name, Ionnides, which is why she didn't come up initially. But God bless Alicia, she kept rooting and found a joint obituary for both parents in *The Columbus Dispatch*."

I said, "The parents died a couple of years apart."

"Maybe the kids did a twofer to save dough. The sister—Katie—is a cook at a chicken joint, so no trust fund."

Or Bankster family dynamics had been interesting.

I said, "How'd she react to Caspian's death?"

"She got pretty overwhelmed, couldn't talk anymore, said she'd call back later. To my surprise, she did but just to tell me she had to work, her break was at noon. You wanna listen in or is the *normal* stuff intruding on your schedule?"

"Nothing normal until tomorrow," I said.

"Wish I could say that."

I was at his office by a quarter to twelve.

He said, "Your crack about if I could see you, you'd be kneeling got me thinking. Why not a face-to-face? I emailed Katie and asked if we could do it on FaceTime and she said sure. Any cyber-shrink tips?"

I said, "Nope. Good thinking, you'll have access to nonverbal cues."

"The remote thing, think it could ever take off for you guys?"

"Tele-therapy?" I said. "It's already done when face-to-face isn't possible."

"And . . ."

"It wouldn't work for a lot of my work. Getting down and playing with kids and being there to reassure them. Talking to adults remotely is better than nothing. But personal contact's a big thing for humans and other species."

"Yeah," he said. "Can't see any reason for it to become the next big thing. But who knows? We might even get those flying cars the experts have been predicting for what, seventy years?"

I said, "Wait long enough, anyone can be an expert."

He half swiveled toward the screen. "You feeling like being on-screen?"

"If you want me to ask questions I should be."

"Okay, let me fool with this." Tilting the screen. Activating the app. Tilting again.

The resulting small box in the lower right corner was nearly filled by his big pale face, with mine occupying a sliver. He adjusted some more, tried to fit both of us in, ended up with two half-faces.

I said, "Keep it mostly on yourself, you're the star. Just introduce me at the outset so we don't spring anything on her. She's stressed enough."

He said, "My face? Not exactly comforting." But he tinkered some more, finally found the optimal angle, and called a number.

Four rings before a woman appeared on the monitor. Late twenties, pudding-faced, with short dark hair, wearing a white apron over an aqua shirt. Raw eyes, downturned lips, dark hair drawn up in a bun. Maybe stress but I suspected only partially and that frown was habitual.

Katie Ionnides was twenty-nine but already sporting wrinkles perpendicular to her mouth.

Behind her was what looked like an outdoor parking lot. Traffic hum in the background. A pickup truck crossed the screen then vanished. Pigeons pecked near a dumpster.

Katie Ionnides's image jiggled. Using a handheld phone. Unsteady.

Milo said, "Hi, Ms. Ionnides. Can you see us?"

"Yes, sir."

"I'm Lieutenant Sturgis and this is Alex Delaware."

I said, "Hi."

She nodded.

I made out a few more blurry details. An unoccupied picnic table, cups and napkins on top. Behind that, a mock-adobe building topped by a sign too distant to read.

Milo said, "Again, we are really sorry about your brother."

She said, "Thanks. Charlie was . . . he didn't deserve this."

"Absolutely not. Is there anyone you can think of who might want to harm him?"

"No, sir."

"When's the last time you and Charlie had contact?"

Katie Ionnides glanced to the right and bit her lip. "He called . . . I want to say a little over a year ago. It was right after my anniversary. Our anniversary, me and Stavros—my husband—we're together three years. Charlie forgot the real date but it was nice he called."

"What about before that?"

Katie Ionnides scratched the side of her nose. Another right-hand glance. "This is going to sound bad, sir, but not for a while. Charlie and me didn't have regular contact. He kind of . . . left the family. Left me, really."

"When did that happen?"

"He actually physically left," she said, "once my parents were gone." She shook her head, dispelling euphemism. "Once they died. He *really* left, like here"—touching her heart—"way before that."

Deep sigh. "It's not his fault. It was really rough for Charlie. I guess you know. Do you? That he was gay?"

"We do."

"So you get it," she said. "It was rough for all of us. Our family. But especially for Charlie. He wanted to be himself but they weren't hearing it."

Milo said, "Mom and Dad didn't want to know."

"They didn't want to know *anything*," she said, with sudden vehemence. "They both drank all the time and got physical."

"With Charlie?"

"With Charlie, with me and Joey—my other brother. With themselves."

"Sounds like a tough situation."

She shrugged. "It was what you'd call hell, sir. I was the first to get out. I had a boyfriend and then I had Stavros. Joey and Charlie stayed but then Joey had a bad accident and they put him in a home. Charlie didn't like the place, he said there were roaches and it was filthy but they weren't changing it because it was cheap. They started using some of Joey's payments for themselves. Then they died from smoking and drinking and left us nothing but debt and Charlie moved Joey out to L.A. I said you're leaving me? He said, I have to. And that was it. The anniversary is the first time he called me in a long time."

Another chest heave. She wiped both hands on her apron.

I said, "Charlie broke off emotional contact long before."

"He was mad at everyone," she said. "Including me 'cause I'd escaped and he thought I'd left him holding the bag. Like I was supposed to stick around and never have a life? Like after I got pregnant and Stavros wanted to marry me I should abort and stick around and be a *punching* bag?"

I said, "Charlie suggested abortion?"

"He didn't have to. He just kept telling me being a mom was going to be too much for me, I'd mess the kid up. Stavros got mad and told him to fuck off—pardon the language. I didn't want anything to happen so I said let's be cool, Stavros. Then Charlie left so I said let's just book, Stavros. So we booked. We just drove west, had no idea. We ended up here, it was warm, Stavros got a job at a warehouse and even though I was pregnant, I got this job, cooking chicken, and after the baby was a year, they gave it back to me. I was always good at chicken. When we could afford it. We had jobs, we had Shiloh, everything was good."

Her lips dipped lower. Vertical wrinkles deepened.

I said, "Charlie didn't acknowledge that?"

"How could he if he didn't even know? The time before the anniversary when he called we had a fight. He said the place he found for Joey in L.A. was no better than the dump in Columbus, he wanted serious money to get something better for Joey, family had to stick together. I said why do you need money, everything's covered by SSI. He said not in L.A., the place he wanted was nicer, it cost extra to keep Joey there. I said, sorry, nothing to spare, and he hung up and that was that. I was surprised when he called about the anniversary. Even though he got the wrong day."

The on-screen image was too indistinct to make out tears but her swiping at both eyes implied them.

"If I'da had money, I'da given it. Even though Joey was never nice to me, he was the oldest, had started acting like *him*."

I said, "Like your father."

Two emphatic nods. "Drinking himself stupid, getting nasty. That's how it happened. He got stupid drunk, crashed his motorcycle into a tree, and got totally messed up."

"And Charlie took over his care."

"In L.A.," said Katie Ionnides. "Where it's expensive. His idea. Like me and Stavros have L.A. money."

"Was the anniversary call the last time you heard from Charlie?"

"Nope, one more time and it was kinda weird."

"How so?"

"Like I said, the time before he hung up mad that I wouldn't give him money for Joey. And to be honest, I was kinda mad, too. That he didn't understand my situation. So we basically had no contact for a while. Then the anniversary call was just . . . short. Then, like six months ago, he calls out of the blue and says everything's great, he's working all the time doing hair, plans to become famous."

"How?"

"Through this new friend, some genius psychiatrist—she's helping him align his spirit or something like that. Also, he changed his name to Caspian Delage. Which I thought was stupid and bogus sounding. I'm also thinking if you can afford a fancy psychiatrist, why are you calling me while I'm cooking chicken to get my money?"

Milo said, "Did he name the psychiatrist?"

"No," said Katie Ionnides. "Maybe he woulda but I didn't care and I wasn't having it." Another eye swipe. "I hung up on him. Now he's . . . so who killed him?"

"We've just started investigating."

"Oh." Another hand-wipe on the apron. "So is the . . . do I need to do something about him? About his . . . you know."

"Disposition of the body will have to wait a while. You have no obligation but if you're interested, I can put you in touch with the coroner."

"Hmm," she said. "Let me think about it. I need to think about it."

26

Wishing Katie Ionnides well, Milo thanked her and ended the session.

I said, "Another link between Cordi and Caspian. Tough family lives."

"Misery lusting for company? Nice insight but unless I'm missing something, she told me nothing I can use."

He got a text. Read, cursed violently, shot to his feet.

Tight lips, hot eyes, white face.

"Mr. Hoffgarden has shown up."

I said, "Great."

"Not so great. Let's take separate cars, don't know how long I'll be stuck there."

The hills above the northbound lanes of the 405 freeway are generally an uncomplicated drive from the station. Sepulveda to Sunset, a quick right, a quick left.

Orange cones due to police activity had stopped the traffic at Sunset and it took me a while to edge close enough to an imperious traffic cop so I could flash my LAPD consultant's badge. It's long expired but I've never bothered renewing because most people have no interest in details.

Luckily, that applied to Mr. Traffic. Grudgingly, he moved a few cones and I cruised past murderous looks from less fortunate motorists.

The hills are softly rounded suggestions of altitude, sometimes green, now bearded with high dry grass that gave them a frosted look. I parked next to an LAFD ambulance occupied by two firefighters eating sandwiches, walked north to a border of billowing yellow tape, and got waved under by a uniform chewing gum at an aerobic level.

Milo stood fifty or so yards up, flanked by Reed and Alicia. Detective Sean Binchy was positioned away from them, closer to the tape. Tall, lanky, freckled, with spiky red hair, Sean wore his usual navy suit, expressive tie, and the Doc Marten boots that evoke a past life as a ska-punk bassist.

I saved Sean's life a couple of years ago, spent a long time with him afterward, arranged for a master therapist named Larry Daschoff to help him with incipient PTSD. All that had changed our relationship and Sean tended to avoid contact with me. But he'd never stopped being friendly. Even the day after nearly falling from a twenty-plus-story building.

He stopped working his phone, flashed a country-boy smile. "Doc. Hey."

We pumped hands.

"Nice tan, Sean."

"Bible camp near Crater Lake, took the family, did the camping thing, some music, awesome."

He cocked his head toward the other D's. "Loot asked me to find the decedent's phone carrier, still working on it."

"Good to see you, Sean."

"You, too, Doc."

I continued up a narrow path that scythed through the grass. Not a planned access, a rut caused by years of surreptitious foot-traffic.

The hillside's a combination of hard-to-access private property that forms the bottom borders of ambitious houses on stilts, along with intermittent patches of county easements that exist for no apparent reason.

Nice to see the grass back, along with clumps of pretty blue statice, other flowering succulents, and seedlings rebounding.

A couple of years ago fires had ravished California, and much of this land had been charred to the roots. Self-labeled experts predicted ten to twenty years before anything grew. As with everything, the issue had turned political and contentious, with blame leveled at climate change, government overreach, government underreach, the failure of greedy rich people to maintain their land, willful suppression of animal habitats.

The real reason turned out to be a cooking fire caused by intoxicated carelessness in a homeless encampment that had escaped everyone's attention.

As far as I knew, the homeless had moved on, but I didn't know much and I wondered how and why Tyler Hoffgarden had ended up here.

As I climbed, I scanned for shoe prints or drag marks, saw none. When I was a few feet from the three detectives, the slope eased into a flat background and activity clarified: a pop-up tent; coroner's investigators and crime scene techs passing in and out; two uniformed officers running metal detectors over the brush; a hard-breathing Belgian Malinois leading a handler in hurried arcs.

In counterpoint to all that, two burly men stood to the right, motionless, taking in the view of the freeway. Crypt drivers waiting to transport yet another body bag to North Mission Road.

Alicia and Moe said, "Hey, Doc," in unison.

Milo nodded and eyed the pop-up. "Feel free to look but my advice is don't."

I said, "Just for a sec," and headed for the tent.

Why? A perverse fear of missing out? Plain old habitual compulsiveness?

In the spirit of being kind to myself, I decided on not wanting to miss a crucial detail.

But who knows?

The smell hit me first and endured well beyond the split-second image that filled my eyes and my head.

Something in clothing. The flesh that wasn't garbed was a weird combination of dehydration in some places and slick, gelled putrescence in others.

I got out of there and returned to the detectives.

Milo said, "Learn anything?"

"To take your advice. Who found him?"

"A homeless couple, looking for a nice place to set up camp."

Alicia said, "Hopefully not with Sterno."

"Well taken, kid, but these two were good citizens. Ran down to Sunset and flagged a motorist who called it in, then stuck around."

Alicia turned to me. "And got compensated by Loo's generosity."

I said, "Lunch money?"

She said, "More like lunch, dinner, brunch the next day."

Milo said, "It's all about working with the citizenry. Anyway, before I got here, patrol showed up, took down the basics, and taped it off. C.I.'s guessing three, four days, sent photos to Basia and she said that sounded right, pending her hands-on. As you saw, the body was left clothed. What you couldn't tell was it was facedown with two bullet holes at the back of the skull and rope burns around both wrists and shins. So he was trussed, maybe even hog-tied. So far, no casings, a careful shooter or a revolver. I.D. was no mystery, Hoffgarden's wallet was in his jean pocket. His face was pretty much eaten away by decomp and animals but the hair color's right and there's not a lot of people his size."

I said, "Sean said he's still looking for the phone server. Wallet on the scene but no phone?"

Reed said, "Nope, and no cash in the wallet."

Alicia said, "Plus still no sighting of the Mini anywhere in the county."

I said, "Robbery taken further?"

Reed said, "That's how I saw it." Alicia nodded.

Milo said, "Or someone wants us to think so."

Both younger detectives flinched.

I said, "Didn't see any drag marks. Did it happen here?"

"The blood says yes."

"So Hoffgarden was marched uphill, bound, and shot? A man his size with mixed martial training?"

Milo said, "We're thinking more than one offender."

Alicia said, "The gangs have been doing team-things for home invasions and street heists. Three, four, five lowlifes swarm, point firearms, and overwhelm the victim. Sometimes they shoot in the air, sometimes they just shoot. Most of what we've seen has been southside or Venice but there was an ADW/attempted homicide in Beverly Hills last year and the idiots who pulled that one off got busted trying the same thing in La Canada."

Reed said, "Mixed martial is fine but an army against you changes everything."

Milo said, "Okay, onward. Moe, you've had contact with Hoffgarden's landlady so you do the victim's warrant and you and Alicia handle the toss. Sean will stay on the phone search and I'll be here until I start to feel useless."

"Got it, L.T."

The two of them left.

Milo said, "Let's take a stretch."

We walked past the pop-up, got back on the footpath until it ended at a surprise: a copse of young sycamores ranging from two feet of tender growth to trees six feet tall.

Scattered planting, not a human intervention. Sycamores are native trees, fast growing, always primed for a reboot. A couple more seasons and they'd be towering.

Ten to twenty years.

Milo stood with his back to the mini-grove, pulled out a panatela, lit up, blew perfectly circular smoke rings.

I said, "The kids think robbery. You're not buying no link to Cordi."

"There's gotta be something," he said. "Don't know what it is, but stuff just doesn't happen."

I wondered about that. A man with temper issues like Tyler Hoffgarden had plenty of opportunities for getting into trouble.

My jacket pocket vibrated; my turn to get a text. Superior Court judge Wendy Abrahamson.

Milo said, "You need to get that?"

"Eventually." I pocketed the phone.

"Any thoughts about Hoffgarden?"

"Not yet," I said. "His phone records could tell you a lot."

He crossed his fingers. "Thanks for that and thanks for coming. Probably a waste of your time but I know you like to look at scenes."

"I do."

"I'll walk you back. Keep you posted."

27

I called Judge Wendy Abrahamson's chambers from the Seville. Her clerk put her on immediately.

"Thanks for the quick get-back, Alex. This is no doubt bullshit but I got a complaint about you from a lawyer. A case you haven't even started."

I said, "Lewis Evan Porer, *Deeb versus McManus.*"

"Something really did happen?"

"He tried to pressure me into changing the way I work."

"How so?"

"He kept pushing for me to sit down with him before I met the principals on the pretext of educating me. You know what he was really after."

She said, "First dibs so he could influence you. Did it get nasty?"

"Not at all, Wendy. I just insisted on sticking with the usual and he didn't like being told no. The funny thing is, he called a couple of days later and apologized."

"Did he," she said. "Sounds like he's being manipulative."

"That would be my take."

"Lewis *Evan* Porer," she said. "You've got to wonder about someone who introduces himself with his middle name."

I said, "Has he appeared before you?"

"Never, I guess there's always a first . . . *entre nous,* he did come across like a tool."

I've always wondered about the derivation of that insult. Tools are, by nature, useful.

"What's his specific beef with me, Wendy?"

"Bad attitude and unprofessionalism leading to potential bias."

I said. "I wouldn't let him bias me so I'm likely to be biased."

She laughed. "The workings of a fine legal mind. So where do we go with it?"

"Up to you. If appointing someone else makes your life easier, no sweat."

Wendy Abrahamson let several moments go by. No surprise; she's habitually thoughtful.

"So," she said, "I'm supposed to let Porer come in and shape court procedure? Naw, I don't think so, it'll be business as usual, Alex. Speaking of which, we're ready to go on this one so you can start interviewing. Porer represents the wife and he impresses me as the type who'll play around with stays and delays. But no reason you can't talk to the husband."

"Bias be damned."

She laughed. "That should be a slogan."

"For who?"

"Everyone."

By the time I got home, a message from "the law offices of Meredith Rinaldi" had been lodged at my answering service. The rest of my calls were follow-ups on ongoing custody cases.

Nothing from Milo.

I called Rinaldi back, got put on hold for a minute or so before a woman said, "Doctor? This is Meredith. I represent Conrad Deeb in his divorce and the judge said it's time to get going. What's your process?"

"I meet with parents, then the children, then whichever ancillary sources I think are important."

"Ancillary being . . ."

"Teachers, babysitters, nannies, grandparents. Anyone I think could be informative."

"Sounds like an involved process," she said.

"Doesn't have to be."

"Okay . . . in this case it's a kid, singular. Three years old and from what I've seen she doesn't talk much. Would you still need to actually meet her?"

"Yes."

A beat. "Okay, your wheelhouse. May I have Dr. Deeb call you personally?"

"That would be best. What kind of doctor is he?"

"Historian," said Meredith Rinaldi, as if she just discovered a rare species.

I said, "Then he should be pretty good at giving a personal history."

"Pardon— oh. Heh. Should he use the same number I did?"

"Yes."

"Thanks, Dr. Delaware. I'm sure you'll do a thoughtful job."

"I'm assuming Judge Abrahamson explained my fee schedule."

"Her clerk did," said Meredith Rinaldi. "Pardon my saying so but it is a bit . . . steep vis-à-vis other consultants I've worked with."

I said nothing.

"Still," she said, "I suppose one gets what one pays for. Hopefully."

◆

By day's end, I still hadn't heard from Milo and did my final check-in with the service. Pauline was on duty again.

"Hi, Dr. Delaware. A Mr. Conrad Deeb would like to meet with you about his daughter, Philomena. Here are a couple of numbers where you can reach him."

"Mr. not Dr.?" I said.

"Actually, he just said Conrad. Sounded like a nice guy."

Two 818 numbers. Voicemail on the first, quick pickup at the second.

"This is Conrad."

"Dr. Delaware returning your call."

"Doctor?—ah, the psychologist. Thanks for getting back. I suppose we need to meet."

I suppose I need to have a prostate exam.

I said, "When's a good time for you?"

"I'm a teacher, only have one course, so my time's pretty open. Anything but Friday. I have to say this is the first time I've done this."

"Spoken to a psychologist?"

"Gotten embroiled in a custody dispute. Is there anything I should bring?"

"Just yourself, Professor."

"Professor?" he said. "Oh, Meredith told you." He chuckled. "According to her it could help make me seem more respectable."

"Being a professor?"

"Yup," said Conrad Deeb. "But I have to say, I'm not sure. You know what people think of academics—heads in the clouds. May I ask what we'll be doing? Overall. Contextually."

"I'll be taking a history and you can offer any additional information you think will help me."

"Help you decide if I get to spend significant time with Philo-mena."

"Let's discuss everything when you get here, Professor."

"No phone chat? Got it, sure, no problem. I am ready, more than willing, and so far, able. When?"

"I've got ten o'clock slots tomorrow or the day after."

"Let's do the day after."

Flexible schedule, able and ready.

Not so much, willing?

CHAPTER

28

Just after eleven the following morning, Milo called from his office landline, sounding light and energetic.

Revived. A man who'd just slurped from the fountain of youth.

I said, "Good news?"

"Sean finally got Hoffgarden's phone carrier to give up his call history for a month and it just might amount to something. Also, Basia put a rush on Hoffgarden's prelim. Markings from what look like rope bindings and a big bruise on his back like someone pinned him down with a knee. No evidence of hog-tying but she can't be sure. Two 9mm slugs entered Hoffgarden's skull from the back and lodged in the roof of his mouth. The angle of bullet tracks suggest he was kneeling, so the killer wouldn't have to be tall."

"Lying prone but brought to his knees," I said. "Classic execution."

"Guy gets it, alone in the dark," he said. "He had his issues, but still."

"What was time of death?"

"Basia's best guess is fifty to sixty hours before the body was discovered, probably closer to fifty. That fits perfectly with the action on the phone stopping fifty-two hours prior. And not much action, at that. Zero the entire day until nine forty-two p.m. when Hoffgarden calls a number and talks for around a minute. Then two more calls to the same phone—ten oh three and ten twenty-eight, number's registered to a female in Venice. The techs are tracing towers as we speak, shouldn't be hard to confirm where Hoffgarden was. We find the damn Mini Cooper and it gives up something, this probably won't go the whodunit route. The car being missing so long makes me wonder if it was an auto theft gone bad."

I said, "Hoffgarden phoned a female but didn't receive a call-back. Maybe he was angling for a date. Was the phone used postmortem?"

"Nope," he said, "and to me that nudges a plain old street robbery a few rungs lower. Most muggers are low-impulse-stupid, right? First thing they do is rack up calls before tossing. The same goes for leaving Hoffgarden's credit and debit cards in the wallet but taking the cash and picking up the shells. A car specialist on the other hand might concentrate on the wheels and the cash."

"Or we've got someone overly clever."

"Meaning?"

"Someone doing an amateur staging. No need for the shooter to be tall but he'd still need to be powerful and large to subdue Hoffgarden, tie him up, and get him up those hills. Who's the female?"

"Twenty-eight-year-old white female named Lisette Montag. It's possible she has nothing to do with it and someone used her phone—stolen, lost, lent. But if she does end up being a dirty-bird, no reason she couldn't have enlisted muscle."

"Any criminal record?"

"No. Her place in Venice is maybe twenty minutes from Hoffgarden's, so yeah, he coulda been trying for a booty-grab. Obviously, I need to talk to her."

Lisette Montag had triggered a trace of recollection. Nothing I could put a fix on but I brought up my online case notes and quickly got the answer.

I said, "Montag could be Hoffgarden's love interest, past or present. But she's also someone who lived in Palm Springs the same time as Hoffgarden and Slope."

"How'd you find *that* out?"

"I bookmarked the *Desert Sun* article on Slope's death. She's one of the people quoted about what a great guy he was. Here's the exact quote: 'The attorney's hairdresser Lisette Montag described Slope as nice, reliable, and super-generous. The two of them were scheduled to have dinner.'"

He said, "Hmmph. I've got it bookmarked, too. Only I didn't think to check."

"You would've once you got Montag's history and found a previous address in the desert."

"Supportive psychotherapy. *Gracias.* So what, she cuts Slope's hair and becomes a big fan?"

"Dinner for two says maybe more. And now that I think about it, she's the second hairdresser we've come across recently."

"Her and Caspian," he said. "Ten paces and draw your scissors? Jesus. Yeah, I'm getting more and more fascinated by Ms. Montag. Gonna comb through her social media and see if I can find out who she hangs with and where she is at various times of day. Then I'll get a face-to-face with her. You have time?"

I checked my appointment book. "For the most part."

"Booked with the normal stuff?"

I said. "We'll work it out."

He said, "We always do. What a life you lead."

I polished two reports, one child custody, the other personal injury, got in the car, drove down the Glen, and dropped them in a mailbox.

When I got back, I began some light background on my next custody interviewee.

Conrad Deeb was a visiting lecturer at Cal State Northridge, teaching a class titled Rock 'n' Roll, Reality TV, and Rust: Shifting Values, Symbols, and Perspectives in Popular American Culture.

B.A., Princeton. Not history, American studies. A year at Oxford, then a Harvard Ph.D. and lectureships at NYU; the University of Florida–Gainesville; Rochester; Indiana U.–Bloomington.

Moving around, no tenure, but this early in the game, no sense over-interpreting.

I brewed coffee, delivered a mug to Robin at her studio, got kissed and hugged and smiled at by Robin and Blanche. Then back to my desk, where I conducted my own dive into the online world of Lisette Montag.

Her pages showed her to be a flamboyantly tattooed hard-body with wide-set, ultra-blue eyes and a lean, angular face built around a longish nose and plump but narrow lips. The clothing she chose to share with the world consisted of thong bikinis and lacy black things. Hairstyle and color shifted frequently, the most recent choice an unevenly hemmed, feathery do with the left side buzzed to the scalp and the rest tinted turquoise and cool pink. Streaks of both hues segued smoothly as if applied by an airbrush.

Given her profession, the variety and the flash weren't surprising. Why not be your own billboard?

I looked for a salon address, found none. No phone number, either, just an email address enabling contact for "personalized styling at home or work."

The rest of her public life was heralded by long lists of favorite TV shows, movies, and musical artists.

At the bottom, a single book: *Perfecting Yourself Emotionally and Physically.*

Recreation consisted of "Living life to the fullest."

Travel meant "getting away to Maui or Kauai," illustrated by more bikini shots.

As I combed through her friends, it became clear that Lisette Montag's social net had scooped up two distinct catches: imaginary pals aka celebrities and a few people she actually seemed to know.

Her real-life contacts were all around her age. Women and men, gays and straights, a level of racial and ethnic diversity that would do a human resources department proud.

Varied every way but in terms of body shape.

The folks Lisette Montag held dear lacked any visible body fat.

Thumbnail after thumbnail of toned, spray-tanned physiques ranging from dancer-lithe to iron-pumper bulging. Lots of posing, flexing, stretching, and just plain being adorable.

No sign of Tyler Hoffgarden.

Had he been erased actually and virtually?

I searched for someone large enough to overpower Hoffgarden and two men jumped out at me.

Identical twin behemoths in flesh-colored bicycle shorts managing to grin as they each deadlifted six hundred eighty pounds.

The near-equivalent of three Hoffgardens.

Rodney and Renny Tabash, aka The Buff Brothers. I switched to their pages.

Not much there, just a single shared Instagram site featuring the ongoing quest to conquer iron. The same hypertrophic flaunting, bulging blood vessels, and the kind of smiles you see on constipated infants straining to fill their diapers.

No friends listed.

Twins are no less adjusted than anyone else but when there's pathology it sometimes takes the form of codependency and a steadily narrowing existence.

Alternatively, Rodney and Renny Tabash were too busy destroying and adding compensatory muscle and had no use for words and sentences. Or human contact.

Numbers, on the other hand, were acceptable. Each brother presented detailed logs of weight-lifting progress and meticulous body measurements.

Rodney Tabash stood five foot eleven and seven-eighths tall and had last weighed in at two sixty-four. Renny was an even six feet tall and a smidge lighter at two fifty-nine, a difference not obvious to the naked eye.

Some twins make a point of establishing individual identities. These two seemed intent on avoiding it. Their bathing trunks varied as often as Lisette Montag's hair but in every photo they'd color-matched. The same went for their hair. Nothing like Montag's chameleon coiffure; two options.

A: skinned heads. B: zinc-yellow faux hawks.

I rolled through their muscle charts. Both had placed in numerous amateur strength contests. Over five hundred pounds of unyielding bulk, between them. Not hard to imagine them subduing, trussing Tyler Hoffgarden, and toting him up the hill to the kill-site.

Neither twin mentioned a source of income and a continued search failed to produce any.

Available to freelance?

I phoned Milo. "There are a couple of guys you should look at."

He said, "The rhinos, just about to call you. Yeah, they could tag-team Hoffgarden into submission even without a gun. And flick Caspian like a flake of dandruff. Plus they've got priors. Nothing juicy: two batteries, one assault, all committed when they were mere lads of nineteen and weighed only two twenty apiece."

I said, "They got arrested together?"

"Every single time," he said. "Bar fights in Fresno where they grew up. No jail time, which could mean anything from good lawyers to insufficient evidence to scared witnesses. Can you imagine getting up on the stand and testifying against them?"

I said, "Not worth getting deadlifted."

"Interesting turn of phrase. They live together in an apartment in Studio City. I just sent Alicia and Sean out there to keep an eye out. The one I really want to talk to is Moses, he knows that world. But his mom just had some sort of allergic reaction, he had to take her to the doctor. The question I have for you is who do I approach first, Lisette or the Gruesome Twosome? I'm thinking her because with their size and proclivities, I'm gonna need an army, and without evidence going in gangbusters is a bad idea."

I said, "Any way to get Montag's pings?"

"No grounds," he said, "unless Hoffgarden's pings show him near her place right before he was murdered and the techs are still working on it. Another problem is that if Montag is involved, she's the contractor. You know how it is with conspiracies. Start with the hired help and get them to snitch."

I said, "You could still start with Montag as long as you do it nonthreateningly. No suspicions, she came up on Hoffgarden's call list, you're talking to everyone he knew. If she contacts the twins right afterward, Alicia and Sean will be there to see if they make a move."

"Hmm. Makes sense. Okay, I'll have a female officer dummy-call Montag, try to sell her magazine subscriptions or something. She's home, I drop in. How are you schedule-wise the rest of the day?"

"Open. Tomorrow, my morning's booked."

"Hopefully it's not gonna take that long," he said. "Two hairdressers and three musclemen."

I said, "Go into a bar."

He cracked up. "Can you see any link between Hoffgarden's murder, Cordi, and Caspian?"

I said, "Cordi doesn't come up in Montag's network but the one book Montag lists is something called *Perfecting Yourself Emotionally and Physically.* That sounds like the kind of thing Cordi might recommend."

"Montag was Cordi's patient?"

"Maybe referred by Hoffgarden."

"Life coaching goes bad?" he said. "Not much of a motive for murder, Alex. Then there's Slope. He did Hoffgarden's divorce, tried to foist Cordi off as an expert, worked *out* at Hoffgarden's new gym in the desert, where he got his hair cut by Montag and ended up strangled in bed. There's something going on, Alex, but it feels out of reach."

"Get Montag or the twins in the box," I said. "If it's the twins, interview them separately."

"Yeah, okay—hold on, Moses is calling in."

Dead air for a couple of minutes before he returned. "Mom ate a kiwi, got an itchy throat, doc gave her a shot, she's okay, he's on the way back. Turns out he knows the twins. Used to work out at the same gym and spotted them a few times when they bench-pressed. Simultaneously. They always lift simultaneously. Wonder if they wipe each other's bottoms."

I made my voice plummy. "There does seem to be a blurring of identities. Moe ever see signs of violence in them?"

"The opposite, he was surprised to hear about the Tabashes' priors, said they're dumb as blocks of cheddar and mild-mannered, except when they're pumping. We've got nothing on them but appearing on Montag's pages and being big, so it could be another dud. In any event, Moses no longer uses that gym, too crowded, but he's pretty sure they do, it's close to their apartment."

"He's been to their place?"

"He's seen them walking home."

"Speaking of which, what do they drive?"

"Hold on . . . no registered vehicles."

I said, "How old are they?"

"Twenty-five."

"The Uber generation."

He said, "No one wants to take the wheel . . . but Montag does. Six-year-old Ford Explorer."

I said, "Plenty of room for a passenger or two. And a captive."

He said, "I'm gonna drive by her place right now."

"If you want, pick me up."

"I want."

Lisette Montag lived on Brooks Avenue off Sixth Street in the converted garage of a twenties bungalow spray-stuccoed Pepto-Bismol pink. Like the main building, a box with a low-peaked tar-paper roof. What a preschooler might produce when asked to draw a house.

A thoughtful conversion: separate driveway perpendicular to the lot, three windows dressing up the front, an eight-foot redwood fence shielding the guesthouse from the rest of the property.

Privacy that could be used all kinds of ways.

Milo said, "I don't see her shooting anyone but you never know." He slipped his hand under his jacket, unsnapped the holster of his Glock. We got out, breathed a curious mix of ocean brine and motor oil, and headed for the driveway where a gray Ford Explorer sat. The SUV's nose was a couple of feet from the door. As we edged around it, Milo touched the hood. "Cold."

He patted the bulge above his right hip and rapped on the door.

No response but a second try produced footsteps and a female voice. "Who is it?"

"Police, ma'am. Incident in the neighborhood."

"What kind of incident?"

"Robbery."

"Oh, shit. Figures."

Flash of badge, creak of hinges.

Lisette Montag, now sporting long, snow-white hair, looked at us with no evident anxiety. Today's black lace ensemble was a bra and shorts under a filmy thing tied at the neck and billowing free. Smooth, white leg-flesh gave way to black leather boots at the knee. Even in stacked heels, she stood no taller than five-three. Unless she had magical mystical ninja training or a handheld nuclear weapon, zero chance of subduing an average-sized man, let alone Tyler Hoffgarden.

The same couldn't be said of the identical hulks testing the springs of a couch a few feet behind her.

The Tabash twins were in a skinned-head phase. Maybe to showcase the riot of tattoos snaking across their crowns. Bare-chested above white shorts, socks, and shoes, they regarded us with wide eyes.

The only evidence of Milo's surprise was a quick blink.

He said, "Hey, sorry if we're interrupting something."

Lisette Montag said, "We're fine," without looking back. "So where was the robbery, Officer?"

Rodney or Renny said, "Oh shit," in a comically high voice. Mike Tyson recovering from a helium spurt. I tried to resist the clichéd assumption: overcompensation. Couldn't fight it.

His brother said, "Cops?"

Lisette Montag whipped her head toward them. Instead of calming them down, her stare made their mouths twitch like galvanized frogs. Her fists clenched. But she was smiling when she turned back to us.

Milo said, "A few blocks away."

"Happens all the time, no one ever gets caught." Faint tremolo in her voice. Her eyes had grown active.

"That's why we're here, ma'am. It happened three nights ago. Were you here and if so did you hear anything?"

Montag fooled with white strands. "Yeah, I was here. But no, I didn't hear anything."

One of the twins made a squeaky noise. Another warning look from Montag.

Milo said, "Were you guys also here?"

"They weren't."

The twin on the left said, "Yes, we were, sir!"

The twin on the right said, "I *told* you, Lise," and stood.

She said, "Why don't you just sit down and chill, Renny."

Hesitation, then obedience. Two massive heads drooped. The pitiful shame of mastiffs caught messing in the house.

Lisette Montag said, "Sorry about my cousins, they're a little—" Eye roll, quick tap of one temple.

"We're not cousins!" said Rodney.

"*We're* sorry," said Renny. "She told us—"

Montag wheeled again. "Shut up and let these guys do their job." Pained smile. "Okay, Officer?"

Rodney said, "It *is* their job."

Renny said, "We're really sorry, sirs, we didn't know!"

Milo took a couple of steps forward, keeping an eye on Montag as he favored the twins with an avuncular smile. "What are you guys sorry about?"

Montag said, "Nothing. They're just talking. They're kind of . . ." Tapping her temple.

"It's *her* fault," said Renny.

"She said it was just to show off." Rodney. "We didn't know what she was—"

"Shut the fuck up!"

Milo kept the smile going. "What was to show off, guys?"

"The gun. We didn't do nothing but bring him. She had the gun."

"She shot him, we're, so so so so so so sorry!"

Montag bolted toward a doorway to the right of the sofa. Still sitting, Rodney reached out and snapped a giant paw over her wrist. She thrashed and gnashed as he held her at arm's length.

"See?" said his brother. "We're helping *you*."

Tears in his eyes.

Milo said, "This sounds like something we're going to need to check out."

"It's bullshit," said Montag. "I promise you. They're retarded."

Wincing; increased pressure from Rodney's mitt.

Milo said, "Thanks, pal, I'll take it from here."

"Yes, sir." Releasing sausage fingers, Rodney sat back as Milo took hold of Montag.

Milo said, "This is for your safety and ours," as he cuffed her. She cursed and spat. A gob of spittle landed on his cheek. He wiped it on his sleeve.

The twins remained on the couch. Terrified to the point of shaking.

Milo said, "Guys, I need you to keep helping me, okay?"

Simultaneous nods.

"Great. Thanks. I'm going to put your friend here in my car. Could you please just wait for me patiently?"

Renny said, "Yes, sir."

Rodney said, "She's not our cousin. She shot him."

Renny said, "We want to be safe."

Milo said, "From what?"

"Her."

Rodney said, "We came here to tell her. We want it to be *over*."

I stood in the doorway as Milo hustled Lisette Montag, still struggling, into the backseat of the Impala. During the time it took to belt her in, close the door and reopen with some sort of warning, shut it again and get on his phone, I'd managed to catch the twins' downcast eyes and smile.

Meager comfort; four giant hands hadn't stopped shaking. At the exact same pace, as if the product of a common nervous system.

I said, "Don't worry, guys, we'll take care of you."

"I hope so," said Renny, doubtfully.

"We need . . . something," said Rodney.

"Mom and Dad," said Renny. "They could help us."

I said, "Where are they?"

"Vacation," said Rodney.

"A cruise on a ship," said Renny. "They're supposed to call us to-night."

"I hope they do," said Rodney.

"Do you have their number?"

Both of them recited a 310 that I copied. "Thanks. We'll do our best to get you in touch."

Renny said, "They're on a ship, sir."

Rodney grimaced. "What . . . it was just supposed to be . . ."

"Protecting her," said Renny. "She said he was dangerous."

"We were trying to help 'cause she cut our hair."

"We *really* didn't know."

Milo came back. "Okay, guys."

His reappearance seemed to calm the twins. I've seen that before. People comforted by his presence.

Families of victims. Others who'd done no wrong.

These two had no idea.

I knew what they'd done but I found myself feeling sorry for them and told Milo about their parents.

He said, "Out to sea, huh? Where?"

Twin head shakes.

"Okay, give me that number."

"Here you go."

He pocketed the credit slip I'd used. "Great. Once we figure things out, guys, we can put you in touch with your parents. Meanwhile, it's going to get a little busy around here. A bunch of people are coming over and guess what, you know one of them. Moses Reed."

Dual blank looks.

"Blond guy, a little older than you, used to work out at Magnet Gym?"

Continued confusion.

Milo said, "Maybe you knew him as Moe? Blond crew cut, around your heights, maybe two twenty-five."

Head shakes.

"He knows *you* guys. Says he used to spot your bench presses."

"Oh," said Renny. "The cop."

"That's him, my friend."

"He's strong," said Rodney. "Relatively." Uttering the word with pride.

"He was a good spotter," said Renny. "But I don't think he could do a full press with it."

"Totally not," said Rodney. "But he could spot." To Milo: "He's your friend."

"Yup."

"Wow."

Milo pulled up a chair and faced them. "Anyway, is there anything else you want to tell me about what Lisette did?"

"She called us and said there was a guy."

Milo said, "Tyler Hoffgarden."

"She didn't say the name," said Renny.

"She said he wanted to rape her," said Rodney.

"She said she needed to scare him."

"She said we're the only ones could do it 'cause he's big."

"Not as big as us."

"No way." Rodney managed a shy smile.

His brother saw it and imitated but with scant conviction.

"She said come here and when I tell you, surprise him."

Milo said, "Surprise Tyler Hoffgarden."

"Yes, sir."

"How?"

Both twins raised their arms and clawed their hands.

Milo said, "Grab him?"

Rodney said, "Grab him and control him."

"Here," said Renny, touching a spot on his own shoulder.

"You pinch it," said Rodney, "then you control."

"He tried to fight us," said Renny.

"We controlled him. We don't like rapers."

"We know girls who got raped. If they wanted us to control a dude we'd control."

"He was big," said Rodney. "No way she could've controlled."

"Didn't take long," said Renny. "Then she tied him up and put a towel in his mouth."

"No, a washcloth," said Rodney.

Renny palmed his own brow. "Right. No way a towel could fit even with his big mouth."

His brother laughed.

Renny said, "It is funny. But not . . ." Looking down again.

Milo said, "Not what?"

"What happened," said Renny.

Rodney said, "She said put him in the Explorer, we're taking a ride. We didn't even see it."

"See what?" said Milo.

"The gun," said Renny. "It's in there." Pointing.

Milo said, "In her bedroom?"

"Right on her bed."

"She just showed it to us," said Rodney.

"To scare us, sir."

"Then she said she'd pay us even more if we didn't snitch."

Milo said, "More than . . ."

"What she first said, sir," said Renny.

"A hundred."

"Dollars?"

"Yes, sir."

"Each? Or between you?"

"Each," said Rodney. "We didn't do it for the money."

"She said he was a raper."

"We wanted to help."

Milo said, "Then she offered you more to shut up."

"Two hundred," said Renny.

"We went home and were scared," said Rodney. "Because of what happened. So we came here to tell her we were really scared."

"She showed us the gun and said 'nothing to be scared of.' Then she said I'll give you five hundred."

"Five hundred, you can stock up on protein shakes."

"We were still scared."

"Then you showed up, sir. Thank goodness."

Milo said, "You guys were scared because of what happened."

"Yes, sir."

"What exactly happened?"

"We put him in the Explorer. In the back part. She tied him up more. More rope and bungee cords that she hooked over the seat."

"She put the washcloth deeper. He made noises."

"I sat in back," said Renny.

"I sat in front," said Rodney. "She drove."

"Where?"

"It was dark, sir," said Rodney. "We didn't know."

Milo said, "But she drove straight to where it happened."

"Yes, sir."

"And then?"

The twins looked at each other.

Rodney said, "It got bad."

"But not at first," said Renny. "We believed her. We really did."

Milo said, "Believed what?"

"It was to scare him, sir."

Rodney said, "Just to scare him."

"To take a little walk and scare him. That's what she said, a little walk."

"She held the flashlight," said Rodney. "Otherwise I'd fall."

Milo said, "You guys were carrying him."

Hesitation.

Milo waited.

Rodney said, "He was pretty light. She said it was just a little walk."

"To scare him," said Milo.

"In the dark, no one there," said Renny. "It *was* scary."

"I'll bet. So then what happened?"

"We carried him."

"Until she said, 'Here.'"

"She said put him down. We laid him on his tummy," said Rodney.

Renny said, "She said put him on his knees."

"Then she said, 'Wait by the Explorer.'"

"Before we got there, we heard it."

Milo said, "Heard what?"

"You know," said Rodney.

"I'm pretty sure I do but I still need to hear it."

"Gunshot," said Renny, barely getting the word out.

"Then another."

"We ran to the Explorer."

"We were thinking get away somewhere."

"But we had nowhere to go."

Milo said, "So you waited."

"Yes, sir."

"And . . ."

"She came back smiling and said, 'Good job, guys. I'll take you home.'"

Rodney said, "She did."

Renny said, "We didn't sleep and we both had to pee all night."

"All night a lot," said Rodney. "And we didn't even protein-load that much."

"It was a light-protein day and we still peed crazy," said Renny. "Maybe our kidneys got scared."

Milo said, "Feeling okay, now?"

"Yes, sir."

"Yes, sir."

"That's great. I gotta tell you guys, you've been really helpful. And if you keep being helpful, we should be able to help you. Okay?"

Twin nods.

"In order to help you, I'm gonna need you to tell your story again over at the police station. Do you think you can do that?"

They looked at each other.

Rodney said, "How do we get there?"

"We'll drive you—Moses Reed will drive you."

"Okay."

"Before that, while we wait, I'ma read you something, okay? Maybe you've seen it on TV. Don't be scared it's just something I need to read to you so I know you understand."

"Yes, sir."

"Yes, sir."

"Here goes, then. You have the right to remain silent . . ."

30

Reed showed up ten minutes later with Alicia. Moments later, a black-and-white screeched up and four officers got out.

Again, I was left with the Tabash twins as Milo went outside and conferred. The Miranda warning had caused the brothers no anxiety. Maybe it was being left on the couch unshackled. Or maybe they didn't get it.

I said, "Some day, huh?"

That seemed to puzzle them. I was still figuring out what to follow up with when Moe Reed came in.

Four eyes lit up.

"Hey, guys." Reed mimed an overhead press.

The twins giggled.

"Hey."

"Hey."

Reed said, "My boss—the lieutenant—said you've been super-helpful. Thanks a ton, guys. If you're ready, I'll drive you back to the station."

"Okay." Renny made it sound like a question. "What will happen there?"

"I'll get you guys something to drink and eat and you can tell the same story you told the lieutenant. Ready?"

Rodney said, "Guess."

The twins exchanged glances and got to their feet. The couch sighed in relief and rose several inches.

Moe stood back and allowed them to pass, then said, "The blue car," and led them to an aqua sedan, not his usual ride.

A pair of monumentally powerful suspects. At worst, accessory before the fact. At best, conspiracy to commit murder. Despite that, no cuffs. Sometimes you need to be creative.

I wondered if some defense attorney might seize upon that. *Is that your usual method, Detective? No? Then obviously, you didn't regard them as true suspects?*

I found myself mapping additional strategy for the twins. Wondering how they'd score on an IQ test, a neuropsych exam . . .

Moe reached the blue car first and held the rear door as the Tabashes wedged themselves in. When he opened the driver's door, a dome light went on and I saw the steel mesh partition isolating the back of the car.

Creative but not stupid.

As Reed drove away, Milo opened the door to the Impala, said something, waited, reached in and drew Lisette Montag out with effort.

No struggle; she'd switched to passive resistance, closing her eyes and going limp and making him work.

Not for long. A couple of uniforms, both females, hurried over and took charge. Carrying Montag with ease as her white hair streamed like cotton candy.

Unceremoniously sliding her in back of their cruiser and belting her in. Milo dismissed the second black-and-white and returned to the house.

I was outside, checking messages.

He closed the pink house's door and said, "Let's go."

I said, "No search?"

"No paper, John says better to wait in case the twins retract or my afterthought Miranda causes problems. Spoke to Sean and by luck Montag has the same carrier as Hoffgarden so he's got a contact to fast-track her calls."

"She say anything?"

"Fuck you, pig. I want a lawyer. Then some really mean stuff. *Then* she tried to bite me, failed but succeeded with another nice load of spit." Fingering a spot on his right cheek.

I said, "Anti-police brutality."

He laughed all the way to the Impala. Stopped and a look back at Montag's house and shook his head. "Talk about weird. I go in prepared to be subtle, find the behemoths right there and they can't wait to express themselves. Would you call them developmentally challenged? Or whatever the acceptable term is now."

I said, "Probably borderline but they're still eyewitnesses with a detailed account. You just got a gift, my friend."

He said, "Yeah, but assembly required."

31

Assembly took the better part of that evening and the following day. Lots of moving parts.

I was home for most of it and got a morning phone report from Milo. Deputy D.A. John Nguyen had consulted with his boss who agreed that the Tabash twins' story and the fact that Lisette Montag was the last person to talk to Tyler Hoffgarden justified an arrest warrant. With that set in place, getting a search warrant for Montag's residence and her Explorer was a formality. Milo, his young D's, and his army of techs worked late into the night.

The front seat of the SUV gave up a rough match to Montag's DNA and that of Renny Tabash, sure to be refined later. The rear offered Rodney Tabash's genetic material and Tyler Hoffgarden's.

Perfect confirmation of the twins' account.

In Hoffgarden's case, sloughed skin cells were also found on the exterior of a size seven sweat sock, with the interior matching Montag's. The final find was a scatter of barely perceptible dried blood on the back of the driver's seat, spied and swabbed by a sharp-eyed tech.

The twins, subdued by incarceration, were represented by a lawyer named Harvey DiPaolo who shepherded their comments. DiPaolo did allow them to confirm that Montag had jammed the sock into Hoffgarden's mouth and that, though restrained, Hoffgarden had struggled "a little" and "by accident" bumped his forehead against the seat.

Dr. Basia Lopatinski had then looked for and found minuscule lacerations—little more than scratches—on the victim's brow.

"Between us," she told Milo, "I probably would've missed it because I was concentrating on some massive edema under the bridge of what the animals left of Hoffgarden's nose and another in his chin."

Both swellings turned out to be resting places for two .32-caliber bullets that had lacked the momentum to exit Hoffgarden's massively boned head.

Milo said, "How come the animals didn't chew over there?"

"Good question," said Basia. "Maybe these are picky Bel Air animals. Or they don't like the smell of lead."

The slugs were too degraded to match to a .32 FÉG PA-63 semi-auto pistol discovered in Lisette Montag's nightstand. Hungarian military manufacture, unregistered, never reported stolen. Montag, repped by a lawyer named Alan Bloomfield, wasn't uttering a syllable.

No need for her cooperation. Toward the end of Milo's compulsive search of the converted garage, during which he discovered weed, cocaine, meth, Ecstasy, a host of prescription pills, and an admirable supply of beauty and hair products, he got an aha moment.

Two .32 casings wrapped in a black silk scarf and stashed in a jewelry box at the rear of an upper bedroom closet shelf. Milo drove them to the lab at six a.m., charmed a senior tech, jumped the line, and got a quick match to the gun.

"Lying on top of earrings and necklaces," he said.

I said, "There are all kinds of adornment."

"Guess she was proud. Must've hated the guy big-time, still have no idea why."

I was playing guitar in the living room as Robin read a book about Amati violins when he called again just before nine p.m.

"Her lawyer claims she has something to offer. I authorized bringing her over from the Pacific Jail, she's en route. Too late for you?"

I looked at Robin.

She laughed.

I said, "On the way."

When I arrived, he showed me a cell-tower ping chart that mapped Tyler Hoffgarden's phone.

Small map: During the last hour of Hoffgarden's life, he'd traveled from his apartment in Culver City to Montag's place in Venice. Then the phone was shut off.

Also available was a transcript of texts between Hoffgarden and Montag for five days prior.

No hostility; flirting advancing to sexting.

The three final contacts were calls, not texts, so impossible to know what was said. But given the steamy tenor of the texts, not hard to imagine.

Milo said, "Like we said, booty-call. Works every time."

He hummed a few bars of "Isn't It Romantic." Better than the ring-tones but not by much.

I said, "She lured him to her place, his guard was down, the twins materialized from the back of the house, blitzed, bound, and gagged him, then stowed him in the Explorer."

"Then they all take a ride. I'd be sympathetic but he still coulda killed *my* victims."

Officially, Hoffgarden was also his victim. No sense getting official.

He looked at his Timex. "Authorized the jail to deliver her an hour ago, hopefully this is gonna happen."

Seconds later, his desk phone rang. "Sturgis. Bring her up."

Milo and I waited by the elevator. A few minutes later, it opened and disgorged Lisette Montag in dark-blue jail clothes. White hair bunned, head down, hands cuffed in front, and shuffling in jail slippers, she was guided by a female uniform from downstairs.

Following closely was a tall, balding, stork-like man in his sixties wearing a black silk T-shirt with a visitor sticker and baggy, stone-washed jeans who introduced himself as Al Bloomfield.

Milo gave Bloomfield my name. It meant nothing to the attorney, which was just fine.

He said, "Pleased to meet you. Considering."

I smiled and he returned the favor, flashing a great set of dentures.

Milo led the procession to the large room he uses for meetings and situations like this. He'd prepped the space, placing two chairs on either side of a small folding table in the center of the room. Asking the patrolwoman to wait outside, he showed Montag and Bloomfield to one side of the table and we took the other.

Montag's head stayed down.

"Evening, Lisette. Mr. Bloomfield. Can I get you something to drink?"

"Thanks but no need," said Bloomfield. "I made sure Lissy was hydrated. Had to, she was looking pretty peaked when I got there, you people should really do better when it comes to caring for your charges."

Milo said, "I'll bear that in mind. So what can I do for you?"

Bloomfield smiled, as if cued by a stooge for a punch line. "At the risk of engaging in an obnoxious cliché, it's not what you can do for us, it's . . ." Instead of finishing, he raised both hands like a conductor evoking a crescendo.

"I'll bite, Counselor. What can you do for us?"

Bloomfield sat back and crossed his legs. Close to ten p.m. but the attorney was chipper and dressed casually. Experience or just a guy going through the motions?

Montag's demeanor remained the same. Grave, defeated, dull-eyed. Less than a day in jail but already pallid and puffy.

Milo crossed his own legs.

Bloomfield said, "Okay. Ms. Montag is ready to truth-tell. I'm aware that officially you can't offer deals, it's a D.A. thing. But of course we both know that a man of your rank, experience, reputation, and rapport with the D.A.'s office is in a position to exert intelligent influence."

"Flattered," said Milo. "Rapport? If only."

"No false modesty, Lieutenant. And *please* no humble-bragging." Bloomfield chuckled.

Bright-eyed and buoyant. Enjoying himself. Then again, he was at no risk of ending up in a cell for the rest of his life.

"What does your client have to offer?"

"Justification."

"For murder."

"For ridding the world of a violent, vicious murderer. We'll be putting forward a self-defense scenario and hope you'll allow yourself to be educated."

Milo put his hands behind his head. "I'm listening, Mr. Bloomfield."

Bloomfield chuckled again. "Before we begin, make sure this is being recorded." He glanced at the one-way mirror. "If you already haven't initiated that process."

Milo got up, left the room, and returned. He'd already set up the equipment in the adjacent room, had just pretended to do it.

"Excellent," said Alan Bloomfield. Shifting his weight, he produced paper from a jean pocket. Folded paper that he unfolded and handed to Montag. Two sheets filled with typing.

She took them but placed them on the table.

Bloomfield said, "Lissy?"

She bit her lip and rubbed her eyes. When she pulled her knuckles away, the irises were pink and moist.

Bloomfield patted her hand. "It's okay, dear, just be honest. I have a good feeling about Lieutenant Sturgis and his colleague—was that Alex?"

I nodded.

Milo said, "Dr. Alex Delaware, our consulting psychologist."

Bloomfield stiffened. "Is he here as some sort of attempted human lie detector?"

I said, "Appreciate the compliment but not that talented."

"What then?" Directed at Milo.

"Dr. Delaware consults on cases where psychological analysis is called for. He's been involved in the Hoffgarden case from the outset. Is there a problem with that?"

Lisette Montag didn't react. I wasn't sure she'd tuned in to any of the exchange.

Alan Bloomfield said, "I need to think about this." He closed his eyes and put his palms together. Seconds later, he snapped to and said, "Sure, no problem. It will help Lisette because any decent psychologist will be able to tell she's not a bad person."

Shifting to me.

I smiled.

Bloomfield wasn't sure what to make of that but said, "Go ahead, dear."

Montag lifted the paper, opened her mouth, tried to speak, produced a hoarse grunt.

Bloomfield said, "This is your time to shine, Lisette. When you're ready."

Montag cleared her throat, coughed once, then again. Her hands shook, causing the papers to billow.

She inhaled and began reading in a monotone.

"I, Lisette Deandra Montag, swear that my story is true."

Turning to Bloomfield.

He said, "It certainly is, dear. Go on."

". . . that my story is true. I formerly lived in Temple City, California, and worked at The Style-Right Hair and Beauty Salon in nearby Palm Desert. During the course of my employment at The Style-Right Hair and Beauty Salon, I met a gentleman named Forrest Slope. Mr. Slope was an attorney who'd just retired and moved to Palm Desert. He had a very good head of thick, wavy hair that required regular . . . attention. He'd tried other haircutters and found them lacking and for that reason came to The Style-Right Hair and Beauty Salon. We'd gone unisex a few months ago and men were coming in more and more because we knew how to treat them with sensitivity."

She stopped, gulped. "I *could* use some water."

Before Milo could respond, I was up and out of the room and filling one of the plastic cups Milo keeps in his office from a lavatory sink. When I returned, no one was talking.

Bloomfield said, "That's something. A doctor fetching H_2O."

I handed the cup to Montag. She drank greedily.

Al Bloomfield said, "Need more, dear? I'm sure the doctor will be happy to fetch you more."

She shook her head, returned to the front sheet, and scanned.

"Take your time," said Bloomfield. "There's no rush."

Montag didn't respond to him. Stayed robotic as she ran her finger down to a paragraph and cleared her throat again.

"So men were coming in more and more and one of them was Forrest and I got him because the day he came in my chair was empty. The cut and style went great. He had great hair and I did a great job. He started coming in regularly, sometimes even once a week for a trim. Then I suggested some skin work because the desert sun can do so much damage and he said let's try it and I gave him an herbal wrap and he really liked it. Then he said he was looking for a place to get his body in shape so I said I work out . . ." Quaking chin. "I work out at this place up the block called The Sweat Box, it's owned by a guy named Tyler Hoffgarden, he really works you hard, like a boot camp but you see results. That's what I told Forrest and he said thanks Lisette and then I actually took him over to The Sweat Box and he liked it and started working out there."

Her eyes shut.

Bloomfield said, "We know it's tough."

She faced him. "It's my fault. I introduced them."

"You had no way to know, dear. Your intentions were nothing but positive."

"I know, I know . . . still . . ."

"Still *nothing*, dear. You shared your own positive experiences with someone out of the goodness of your heart. That's nothing to regret, absolutely nothing."

Talking to us as he made a gym referral sound like something in Mother Teresa's appointment book.

Milo knows keeping them talking is the big thing so he said, "Sounds like it started off pretty innocently."

Lisette Montag said, "Not pretty. *Totally.*"

Bloomfield said, "No malice, no hidden agenda, she was being nice and the fact that things happened is not her fault."

I pictured Montag directing the Tabash twins as they overpowered, transported, and lugged Hoffgarden to the kill-spot. Telling them go and wait by the Explorer, then finishing the job.

Milo said, "Got it."

Bloomfield touched Montag's hand. "Go on, Lissy."

Her finger landed at the bottom of the first sheet. Her eyes moved back and forth.

Sighing, she said, "We became friends, a group. Me, Tyler, and Forrest. We went out for Mexican food, which we all liked. We all liked margaritas so we tried different places for margaritas. We liked Italian so we tried that, even though Tyler was a fitness guy he was pretty normal in his eating. We hung out. Then . . ."

Shaking. "Then . . . then Forrest and I became more than friends. We . . . got close. We . . . started making love. We fell in love. He was divorced from his second wife, came to the desert because he was lonely and wanted to start over and I had broke up with a loser boyfriend so we started a relationship."

The shaking got worse. She slapped the paper down. "I can't do this."

Al Bloomfield said, "Easy and slow, dear."

I said, "You had a relationship with Tyler at the same time as Slope."

Montag stared at me.

Bloomfield's smile turned sour. "Psychology." Still showing off his bridgework but his voice had steeled.

I said, "Am I wrong?"

"Yes!" said Montag.

Milo said, "You and Tyler were just friends."

"Yes. No. It's . . . I don't know what to say."

Bloomfield said, "Why don't you just read, dear."

"I don't want to read," she said. "I just want to speak truth to power. I just want . . ."

Her shoulders dropped. "Okay, yes, Tyler and I slept together. Before and later. But only a little."

Milo said, "Before you met Forrest and afterward."

"I never cheated on Forrest," she said.

"Forrest knew."

"No, no, he didn't, and there was really nothing, with Tyler it was just fu— just sex, Tyler never had my heart, never once. Forrest had my heart. He was older, he knew how to treat a woman. He was . . . nice."

"Tyler wasn't."

"Tyler just wanted to jump my bones."

"No emotional attachment," I said.

"Exactly."

"Did Tyler get jealous?"

"No! That was me, *I* did!"

Milo and I looked at each other.

Al Bloomfield pointed to the paper. "It's all in here, gentlemen. We took time and pains to be accurate so I suggest she reads and you listen."

Milo said, "Sure, if she wants to."

"Lisette? Please. For your sake. Talk truth to power."

Looking unconvinced, she picked up the paper. Put it down and resumed reciting in a softer, weaker voice. ". . . I had broke up with a loser— . . . I already said that . . . okay . . . Forrest and I were in love and Tyler was our friend but then Tyler and Forrest started something."

Milo's eyebrows rose.

Lisette Montag saw it. "Not that, don't be gross. Money. They started to talk about money. All the time. Forrest investing in Tyler's gym and then building a whole bunch more. A whatyoucallit . . ."

Looking at Bloomfield.

He said, "A fitness franchise."

"A franchise," she said. "Like McDonald's, they were going to be huge."

Milo said, "You were jealous of that."

"No, not getting rich. The time they spent together. It was money this, money that, the two of them meeting. Money money money. They were always looking at maps, planning, Forrest used to show Tyler articles about money. They never included me. Not once. I even said hey, Forrest, if you do that for Tyler can you do it for me—let's make a franchise for salons and skin care, out here in the desert people's skins get fucked up, it's perfect."

She shook her head.

I said, "Forrest said no."

"He said it was a different financial model, one thing at a time, maybe one day but right now the gym thing was the thing. The thing. Like it already *was* a thing. He said if I needed money, he could give me some. I said okay, whatever you want but it's not the money. I could tell he didn't believe me."

Milo said, "How?"

"The way he smiled at me," said Lisette Montag. "I've had lots of guys smile that way. Like you're just a stupid girl, you don't understand, you're not smart, you don't get it. But I didn't get mad at Forrest, he was an older guy, from a different place. To him women were to be protected. He held doors for me, brought me flowers, never let me pay for dinner, never did the I-left-my-wallet-at-home. I understood his soul. I didn't get mad."

"But you were still jealous."

Al Bloomfield said, "Lissy, I think you should go back to reading."

The iron in his voice caused Montag to shift her eyes toward him. He remained stony-faced.

"Yes, sir," she said. Back to the second page. ". . . so . . . could I smoke?"

Milo said, "Sorry, no smoking."

"Not *that*," she said. "Some weed or an edible. It's legal, right?"

"It is, Lisette, but we haven't come that far policy-wise."

"Why not?"

"You know," he said, "I'll have to ask someone. Now if there's nothing more you want to—"

"*Read,*" said Bloomfield.

"Yes, sir, sorry . . . so . . . Tyler and Forrest planned their franchise and I was left out of it but it was okay. Forrest and I were in love and I figured it's time to stop having sex with Tyler because it could be complicated. So I told him. And he was cool with it. Said the main thing with him and Forrest was the franchise, I was a great person and he was happy for me to be happy."

She rolled her eyes.

I said, "Tyler's reaction surprised you."

"Totally. He was always . . . like a hungry animal. He wanted it, he went for it . . ."

Bloomfield said, "*Please.* Stick with reading."

"Okay, okay, sorry . . . so . . . so I told Tyler and that was that and we kept doing Mexican and Italian when they had time off from their franchise-talking and then Forrest changed his mind about doing the franchise. He never said why, he never told me anything to do with it, so when he stopped I learned it from Tyler who was mad."

She looked up. "Tyler had anger management issues. He could get mad like that."

She snapped her fingers. "Like *that.* He'd just get this look and that's the look he got when he told me about Forrest. But first he got mad at me. I was in the gym and he said come into my office and then he got really scary and started freaking out. Forrest had fucked him over, Forrest had played him like a stupid asshole and did it happen because I convinced Forrest?"

She shuddered. "That's when he came up to me and held me here." Touching her shoulders. "His eyes were like . . . these red dots. I thought he was going to kill me. I said why would you think that, why would that be in your fucking head? And he's like because Forrest is obsessed with your pussy, you could get him to drive his car off a cliff and I'm like it's not like that, it's normal love and I'd never tell him to go off a cliff or do anything he didn't want to do and he said he didn't believe me and I started crying and then he believed me. Said the fact that you're crying shows me you're being straight. Then he let go of me and said go back to your elliptical machine, I'm going to Forrest and we're going to have a talk."

Tears pooled in her eyes and flowed down pale cheeks. "The next day, Tyler came to me and said Forrest was dead, it had been an accident."

Milo said, "What kind of accident?"

"A heart attack, they were talking and getting angry and all of a sudden Forrest collapsed and Tyler tried to do CPR but it didn't work and I needed not to tell anyone because if I did I might get in trouble myself."

"Why?"

"Because I was the girlfriend, the cops always look at the girlfriend or the boyfriend. I said that's crazy and Tyler's like I'm telling you, your life's going to get turned over, they're going to find your dope and make like the bad girl who did corruption to a rich older guy and even if they stop, you'll lose your job and your apartment and be totally fucked up."

"Heart attack," said Milo. "Did you ever learn differently?"

"Just from the papers," she said. "They said it was a gang thing, a home invasion. They never said more. I figured he got scared."

"You never talked to the police."

"They never talked to me and Tyler scared me not to."

"Did you ever suspect Tyler had murdered Forrest?"

Her eyes drifted to the left and back.

Bloomfield said, "I can't help you if you don't help yourself, Lisette. Please. Read."

"Okay, okay." She looked at the second page, seemed lost. Bloomfield poked a spot. "You were here but skip that, we've covered it . . . here."

"So . . ." said Montag. "Tyler moved back to L.A. and I stayed there. Then The Style-Right Hair and Beauty Salon closed because the owner, Mrs. Tranh, decided to retire. She only told us a month before, I was already late in my rent and without Forrest I was totally messed up inside. So I also moved back to L.A. and got a chair in a place but it was all the way in Alhambra and I was living in my aunt's place in Venice and the commute was difficult. So I finally made some contacts and started to freelance and soon after I heard from Tyler. He was back but still looking for work but he had some money saved up, he never said from where. But he was saying the truth because he was wearing a Rolex watch."

Milo said, "Several watches were taken from Forrest's house the day he was killed."

"I know that now. Tyler told me. And that's why it happened."

"Why what happened?"

"What happened to Tyler." She pushed the papers aside. "That's why."

Bloomfield said, "I give up, just tell it the way you want, dear."

"Okay," she said, suddenly perked up and eager. "Tyler and I started to . . . you know. Not regularly, he'd call, if I was free, why not? Then last week, it happened. He got crazy stoned on meth and got that same look he had when he grabbed me in his office, the red dot eyes. And he did it again. Grabbed me. Not mad, just . . . you know, intense. I said what's going on? He said, I need to tell you. I'm like about what? He's like about Forrest. Then he gives a creepy smile and says Forrest didn't die of a heart attack. I snuffed him, Lisette. I snuffed him while he slept because he was an asshole and a traitor, even when he did my divorce he fucked me over, someone else would've got me more money for the gym."

Her hands rose to her temples. "I was so so so so scared. And yeah, mad, I loved Forrest, Forrest was going to make my life better and look where my life was, living in my aunt's garage. I could've had that house in Palm Desert, Forrest had a pool and a sauna and an eighty-inch high-definition Sony and . . . whatever I wanted. And Tyler had ruined everything. For what? Because he didn't get his way and had anger management issues? Because Forrest changed his mind? But I said nothing, with Tyler if you said the wrong thing when he was on meth, anything could happen."

Al Bloomfield said, "Exactly, anything. It's a narcotic with unpredictable side effects but violence isn't uncommon and the person in question was violent, unstable, and had shown himself capable of becoming cataclysmically enraged."

As good a summation as I've ever heard.

Milo said, "So you did nothing."

"Yes, sir. Not that time. Then I started thinking. And that's what happened."

"You decided to kill Tyler."

"I was scared, sir. He killed Forrest, I was terrified he'd kill me because now I knew and when he came down from the meth, he'd think about that."

"You didn't call the police in Palm Springs."

"They never spoke to me, sir. They said it was a gang home invasion. Why would they believe me? And even if they didn't, Tyler would find out I snitched and snitches end up in ditches? Don't they?"

Milo said, "See your point, Lisette. So what actually did happen to Tyler's demeanor when he did come down?"

"Back to the same," she said.

"Meaning?"

"Wanting to put his dick in me. I got texts, you can read them."

We had.

Milo said, "So back to normal."

"But he could change anytime," she said. "What if he got loaded again and started to think? He already killed Forrest for nothing, Forrest didn't deserve that. I didn't deserve anything but a good life so why should I let Tyler kill me?"

"Obvious threat," said Bloomfield.

Milo said, "So you got the Tabash twins to help you. How do you know them?"

"I cut their hair. I cut their caretaker's hair."

"They have a caretaker?"

"Not a nurse, just a nice woman their parents hire because Rod and Ren are kind of retarded. Not real retarded, they just need a little help."

"What's this woman's name?"

"Siobhan," she said. "I cut her hair and she said I could cut the boys' hair, it was basically skin them or do a faux with color when they wanted to let it grow out. They changed their appearance to do muscle shows."

"Ah. They pretty nice guys?"

"The best. Sweet. I'm so so so so sorry for getting them involved. They didn't do nothing except help. I did it. The shooting part, they didn't know. I had to. I was saving my life, Tyler already killed Forrest. I had no choice."

"Obviously exigent circumstances," said Bloomfield.

Milo said, "You're making a point, Counselor."

That startled Bloomfield.

Milo turned back to Montag. "Where'd you get the gun, Lisette?"

Smug smile. A question she welcomed. "I was just going to tell you. From Tyler. How's that for ironism?"

"Tyler gave you the gun."

"Yes, sir. Last year, back in the desert. I told him I was scared living alone. The next day he gave it to me and told me not to use it unless I had to."

Bloomfield said, "Beyond iro*ny*."

Milo said, "Lisette, we found the casings from the bullets you used to shoot Tyler in your closet, stored with some jewelry."

Montag began gnawing her lip.

Bloomfield said, "What's the difference? Doesn't change the basics."

Milo said, "It might be good to know."

Lisette Montag said, "I kept them to remind me. That I was strong."

"Kind of like a trophy."

"That's not what she said, Lieutenant. Just a reminder."

Milo said, "More like a battle ribbon."

"Yes!" said Montag as Bloomfield shook his head. "I sometimes still feel weak. I need to remember and feel I can take my own life back."

Al Bloomfield said, "Lieutenant, I think we've meandered along this pathway sufficiently. As you said, I made a good point." Speaking louder and eyeing the one-way glass. "And let's establish some perspective, Lieutenant. Lisette has absolutely no criminal record. Which is why you've never encountered a more forthright, honest, abjectly remorseful suspect. This isn't who she is. She was coerced." To me: "Coerced psychologically. And please note that she's just ripped open her chest and showed you her heart. Surely you can't be asking for all of her blood."

"God forbid, Counselor. But I could use some information about Cordelia Gannett and Caspian Delage."

"Who?" said Lisette Montag.

No eye-dancing or shifting posture. Meeting Milo's eyes straight-on. He repeated the names.

She said, "I have no clue what you're talking about."

Meaning it.

Devastatingly honest.

Alan Bloomfield said, "These are obviously other murders. Am I correct in assuming you suspect Hoffgarden for those, as well? All the better."

"It's not that simple," said Milo.

"Maybe in your mind, Lieutenant. In my mind, my initial premise has just grown significantly stronger."

Lisette Montag said, "What the *fuck* are you guys talking about? It's like hearing a foreign language."

32

Milo and I watched the uniform, Montag, and Bloomfield head for the elevator.

Bloomfield stopped and saluted. "Thanks for your time, Lieutenant. I know you'll do the right thing."

When they were gone, Milo said, "Oh sure, I'm a white knight."

We returned to his office where he speakerphoned D.D.A. John Nguyen. It was pushing eleven p.m. but Nguyen answered, sounding alert.

"Dude, do you know what time it is?"

"I thought you'd want follow-up."

"On what?"

Milo recapped.

Nguyen said, "Wonderful. Guess I should've warned you about Bloomfield. Not that it would've made a difference, he can't take credit for her not knowing squat about Gannett and Delage. Allegedly. You believe her?"

"Unfortunately, I do."

"What does Dr. Shrink say?"

"Same thing."

"Hmm," said Nguyen. "At least you solved one."

"Gonna be a process," said Milo. "What's Bloomfield's story?"

"Major guy at the Scranton, Pennsylvania, D.A.'s office," said Nguyen. "Rose to second in command then became a honcho at the state attorney general's office before going private. He defended some of the heaviest bad guys, including mob murderers and union racketeers, won a lot more than he lost. When he turned seventy, he retired, moved out here, and got himself an estate in Hidden Hills. Horses, the works. Then he got bored, took the California bar with no prep, passed the first time, and started doing defense work again, pro bono."

"Montag lucked out."

"Yup. Next name on the list. So what do you think for her? Voluntary manslaughter?"

"You've got to be kidding, John."

"You hear laughter?"

"She sets Hoffgarden up, gets the twins to bind and gag him, drives him to the kill-spot, shoots him twice, and takes the casings for a souvenir?"

"I am aware of all of that," said Nguyen. "Except the casings. Which don't change anything. We're talking a lowlife like Hoffgarden with a prior history of violence and a probable murder under his belt and she's what, five-two, hundred pounds with absolutely no record? I can just see Bloomfield bringing in a parade of people that Hoffgarden terrorized. Some of them might even be righteous. I don't play, I could lose."

Milo threw up a hand. "I think it's insane, John."

"I'm thinking she pleads out," said Nguyen, as if the last comment hadn't registered. "Bloomfield asks for time served, I say no way and demand a serious sentence, he whittles, I whittle, eventually we reach a meeting of the minds. Like voluntary manslaughter."

"What's the sentence gonna be?"

"I'm a prophet? Last time there was anything remotely like this we got a tenderhearted judge who called it at four years and half of that suspended."

"Jesus."

Nguyen said, "Jesus was into forgiveness. Bloomfield applied for her bail this morning, I'm figuring not to argue but we'll put an ankle bracelet on her."

"What about the twins?"

"Even iffier prosecution-wise. Their parents are rich, called from the cruise ship to engage Harvey DiPaolo who does *not* work pro bono. He called me, laid on a whole thing about them being mentally challenged and he can prove it with as many shrinks as he needs. On top of that, Montag's not disputing their account. She planned it, recruited them, didn't let on what she had in mind, and they never directly hurt the victim."

"Binding and gagging isn't hurting."

"She did the gagging. I'm figuring accessory before the fact, couple of months in jail, then time served and they can go back to getting inappropriately strong."

"Law and order," said Milo.

"Mostly order, dude," said Nguyen. "We both know all that bullshit about every victim counting the same is just that. The way I see it, we lucked out. Neither of us will have to prep and go to court and the city's down one anger-issue murderer. Maybe a mass murderer if he did your other two. Maybe it's not hopeless, you do have probable offender blood."

"Still waiting on DNA, John. I'll ask Basia to do an ABO but the offender blood's O positive, the most common type. It differed from Victim Delage's O positive but the offender's was the most common pattern."

"Hoffgarden matches, it means nothing, got it. On the other hand, it doesn't eliminate him. What's the ETA on the DNA?"

"Twelve to twenty weeks," said Milo.

"Not bad, I've had worse."

"Glad you're so buoyant, John."

"One life, why ruin it with worrying?"

"Yeah, right. Can you put in a rush for analysis?"

"See what I can do. Though the justification isn't much. The only link between Hoffgarden and Gannett and Delage is he's a likely prior offender. So you'll probably need to wait in line."

"Just try, John."

"Sure, but Yoda won't approve."

"What?"

"There is no try, only do."

"Then do."

Still no fatigue in Nguyen's voice but he yawned dramatically. "Okay?"

Milo said, "I can't believe Montag's gonna get off so easy."

"Couple of years in jail is worse than it sounds," said Nguyen. "Especially for someone who's never been in the system."

"She committed premeditated *murder*!"

"Of a *bad* guy," said Nguyen.

"Unbelievable. Talk to you later."

"Hey," said Nguyen. "Did I ever tell you about my sister in the bathroom?"

"Must've missed that one."

"Then catch it now. Back when my folks were living in Hanoi and the commies took over the whole country, there was no currency. Literally. No money, everything was chits like in an arcade, you had to hoard them and wait hours to get food. People tried to raise their own food, we're not talking gluten sensitivity, there was a serious risk of starvation. Anyway, my sister Anne, she's the older one, she wants to play with a friend. We're living in a shit-ass hovel but her friend's father was a petty dignitary for the commies so she lives in one of those soulless commie high-rises. Anne goes there, eventually she has to use the john, there's no electricity, it's pitch dark. She gropes around, is about to squat over the hole when she hears this god-awful grunt then a squeal. Turns out they're raising a pig in the john—not for fun, for pork chops—and Anne just sat on it and pigs are total wimps, they make noise about everything. The fucking piece of lard started butting her around. She was eight, almost died of shock."

"Great story, John," said Milo. "The point being?"

"She went back there, anyway. To play with her friend. And if she needed to pee, she went to the john knowing what was in there. And not knowing if more had been added to the farm. Like snakes or toads or scorpions, 'cause they were being raised for food, too. Everything that moved was. She's a neurosurgeon now, raking it in big-time. She learned to live with uncertainty and unpleasantness and grew from it and so did the rest of us. So why not you?"

CHAPTER

33

I left Milo in his office, glum and silent but for a muttered, "Thanks. Onward. Wherever."

Humans are programmed to detest uncertainty, and nothing ruins a detective's life more than too many question marks. My friend was great at what he did, with a near-perfect close rate, but the murders of Cordi Gannett and Caspian Delage were looking like the exception.

I had nothing to offer him.

I drove home trying not to think about that and ready to focus on my ten o'clock the following morning.

Even with being abused as a child and spending a good deal of my life trying to patch up other people's misery, I tend to be trusting and optimistic, willing to be disappointed rather than concede my life to suspicion and dread.

Why? Who knows? If I could claim some sort of psychological magic bullet, I'd write a book and get my own talk show. But I suspect it's just good luck: the temperament I was born with. Maybe even something I got from my father. Unlike my mother who was invariably dour and pessimistic, when Dad wasn't drunk and enraged and beating me, he could be a jolly guy.

Working as a child psychologist synced with my positive attitude, starting with a belief that people can change. That's especially so for kids. They want to get better and don't play resistance games the way adults do. If you know what you're doing, you can guide them there.

Child psych's a high-success endeavor. A friend who's a pediatric psychiatrist once told me, "Let's face it, Alex. We do it because we want to feel like heroes."

Yet I'd given up doing therapy with kids long-term, substituting short-term consults and relying upon injury cases to bring quick, positive results. Why? In the beginning, it was burnout. Years later, I'm not sure.

Even working with Milo and seeing the worst of humanity meshed with my temperament. Homicide detectives speak for the voiceless and when everything falls into place, they achieve justice or something close to it. Playing a role in that process—seeing bad people held accountable—was immensely satisfying.

Then there was child custody work.

Innocent until proven guilty is a great principle, worthy of being sanctified. But when I embark on a custody consult, optimism falls by the wayside and I assume everyone's going to lie to me.

I don't think about that much anymore, it's just there, flavoring my perception, like a movie soundtrack.

And I keep editing scripts.

By nine forty-five the morning after Milo hit a wall on Gannett/Delage, I was open to being surprised by Conrad Deeb but not prepared to bet on it. Five minutes later, the doorbell rang. Ten minutes early. I'm not one of those shrinks who interprets everything. Waste of time. Maybe he'd hit light traffic.

I opened the door to find a man on the entry terrace, facing me, hands at his sides, smiling with obvious effort. A black Toyota Celica was parked down below. In need of a wash but he wasn't. Quite the opposite: freshly shaved and rosy, spotless clothing, shiny shoes.

"Professor Deeb?"

He said, "Conrad's fine. My friends actually call me Con but I don't imagine that would be a good start."

I smiled. He smiled back. Then he looked me over from head to toe.

I was wearing a pale-blue button shirt, jeans, and brown loafers. But for Nikes on his feet, his clothes were a match.

We saw it at the same time and our smiles widened.

Conrad Deeb said, "Guess I got the uniform right," and followed me to my office.

In custody evals, I'm the director and I set things up with a reason. The battered leather couch was the only place for Deeb to sit and he perched close to the edge. Not as relaxed as he was trying to project.

He said, "Nice place—am I allowed to say that?"

"Why wouldn't you be?"

"I don't know . . . I guess I wouldn't want to be construed as trying to influence you unduly."

"No?" I said. "Everyone else tries it."

He stared at me. Broke into laughter. "Okay, this is the greatest office I've ever seen and your awesome house should be in a design magazine."

"There you go." I turned to my computer, typed a bit, let him settle. And stew. When I faced him again, I held my pad and pen and his hands rested on his knees and he'd edged back a bit.

He was forty, around six feet tall, with a solid, broad-shouldered build running slightly to paunch. Sandy hair was thinning but his jawline was holding up well. Clean-shaven but for a gingery soul patch.

His eyes were light brown, beginning to crinkle. As he crossed his feet, I saw that the soles of his sneakers were crisp. New shoes. Box creases on the shirt, immaculate denim.

More than good grooming: dressing for the occasion. Motivated. That could go either way.

He said, "Old school—pen and paper? I like that, refreshing." He blinked. "Sorry if that sounded like kissing up. I really do mean it."

I said, "Tell me about yourself, Con."

"It's about me, not Philomena, huh? Yes, of course it is. It would have to be . . . I'm prattling, aren't I? I have to say, this is a little bit nerve racking."

"Being here."

"Being judged. I suppose that makes me no different from all the other people you evaluate. I guess the closest I've come is student ratings. And before that, of course, school grades. But this? It's . . . a bit disorienting."

"Take your time."

"Thanks, Professor Delaware."

He'd researched me. My eyebrows rose and Con Deeb colored a bit.

"Okay, cards on the table. I looked you up and found out you're a prof at the med school crosstown. Your being an academic gave me momentary relief. Then it gave me pause."

"How so?"

"The relief came from hoping you'd understand the whole academic thing. Then I wondered if you'd bend over backward not to account for it."

"Why would I need to understand the whole academic thing?"

"Because Toni's going to try to use it against me."

"She feels being an academic will work against you in this situation?"

He scooted forward, returning to the edge of the sofa. "As a matter of fact, that's exactly what she feels. You know how it is with divorces—I mean, obviously you do. Toni and I started off great. Part of what she liked about me was what I did. I met her at Indiana U. She was a grad student. Not in my department, in nutrition, but then she gave up because her dad's wealthy and she didn't need to work."

That hadn't answered the question. I said nothing.

Con Deeb said, "Sorry. I really am prattling. This is doubly hard for me because frankly, I'm feeling like a failure. This isn't my first divorce. Fortunately, there were no kids produced from my first marriage but still, you view it as a failure. It *is* a failure. I never thought I'd be in this position."

Long, slow head shake. He played with the soul patch.

I said, "I'm still wondering how Ms. McManus hopes to use your profession against you."

"Oh. Sorry. I'm all over the place . . . well, first of all there's the financial end. She's probably going to make a case for being in a far better position to have primary custody over Philomena because her allowance from her dad is many multiples of what I can ever hope to earn. Then there's the issue of the transitory nature of my employment. If you've done any sort of background, you've learned that I haven't stuck around anywhere for a while. But it's not due to transgression, Professor Delaware. That I can assure you and I have no problem with you contacting any of my previous employers and asking them. I'll sign consent forms, whatever it takes."

"Appreciate it," I said. "So what led to your moving around?"

"Toni will try to blame me—I'm flighty, I don't buckle down. The truth is, the job situation for anyone teaching semiotics isn't exactly booming. Do you know what that is?"

"The study of symbolism?"

"Among other things," he said. "It's the study of what we call semiosis. Processes involving the establishment of signs. Yes, symbolism is part of it, but so are metaphor, allegory, indication, and designation. It's all about the ways we communicate and sometimes they're not obvious."

Talking about something he felt comfortable with had relaxed him. But he tightened up almost immediately.

"That must sound like utter bullshit to you."

"Not at all," I said.

"It really *is* interesting. Has implications all over the experiential map. Anthropologically, sociologically, economically, and yes, psychologically. Even the bio sciences. Semioticians try to discover what leads the world to communicate the way it does. We sometimes get tagged as new-age flakes, which is patently unfair. Plato and Aristotle wrestled with signs. So did every philosopher of note. We look at the interplay between the inner and the outer worlds—"

He stopped abruptly.

"Whoa, Con, put the brakes on, this is not what he wants to hear."

I said, "No need to censor yourself and for the record I've never found choice of occupation to be relevant to child custody. Unless the job's immoral or illegal."

"Well, I'm not a jewel thief," he said. "I may be esoteric but I sure don't act out." Uneasy smile.

"Tell me about your child-rearing style."

"My style . . . never really considered it in that sense. I suppose I'd be characterized as a lax dad. I don't believe in punishment and I feel kids have an inherent wisdom that needs to be respected. If we don't mess them up, they'll do fine in the long run. Which isn't to say I don't hold Philomena's hand when we cross the street. Or I let her eat unrestricted amounts of junk or . . . you get the point. I'm just not much of an arbitrary disciplinarian."

"Is Toni?"

He thought. "I want to be fair. No, not really. She's stricter than me, but that's a low bar. I suspect she's going to tell you she's the primary parent and the adult in the house. That she spends a lot more time with our daughter than I do. That I can't argue with. I'm away from the house teaching and when I'm home I'm grading papers or writing them. So yes, in a technical sense, Toni spends more time with Philomena but I don't see that as justification for her taking Philomena away from me."

"She told you she intends to do that?"

"Not in so many words," said Con Deeb. "But when she gets pissed at me, she threatens. '*I'm* not the one who needs to live in L.A.' '*I'm* not the one bound by wherever your little precious world takes you.' She's from Louisville and wants to go back there. Her parents own a huge horse farm and a bourbon distillery and all sorts of commercial property—the main source of their dough is a slew of rental properties. I have no doubt she's going to try to move back there and if I protest—*when* I protest, because I surely will—she'll say just find yourself a job in Kentucky, you've always moved around. When she gets on that tack, I tell her college teaching jobs aren't exactly in massive profusion and she has three stock answers. A. Switch professions, B. Teach high school or elementary school, or C. Work at Walmart."

Quoting his wife had raised his voice.

He exhaled. "Sorry."

I said, "For what?"

"Getting worked up."

"It helps me to understand your situation."

"Does it? Good. I guess. I mean am I being unreasonable wanting to play a role in my only child's life? Philomena's only three but she's super-smart. Already picking out letters in books. Physically, she's also precocious. Super-coordinated. Though I have to admit that's probably to Toni's credit. She was a dancer and a competitive skier and a champion equestrienne. All that's what got her into nutrition. That and taking care of thoroughbreds. So yes, she makes sure Philomena engages physically. Kiddie yoga, a preschool that offers ample playtime, pony rides. She's got a long view of directing Philomena toward dressage and jumping. She's told me so."

He frowned.

I said, "Where better than in Kentucky."

"Exactly, Professor Delaware, exactly. I may have messed up as a husband but I think I've been a darn good dad and the thought of Philomena being whisked away . . . obviously if through some miracle I find an appointment near the horse country—even a city other than Louisville if it's reasonably close—obviously, I'd opt for that. But I don't see why I should be forced to make that choice."

"How long does your current contract last?"

"Another year and they assure me there's a good chance of renewal. Barring unforeseen circumstances. Which do tend to pop up . . . I know that doesn't sound ironclad but it's the best I can offer and I'm not asking Toni to be tied down indefinitely. I simply don't want to have the rug swept out from under me because our marriage went south."

"Let's talk about that," I said.

"Must we—just kidding, of course we must."

The remainder of the session was spent listening to him discuss the gradual deterioration of a two-year marriage. He had an affinity for confession and apology and that included an admission that Philomena had been conceived during an extramarital affair with Antoinette "Toni" McManus.

I said, "Extramarital for both of you?"

"No, just me, Toni was single. And gorgeous and sexy and alluring and she threw herself at me and that's no excuse. I cheated, plain and simple. What my colleagues would label a lucid signal."

"Of what?"

"That my other marriage was failing and that on some level I knew it," he said. "But at the time what entranced me about Toni was that she was gorgeous and sexy, et cetera. So bottom line, I was a total jerk led by my penis."

I wrote, *Easy confessor. ???*

He said, "You're quoting me on that?"

I said, "I'm not. But let's try to stay away from talking about me."

"Of course . . . so what else do you need to know?"

"Whatever you feel like telling me."

"Plunging headfirst into the great beyond?" he said. "Utterly terrifying . . . I'm not one for randomness."

"No need to be random. Take your time."

"Okay," he said. "Here goes: To me the issue is simple. I love my daughter and wish to remain in her life. Toni wants to take her anywhere she pleases. Robbing me of parenthood, the slightest semblance of bond. My attorney informs me that without extenuating circumstances, a parent can't legally move a minor child out of reasonable visitation distance."

I said, "That's true."

He fooled with his fingers.

"What specifically are you worried about, Con?"

"Toni's family has money and money talks."

"Not to me."

"No, no, that's not what I meant, I'd never suggest any potential mendacity on your part. It's simply that her side can afford to keep the conflict going indefinitely and I can't."

I said, "You're concerned about a war of attrition."

"I am. It preoccupies me."

"What does your lawyer say?"

"Not much, that's the problem. When I bring it up, she tells me to concentrate on the here and now. The ongoing *process*. But let's face it, she's not going to spend a single unbillable minute on my behalf. Once my funds run out, she'll run out."

I said, "Did that happen during your first divorce?"

The question made him flinch. "Bravely into the past, huh? No that was different. Neither of us had any resources; nor was there a child at stake. We did it no-fault, quick and easy. This time it's proving to be anything but, Professor Delaware. All the signs are there."

"By signs you're speaking professionally?"

His head moved back. His smile was shallow. "Touché. I suppose I am. Even before the process heated up, Toni engaged in what I'd have to call malignant metaphor. Pressuring me to leave the home, tossing whatever belongings I couldn't take with me. I told Meredith about it and, again, she said not to get distracted, it's merely conflict one oh one, the key was to build up my own fitness as a parent without disparaging Toni. Which, as you can see right now, I'm trying hard to do."

"Malignant metaphor," I said. "The metaphor being . . ."

"Ex as garbage. You're a bum, I'm going to treat you like a bum because to treat you as a decent human being would send a faulty signal."

I was trying to unravel that pretzel when he said, "By point of illustration, Professor, there was a three-day period between the time I left the house and my new lease began. I requested from Toni that she delay my expulsion. She laughed in my face and I ended up sleeping on a couch in my office."

He patted leather. "Not as comfortable as this one. She sees me as a guy who should sleep on an uncomfortable couch. It harmonizes with her worldview because to her I'm more than the spouse she's ditching. I represent her own relationships gone awry."

I said, "You moved because the lease is in her name."

He wagged an approving finger. "You understand what I'm contending with."

My computer dinged the end-of-session cue. I said, "That's it for today."

"For today? There'll be more?"

"There will be. Take your time to assemble your thoughts so the next time we meet you can tell me anything else you think is relevant."

"What about emailing, texting?"

"No," I said. "I rely totally on face-to-face."

"Why's that?"

It gives me the nonverbals.

I said, "It allows me a fuller picture. In any event, before we meet again I'll be talking to Ms. McManus."

"Alternating between us?" he said.

"That's right."

"May I ask why?"

"I find it useful."

"Do you? You certainly seem like a man with consummate confidence."

I smiled.

He said, "Sorry."

I wrote, *Prone to apologies ????* and saw him out.

CHAPTER
34

I was finishing my notes on the interview with Conrad Deeb when Milo phoned.

"Not sure if this is good news or bad. Basia did a quickie blood type on Hoffgarden. He's A positive so the offender blood wasn't his."

I said, "The good part is you don't have a murderer you couldn't bring to justice. The bad part is the offender's still Mr. X."

"Perfect summary, you do have a gift," he said. "Anyway, I've hit the wall and still need to get my paperwork in order on Montag and the twins. And guess what, big shock, the amiable Mr. Bloomfield no longer is. Not taking my calls and neither is the twins' mouthpiece, DiPaolo. I've got zero tie-in between Montag and the twins and Cordi and Caspian. But last night I woke up at three a.m. and got to thinking. The twins could toss Caspian around like a rag doll. So I asked John to get me blood work on them. He said it's low-priority because there's no indication they were involved but he'd do what he could. Meaning don't hold my breath."

"Not a good idea, anyway," I said.

"What isn't?"

"Holding your breath."

A beat. "I'll keep that in mind the next time I'm feeling oxygen-deprived. Which is gonna be soon. As in waking up at three a.m. with a tight gut and thinking too much. You ever do that?"

"Sure."

"Good to hear," he said. "I guess."

Later that day, I picked up a message from "the law offices of Lewis Evan Porer."

A distracted-sounding receptionist said, "Hold on," and moments later Porer said, "Doctor, lovely to talk to you again."

"What can I do for you?"

"I hope we didn't get off on the wrong foot."

I said, "Not at all. What's up?"

"My client needs to see you posthaste."

"I'm free tomorrow at ten."

"Excellent, I'll tell her. She's Antoinette McManus, goes by Toni with an i, bright, charming, sophisticated, and, most important, she has first-rate mothering skills."

"Looking forward to meeting her."

"Great, great," said Porer. "Has the other party in the arbitration been to see you?"

I said, "Let's concentrate on your client."

"Sure, sure. Though I'm sure you realize it can't be kept confidential because at some point you're going to submit a report along with, I trust, detailed notes, which I assume will include specific dates of contact. What I'm getting at, Doctor, is eventually I'll know."

"Yes, you will. I'll see your client at ten o'clock tomorrow."

"Very well," said Lewis Evan Porer, not sounding the least bit sure of that.

◆

Conrad Deeb had arrived ten minutes early. The following morning, as if some sort of cosmic balance was being laid in place, my doorbell rang ten minutes late.

I opened, expecting a woman, saw a man.

"Doctor? Lewis Evan Porer." Outstretched hand. I took it briefly, remained in the doorway.

Porer was younger than I'd expected. Mid-thirties, narrowly built, sporting slicked-back dark hair and an extravagantly curled handlebar mustache. He wore a red candy-striped shirt, a floppy blue bow tie, gray twill pants with generous cuffs, suspenders patterned with birds, and brown-and-white saddle shoes.

One quarter of a barbershop quartet.

Parked down below was an iridescent, lime-green Porsche 911 Targa. Behind the Porsche sat a silver Range Rover.

He said, "Toni's in the Rover."

I said, "Please tell her to come up."

"I was wondering if we might chat a mite beforehand."

"We might not."

I looked at my watch. Lewis Evan Porer extracted an engraved gold pocket watch from a slit below his waistband. Antiquarian tendencies? Not when it came to his ride: The Porsche was the latest model, still sported paper plates.

He moved his lips, turned his mustache into a writhing snake. I stood there. He sighed. "If you insist."

Rather than go downstairs and fetch his client, he whipped out a phone and said, "Time, Toni."

A blond woman in all-black stepped out of the Ranger Rover's driver's side, hurried to the staircase, and jogged up athletically.

When she arrived, I looked past Porer and said, "Ms. McManus, please come in."

Porer said, "So where should I wait?"

I said, "If you need to wait, your car."

"It can get a little warm. You don't have a waiting room?"

Toni McManus squeezed past him. "Lewis, I told you, no need to stick around."

Porer unfurled a mustached end and recurled it. "Very well." Shooting me a sharp look, he descended.

Toni McManus said, "Please don't hold him against me. He wasn't my idea."

I smiled.

She said, "Thank you," and followed me to my office.

35

My job has trained me to conceal surprise. This morning would be a test of that.

Nothing in Toni McManus's demeanor said I'd blown it.

First surprise: I've seen her before.

The all-blond member of the duo that had buttonholed Moe Reed the morning of the Gannett/Delage murders. Her companion, platinum with black streaks. The two of them pressuring Reed to open the street so they could get their days going. Eventually, Milo had pacified them.

She didn't recognize *me.* I'd been standing well away, no reason for her to notice. But just in case, I fussed with papers and gave her time to recall.

No reaction other than the typical tense face of someone facing first-appointment judgment.

She lowered herself smoothly to the battered leather couch. Yet another one with yoga-grace. Took the exact spot where her soon-to-be ex had sat yesterday, crossed jegging-sheathed legs, fluffed her hair, tugged at a hoop earring, smiled prettily.

Trying to calm her jitters. The smile went no further than her lips and then faded.

My smile lingered. "Good morning."

"Nice to meet you, Dr. Delaware. Though I wish it were under more ideal circumstances." Soft voice; soft southern accent.

I said, "Likewise," did a bit more paper-shuffling as the second surprise hit me.

Toni McManus bore a striking physical resemblance to Cordi Gannett.

The same oval, pointy-chin face, the same luxuriant honey-colored hair. Even the styling matched what I'd seen on Cordi the day in chambers and on her videos. A carefully sculpted mass of waves that managed to look natural.

If Toni McManus told me Caspian Delage was her hair guy, maintaining my composure would be an interesting adventure.

As I readied my pen and pad, I wondered if I was making too much of it. Good-looking blondes in L.A.—on the Westside—weren't in short supply.

Still.

I said, "Tell me about yourself."

Toni McManus said, "Pen and paper, huh? You know, for some reason I find that reassuring. Maybe because my dad's like that. Old school, has his ways, sticks to his guns. Not that you're from his generation—sorry for prattling."

Same phrase Con Deeb had used. Who'd taught who? Or was it just one of those things couples develop? Coming to share expressions, speech patterns, spontaneous utterances. During the good times.

I said, "It's normal to be a bit anxious."

"Well then, I'm normal." Her fingers moved restlessly. "This is going to sound flirtatious but it's not. You have a warm, kind smile. I can see your patients being reassured."

"Thank you."

"So," she said. "Talk about myself. If you've already met my ex, I'm sure he had no problem with that but it's not really my thing, Doctor. At heart, I'm a country girl. Kentucky. We don't brag, we communicate through our behavior."

I said, "Don't get above your raising."

"One of my dad's favorite expressions." Deep-blue eyes studied me. "Okay, here goes—I assume we'll get to Philomena, eventually. Because she's who's important."

"Of course."

"Good," she said. "So how far back should I go?"

"Whatever you think is relevant."

She tapped her fingertips together. "That's kind of open-ended. Which I guess is the point. Like one of those tests you guys use— inkblots, whatever. I didn't take a lot of psych in college but I remember those from Intro. Bats and flowers, the deal is they're ambiguous so you put your personality into them."

I said, "We won't be using any inkblots."

"Well, that's good." Nervous laugh. "Okay, little old me. I was born near Louisville on a horse farm. You're probably going to learn this anyway, so I'll come right out with it. My parents are wealthy and the money goes back generations. Hopefully, that won't damage my case."

"Why would it?"

"You know how it is, nowadays. The whole privilege thing? And this is going to sound obnoxiously privileged but I can't see why anyone should be discriminated against, lucky or unlucky. Which is what it comes down to, right? The luck of the draw."

She laughed softly. "Pick your parents carefully, I guess I did okay in that department. So yes, I had an *über*-privileged life and a great one in ways that have nothing to do with privilege. My parents have been married thirty-nine years and they still love each other madly. For some reason, that's one gene I didn't inherit. I'm thirty-six and have two failed marriages."

"Like your ex," I said.

"So you did see him. Is that what he told you? Figures he'd downplay. No, Doctor, Con's been married *three* times and he's only three years older than I am."

I wrote. She looked on approvingly.

Got him!

I said, "Kentucky."

"Beautiful country, bluegrass, rolling hills, absolutely gorgeous," she said. "I went to Catholic schools, including college. Bellarmine University, a really great place."

An edge had come into her voice. Trying to convince me.

"Con, on the other hand, went to *Prrrinceton*. And if that wasn't enough, *Hah-vahd*." Flourishing a hand. "A fact he never stopped reminding me of. When we had conflict."

I said, "Pulling rank."

"Not in so many words, that would be way too direct for Con."

"He hinted at it?"

"Not exactly—okay, I'll set the scene. We'd be tiffing about something and I'd be trying to make my point and he'd just sit there and not respond and when I'd lose my cool and say, 'Answer me,' he'd give this smug smile, get up and go into his office, and return with two coffee mugs. One from Bellarmine, one from Princeton. Sometimes, he'd bring three—Princeton *and* Harvard. Either way, he'd just plop everything down in front of me and look through me. Letting me know he was way smarter, there was no point going on. Like I was a waste of time. He likes to use riddles and all sorts of head games. He studies symbolism!"

Deep breath. "Until I got wise to his ploys, it pissed me off, which was exactly what he wanted."

She shook her head. "Ninny that I was, I'd get defensive and holler at him. 'What the hell does *that* prove, Mr. Ivy League? *I'm* the one who supports this family financially and in deed. I do everything!' And he'd just sit there, ping the mugs with a fingernail, then get up and take them back to his office and lock himself in for hours."

From the way she'd bounded the stairs, she was an athletic woman but ire had robbed her of breath and now she was panting.

I said, "Would you like something to drink?"

"No, thanks. I guess I just went off the rails, huh? But I can't help it, Doctor. You asked about me and I want to be truthful. *He's* the reason we're in this situation. He probably came across as a real nice guy. Unpretentious, aw shucks, agreeable. That's his act. Pretend to be Joe Average then use Prrrrinceton on me when he needed it. Making sure no one else sees him for the Ivy League twit he is—oh crap, there I go again."

"No problem," I said. "I'm here to learn."

"Are you? I sure hope so." She leaned forward. "I'm not going to insult your intelligence by saying it's all him, I know it takes two to tango. But honestly, Dr. Delaware, I truly do believe it's *mostly* him."

She sat back. "Though sometimes I do feel I'm getting paid back."

"For what?"

"What I did to Judy. We were in grad school. Indiana U., nutritional sciences, she was a year ahead of me and we became friends."

She folded her lips inward. Slowly released them. "So how did I pay her back? By wrecking her marriage. Sometimes I rationalize it by thinking I did her a favor but at the time I wasn't thinking of her in the least, just of myself. I was going through a rough patch, not that it's any excuse."

"What kind of rough patch?"

"My first marriage had crashed and burned because Cliff—my college sweetheart, he was a law student at Indiana—Cliff cheated on me shamelessly and just about drained me of self-esteem. But that's no excuse for doing the same thing to Judy. I was a home-wrecking bitch and sometimes I can't help think God's paying me back."

More panting. "Not that I'm religious. I wish I could be, that would be comforting."

She cried a bit, accepted the tissue I offered with a rueful nod. "Thank you, sir. If you don't mind, I could use some water. Or a Diet Coke, anything with bubbles, whatever."

I went to the kitchen and brought back a can of Pellegrino.

She said, "Little Italian bubbles. I drank this for the first time in Rome, a trip with my parents. Everything tastes better there."

Three swallows later, she looked for a place to put the can down, spotted the agate coasters I keep on a side table. Sometimes people don't bother and that's part of the evaluation.

"So that's my sordid past," she said. "I cheated on Judy with Con and got pregnant—*here's* something relevant. Con wanted me to terminate, I said no way. I may not go to Mass anymore but that much of a Catholic I am. Besides, I felt good about it. Having a baby. Philomena was totally wanted from day one. I had a feeling, this baby was going to be an important part of my life. And she is. Nothing else matters but her happiness, Doctor. *Nothing.*"

I said, "How did Con react to your refusal?"

She sighed. "I wish I could say he made a big deal about it but he didn't, he just dropped it. As if it hadn't been important in the first place. Which is his style. It carried over to the pregnancy. Minimizing. He wouldn't participate in any prenatal program."

"How did he relate to the baby?"

She smiled. "I guess I need to be honest. You seem like a guy who can figure out when someone's not being honest. He was decent. Never changed a single diaper but he actually seemed to like her."

"Seemed."

"Okay, he liked her," said Toni McManus. "Porer told me to make Con out as some kind of ogre but Porer's an idiot and I'm not going to do that. Was Con ever a doting father? Not really. In his world, it's all about him. But when he is with Philomena, they do have fun. He lets her do her own thing, never loses his patience. Not that she tries his patience. Or mine. She's a very easy child, a darling, darling little sweetie, I've been blessed. All I want is for her to have stability, Dr. Delaware. Which Con *cannot* supply. He's a gypsy, can't hold a job, moves from campus to campus taking low-salary lectureships. Not because he's stupid, quite the opposite. I've come to think he doesn't *want* stability. So inevitably, he screws up."

"On the job?"

Emphatic nod.

"How so?"

"Chronic absenteeism, not grading papers, lax about answering his email. Then, when he's called on it, he pulls the I'm-above-all-that attitude. The crazy thing is, he's a good teacher. Gets high ratings from students when he bothers to show up. The same goes for his writing. He won a dissertation award at Harvard, so he must know how to write. And like I said, he goes into his office but there's no follow-through."

"What does he write about?"

"He's been *talking* about writing a book since we met. Some highfalutin thing on signs and symbols, his plan is to get Harvard or Oxford or whoever to publish it."

Dismissive hand-wave. "Three-plus years we've been together and I still don't understand what his thing is. Even with his teaching screw-ups, a book would help him professionally, right? That's what professors do. Put out books no one reads but it gives them status."

I said, "Con's book has stalled."

"That would assume he started it," she said. "He goes into his office for hours at a time and comes out looking as if he's accomplished something. When I ask him about it, he chuckles and shakes his head and ignores me. Like *no way someone of your IQ could hope to understand.*

She recrossed her legs, looked to the right, then down, finally at me. "Confession time, Doctor. A couple of times when he was at work, I went in there searching for some sign he'd written anything. Never found a trace, not on his computer, not on paper."

She colored. "Now you know I snooped in his computer. Unfortunately, I didn't find anything incriminating that I could use now. Nothing at all, really. Not a single bookmark, just a few emails from his work that he hadn't answered. Why he even has a computer, I don't know."

I said, "You see him as someone with a case of chronic inertia."

She stared at me. "Well, yes. That's a great way to put it. So you won't hold it against me? The snooping? Because he gave me good reason. Leaving and being gone whenever he feels like it, walking out without explanation. And when I ask about it, he goes back to that obnoxious, know-it-all smile so of course, I lose it and say if you bring those fucking mugs out, I swear I'll . . . this isn't helping me, is it?"

I said, "You feel Con doesn't care enough to engage."

"Yes! Exactly! I mean, c'mon, people disagree, that's life. Man up and engage, even if it means yelling back. Don't just . . . be a . . . big blob of inertia."

"You have your suspicions about his absences."

"Of course I do," she said. "He cheated on Judy with me so he probably cheated with Judy or someone else. So yeah, I do think he's going out and meeting chicks. Can I prove it? No. And I'm not going to try to prove it even though Porer wants me to hire a private detective to dig up dirt. Because I know where that came from."

She frowned.

I said, "Where?"

"Where else? My dad. He's all about control, talks about money buying freedom, mobility, and control. I am not going to play that game, Dr. Delaware. It would hurt Philomena. Right?"

I said, "It is a good idea to concentrate on Philomena."

"That's what I'm really working at," she said. "She's *everything* to me and that's the reason I want to take her back to Kentucky. Not to deprive Con, so Philly can live an amazing great life. I have no interest in keeping her from Con. But who knows where he'll even be next year, given his work history? He claims he's got another year on his contract with CSUN but there's no tenure, so anything could happen. Eventually, he'll be gypsying off to God knows where and then what? Philomena and I are expected to tag along? I want to settle her and give her stability and back home's where that's most likely to happen. It's beautiful country, my folks own a gorgeous place with horses and farm animals and tons of space to explore and ride and just be a kid. Plus three guesthouses. We could have our privacy. Con could visit and have *his* privacy."

I said, "Con's resisting that."

"He says he is but I suspect he's really holding out."

"For . . ."

"A huge payout from Dad. He couldn't get that from Judy because her parents were working-class but my family? Golden goose."

She looked down at her lap.

"I probably shouldn't say this, Doctor, because it makes me sound like some entitled airhead heiress but we made him a generous offer. Including free transportation to Louisville plus lodgings anytime he wants to visit, no questions asked. First-class airfare, five-star hotel, a car to use. We even said that if there's no convenient commercial flight and the distance wasn't too great, at least once a year we offered him a ride on the farm's private jet. It's a Citation Ten, nearly supersonic."

I said, "It sounds as if you're motivated to make it work."

"I am, I really am, Doctor. On top of all that, he can have Philomena for any holiday other than Christmas because Christmas is a big, big deal at the farm. But any other holiday? Go for it. *Plus* if he did agree to come out to Kentucky, while he was there I'd stay out of his face and he and Philomena could have twenty-four seven together. Doesn't that all sound reasonable, Doctor? Am I deluding myself when I truly think it is?"

I said, "Con doesn't see it that way."

"Con's being Con. If he at least objected, I could respond and we could have a conversation. Instead he ignores me and so does his lawyer. Porer says it's a ploy to keep wearing us down so we up the ante. I didn't think so at first but now I'm inclined to believe him."

"You didn't think Con was interested in money."

"Yes, because money never seemed to matter to him, Doctor. He drives a shitty old car, doesn't really buy anything except books. Maybe he gives gifts to the women he cheats with, I don't know. But they're sure not expensive gifts. Nothing like that comes up on his credit card bills and I know because I pay them."

"You're pretty certain he cheats."

She folded her arms across her chest, released them, looked at the ceiling. "Do I have ironclad proof? No. It's just that . . . okay, let me give you an example. A month after Con moved out, so let's say . . . two months ago, he came by to see Philomena. Which I've never blocked. In fact, it was his idea to move out. Though I'm not saying I argued . . . eventually it would've come to that and since my dad's paying the rent . . . anyway, he came by to see my little sweetie and I came out front to see her off and saw his car but not him. Then, I spotted him walking up the block from one of the neighbors. A woman neighbor and they looked . . . chummy. I thought it was weird. Then I wondered, has this been going on all along? But I didn't want to start anything in front of Philomena so I just raised my eyebrows. Besides, at that point I just didn't care anymore. And he smiled and said, 'Having a scholarly chat.' I thought, *About what? Your dick?* But I said, 'Okay.' And he just waltzed by and took Philomena to the park and that was that. But if he was that blatant, a few houses away, middle of the day, who knows what he did at night?"

I said, "Is the neighbor someone you'd socialized with?"

"Not at all," she said. "I've seen her coming and going, she's some sort of doctor. Was some sort of doctor. Because listen to this."

Another scoot forward.

"This is crazy, Doctor, but she actually got murdered a few days ago. Isn't that horrible? Dad did research before we signed the lease and the neighborhood's one of the lowest in L.A., crime-wise. So who'd expect? But I must admit I'm a little freaked out. All the more reason to get out of here and go back home."

I said, "That is upsetting." *And the Oscar goes to . . .*

"Exactly," said Toni McManus. "Poor thing, losing her life in her own home? Even if she was fucking Con. And maybe I am being paranoid about her fucking Con, maybe he was just flirting, he's all about that. Either way, I just have a feeling Con's *never* been faithful. Obviously not to Judy, so probably not to his first wife. Or me. What I need, Dr. Delaware, is to put a fork in this marriage and move on. And I'm willing to do whatever it takes—psychologically, I mean. Whatever's best for Philomena."

My computer dinged. I said, "Time's up."

"So soon?" She frowned. "Oh, yeah, we started late. Sorry. I told

Porer to be on time. Got here early and sat there waiting for him because he said to. I should probably think for myself, huh?"

I walked her out. At the door, she gave my hand a short, forceful
squeeze. "Please help me, Doctor. Help Philomena."

The green Porsche was gone.

She said, "No Lewis, thank God. Though I'm sure he'll bill for
travel time."

36

I returned to my office with a brain that itched maddeningly. Sat for a long time trying to suppress the sensation. Instead, the feeling ballooned. Blossomed into a high-octane headache.

When the discomfort grew too strong to tolerate, I went to the kitchen, brewed my favorite medicine in the coffeepot, filled one mug (no logo) and another (Martin guitars) for Robin, pocketed salmon jerky for Blanche, and headed out back to the studio.

Nothing in my head had changed but moving around relieved unwelcome focus.

Robin stopped her work and kissed me. When we broke, she said, "What's wrong, honey?"

"Who says anything is?"

She laughed.

I told her.

As my theory unfolded, her eyes got huge. When I finished, she said, "That would be beyond strange."

"It's probably nothing."

"I'm not saying that, baby. Nothing doesn't usually preoccupy you."

"I should tell Milo?"

"Maybe do more research and see what comes up?"

"The case has stalled. Last thing he needs is another dead end."

"You'll know what to do," she said. "You've always been a perceptive boy."

Back at my computer, I began as deep a dive as possible into the life and times of Conrad Deeb, found a birth record forty-one years ago and an article in *The Harvard Crimson* he'd published while a doctoral student.

Review of Jean Genet's *The Maids.* Genet was a career criminal who'd morphed into a literary darling. I knew the play and like much of Genet's work it wallowed in sadomasochistic violence. Deeb's review was airy and irrelevant and his final line made me wonder if he'd ever actually seen it.

"As the millennium rears its dystopic head, symbolism may evolve as the authentic realism."

Searching the *Boston Globe* archive during that same period pulled up nothing. But a *Boston Herald* piece revved up my pulse rate.

Beyond strange.

I read, re-read. Printed. Then I kept hunting.

When I'd found enough and my brain had settled, I called Milo.

He was just about to leave the office, sounded exhausted.

I said, "You're not going to believe this, but . . ."

Fifteen minutes later, he was in my office, sharp-eyed and antsy as a stag during hunting season as he studied the page I'd just handed him.

"The guy stabbed someone and became a professor."

I said, "Bar brawl, self-defense, initial consideration of an ADW charge but the Boston D.A. decided not to file."

"Self-defense," he said. "Or Harvard dude versus Southie plumber is no contest . . . Jesus, sounds like he carved the poor guy up." Touching the side of his neck, then his abdomen.

I said, "Knife-wielding Harvard dude."

He put the clipping on the couch. "You checked him out because he gave you a feeling?"

"Not when I met him. He came across mild and accommodating, made a big thing about being nonconfrontational. I wasn't necessarily buying it because once a case gets to me there's been serious conflict. But no reason to think he was anything other than a bit of a suck-up. Then this morning I met his wife and recognized her from Cordi's crime scene. You met her. She was one of the women trying to get Moe to speed things up so she could get out of there. She told you Cordi had been flirting with her husband."

He nodded. "Coupla blondes getting pushy. Didn't notice any resemblance."

"Your mind was on other things and at that point Cordi's face was covered in blood."

"You recognized Cordi that way."

"I had prior dealings with her."

He waved that away. "You notice things other people don't, fine. I'm used to it. Though sometimes I wish I could wear your eyes. Go on."

I said, "The time Toni—the wife—complained about was when Deeb had already moved out. He came by to pick up his daughter but instead detoured to Cordi's house. When Toni confronted him about it, he admitted being inside for an 'academic discussion.'"

"You show me your doctorate, I show you mine," he said. "So he'd know the layout."

"And if there'd been a prolonged affair, he might have a key. Or lifted one."

He thought about that. Nodded. "But not sure how that leads to evil."

"I'm not, either, but the physical resemblance between Cordi and Toni isn't casual. It's striking. And that got me thinking about Deeb's academic work—signs, symbols, analogies, metaphors. Displacements of reality. I still figured I was being over-imaginative but kept digging and came up with the Boston stabbing, then this."

Page number two nearly lifted him off the couch.

"Bloomington . . . who's Randi Walenska?"

"Someone who looked an awful like this woman." I handed over an image I'd found.

He said, "Judith Deeb, registered dietitian in Indianapolis . . . the first wife?"

"Second. This is his third divorce, each marriage lasted around three years. He and Toni had an affair while he was married to Judith and Toni got pregnant."

His eyes moved back and forth between the headshots. "Judy Deeb, Randi Walenska . . . shit, they could be sisters. Do you have a shot of Toni?"

"No."

He fooled with his phone, retrieved a DMV photo. Sat back and said, "She and Cordi are more like twins—oh, man, you've just taken me to crazy-town."

I said, "There's more. Just before you got here, I found the date of the second divorce. Randi Walenska was stabbed to death in her apartment six weeks before Deeb and Judith finalized their divorce."

I pointed to my screen. He came over and had a look. Pushed the print button, collected the paper, and sat back down. Sweat beads had collected at his hairline. He wiped them with a handkerchief. Flexed his jaws and his nostrils. Looked at me.

"So what're we saying? Guy's marriages fall apart and he takes out his rage on surrogates? Why not the women who actually piss him off?"

I said, "Don't know for sure but my best guess is displacement.

Projecting anger and other emotions onto substitute targets. It's the basis of racism and it's also common in borderline personality. So are inappropriate anger and a distorted self-image. Grandiosity, seeing yourself as above the rules, which is how Toni describes Deeb's approach to his superiors. His career's been based on the study of symbols and that could be rooted in more than scholarly interest."

"No such thing as accidents, huh?"

"Oh, there are," I said. "But rarely when it comes to murder."

"What about the first wife? She healthy?"

"All I've got is a first name, Adele, was about to trace her when you got here. I figured I'd start with the University of Rochester because that's where Deeb taught before he moved to Bloomington."

He got up again and pointed to my monitor. "May I?"

Milo's LAPD password gives him access to the usual databases and several beyond civilian reach.

It didn't take him long to find an eight-year-old address for Adele and Conrad Deeb on Raleigh Street, in Rochester, New York. Nor to learn that Adele's Social Security number now traced to Adele Banerjee, Ph.D., associate professor of classics and women's studies at Barnard College in Manhattan.

Banerjee's faculty headshot showed a pretty, bespectacled redhead in her forties with an open smile. Primary interest: re-contextualizing the writings of Edith Wharton to make them compatible with post-feminist perspectives. She'd been at Barnard for eight years, had earned tenure after four.

I said, "She did a lot better than Deeb."

Milo said, "Another reason to be pissed off. Okay, let's see if he symbolized anyone else."

◆

A woman had been butchered a month and a half prior to Conrad Deeb's second divorce. Finding the date of his first divorce, Milo worked backward, beginning with two months earlier. NCIC gave up four women slain in Rochester during that period.

Three were the victims of gunshot homicides in high-crime neighborhoods. Two of those cases had been solved.

The fourth victim was a twenty-nine-year-old secretary in the university's chemistry department named Christa Leanne Wurtz who'd been found stabbed to death in her apartment.

Basement flat in a house on Raleigh Street.

Three blocks from where Deeb and Adele had lived.

No image of Wurtz on NCIC, newspaper accounts, or the Web. Milo got on the phone to Rochester PD Homicide and was put in touch with a detective named Elizabeth Stoller who recalled the case, but not as an investigator.

"I was a rookie on patrol," she said. "Happened to be riding along when that call came in. The D was a wise man named Cohen, very fatherly, tried to convince me not to look at the crime scene but I was stubborn so he let me. Nasty, near-decapitation. Poor thing was blitz-attacked in the hallway outside her bedroom. Like she'd woken up and got slammed by a prowler. A few things were taken, phone, some cash, a few trinkets. Looking at it made me sick to my stomach but I couldn't show Cohen. An hour later, I decided I could handle it and was going to be a murder gal. I even tried to cold-case Wurtz around three years ago when I got promoted but the boss said no. So this is very good, Lieutenant. Weird but good."

Milo said, "No promises but if I get you some satisfaction, you'll be the first to know."

"That would make you my Prince Charming. What's the deal? Can you give me some details?"

He gave Stoller a sketchy summary.

She said, "Professor type? Interesting. There actually were some questions about a chem prof, real weirdo, peed into jars and kept them around. But he alibied out. So how can I help this along?"

"Love to see the case file."

"It'll be expressed out today. Address?"

Milo gave it to her. "Do you remember what Wurtz looked like?"

"In terms of body position?" said Stoller.

"No, general physical appearance. Starting with hair color."

"That's easy. She was a carrot-top, bright-red hair. Curly. Nice looking, all her photos showed her smiling. That work for you?"

"Oh yeah," said Milo. "Don't open the champagne yet, but start thinking about your favorite brand."

"I'm a martini gal," said Elizabeth Stoller. "But you close this, I'll drink any darn thing you want."

He hung up, wiped his brow, sat back. "Crazy has just turned rational. Okay, I need to get DNA on Deeb and match it to the unknown blood at Cordi's house."

I said, "He's due for another appointment. I'll offer him something to drink. If he says no, I'll observe what he touches and—"

He sliced air with a big hand. "Not. Gonna. Happen."

"I don't see the problem, Big Guy. I realize he's dangerous but he's due here anyway and he'd have no reason to suspect—"

"His ass is *not* gonna rest here, Alex." Slapping the couch. "If your self-preservation IQ isn't high enough, think of Robin. Hell, think of the pooch. Do you really want someone like Deeb to find out you betrayed him? What if I can't get enough to file on him? What if he gets bail—yeah, it's unlikely but that's what self-preservation's all about: figuring on unlikely. Nope, we're doing it the old-fashioned way. Surveillance, he discards something in plain view, we snatch it. He doesn't, we become intimate with his trash."

He picked up his phone. "Gonna sic Moses and Alicia on that right now."

"Not Sean?"

"Sean's been through enough. There's plenty of paperwork, he won't be twiddling his thumbs."

37

After Milo left I headed toward the rear of the house, ready to catch Robin up. Before I got there, the service door swung open and she stepped in with Blanche heeling.

Reading my eyes like the top line on a vision chart. "What did he find out?"

I told her.

She said, "That's absolutely terrifying." She touched my cheek. "Your instincts were spot-on."

Then she stepped back. "You're supposed to evaluate this psychopath. Obviously, he's not coming back here."

"Of course not."

Best supporting actor in a dramatic role.

She entered the kitchen and poured herself a glass of orange juice.

I said, "The thing is—"

She swung around. "There's a thing?"

"Normally, I'd be scheduling another appointment with him. If I just stop working the case, it will attract attention."

"Who would you normally be talking to next?"

"I had planned on him, then another session with her. But I can schedule the daughter."

"There you go," she said. "As long as the mother brings her."

I phoned Toni McManus to set up the appointment.

She said, "Great to hear from you, I'm ready to finish with this ordeal. He keeps calling me, putting on the nice-talk. Like I'd fall for it. So when can you see my little sweetie?"

"How about tomorrow at ten?"

"Ten's her yoga class but this is more important. I'm not sure she really appreciates it, anyway."

"Yoga?"

"Having to sit still."

Unburdened by Porer, Toni McManus arrived at ten on the dot. All-black, per usual, hair flowing, lips set grimly.

The little girl holding her hand wore all-pink, down to frilly socks and tiny bejeweled sneakers. Small for her age. Her mother's pointy chin adding to pixie cuteness.

Toni said, "Dr. Delaware, this is my precious Philomena. Philly, this is Dr. Delaware. Remember what I told you?"

"No shots." Soft, tinkly voice. Clear diction despite Deeb's lawyer tagging her as unworthy of conversation.

"Exactly, baby dolly, this is the doctor who never ever gives shots."

Philomena's searching blue eyes swept from her mother to me and back. Not quite sure she was buying it.

I kneeled to her level and smiled. "Your mom's right, Philomena. No shots, ever. I won't be touching you anywhere."

"Okay. Thank you."

"What we are going to do is play and maybe talk. But only if you want to."

Stating, not asking. Careful, as usual, to avoid the "Okay?" adults often tack on when they offer children non-questions and false freedom.

It's not honest and kids hate it.

Philomena nodded. Small hands grabbed each other and both arms began swinging back and forth.

Toni said, "Sweetie? Did you hear the doctor?"

Philomena looked directly at me and whispered, "Yes, sir."

Toni said, "The sir part she learned from her grandpa." To Philomena: "Gramps was once a colonel. Do you remember what that is?"

"In the army."

"Yes, baby. I guess Gramps can get pretty military, huh?"

Philomena shrugged and continued to look at me. As if searching for a solution to a problem she hadn't quite identified.

Pretty child with delicate pale skin and a tenuous mouth. Golden hair was gathered in a single plait that reached her waist.

Miniature of her mother.

I stood and pointed toward the office and said, "That way."

As the three of us walked there, I saw that the mother–child resemblance extended to gait. Philomena keeping in perfect step with Toni.

My brain clogged with a storm of strange irrelevancies.

Did Cordi Gannett look like this at three?

Did the resemblance between Con Deeb's latest wife and his latest victim begin that early?

Do baby photos of Cordi exist? Renata Blanding has amassed albums full of Aaron, I am willing to bet . . .

Then my mind shifted to the future and it got worse.

The terrible truths this little girl would confront one day.

Perhaps the lack of resemblance to the monster who'd wreaked havoc would turn out to be a smidge of good luck.

Or it would make no difference at all.

As we neared the office doorway, Philomena put a bit of skip into her stride.

Happy child.

How far would resilience take her?

Therapy needs to be honest, but like any relationship, a bit of play-acting can help smooth out the bumps. So I tried to clear my head and put on a smile and by the time we were inside the office, I was pretty sure it looked authentic.

Then again, Robin had read me like a primer so maybe I was slipping.

I said, "Here we are, Philomena. This playhouse is for you."

Toni McManus said, "Wow, that's a cool one—so I can come in, too?"

"Of course."

You have no idea how much she'll be needing you.

Philomena played steadily for twenty-five minutes, when her attention began flagging.

I said, "Great job, we're finished for today."

Tiny smile. Allowing herself a bit of self-satisfaction.

Toni McManus had begun the session as an observer but had switched soon to working her phone. She said, "That's it?"

"It is for today."

"Will we be coming back?"

Oh yeah.

I said, "Eventually. I'll call to schedule."

"So nothing urgent."

Is my child normal?

I said, "None. Philomena, you're a very smart girl."

"Thank you. Sir."

She saluted.

Toni said, "Gramps again. I'm going to have to speak to him."

At the doorway, Toni distracted Philomena with a kiddie game on her cellphone and leaned in close to me.

"Doctor, is there anything I need to look out for? I mean, if it gets stressful. I hope it doesn't, but if."

I said, "Changes in sleep patterns, appetite, mood. Call me with any concerns."

"I will. Thank you."

From several feet below: "Thank you."

Toni McManus said, "Oh, Gramps—that's not a problem, is it, Doctor? Being too polite? I promise you she's not overly restricted."

I said, "Courtesy's a good thing."

That didn't seem to help so I said, "Philomena's a wonderful girl."

That did.

After they drove away, I returned to the office, closed up the playhouse, sat at my monitor and charted.

Bright 3 y.o., exc. attention span, approp. play and separation, some evid. of awareness of situation.

Philomena had begun by uniting the parent dolls but didn't take long to separate them. Placid Caucasian dolls not unlike the people she'd grown up with. I keep them in a variety of shapes and hues.

She began by allotting Mom and Dad equal time, shifted gradually to spending more time with Mom, finally moved Dad out of the picture by placing him in a corner of an attic room where he remained in the company of random, plastic furniture.

At some level, grasping the basics.

So much more was yet to come.

◆

Just as I finished my notes, I got a call from Sean Binchy.

Assigned to paperwork. Had something new emerged in Conrad Deeb's background?

I said, "Hey, Sean, what's up?"

"Doc," he said, "would it be okay if we could talk? Just for a few minutes."

"Sure. Go ahead."

"Um, I was thinking in person?"

"No prob. What works for you?"

"Well," he said, "I'm actually on my way home and Waze says the Glen's the best way to get to the Valley, so I thought . . ."

"I'll be here, Sean."

"You're sure, Doc? Don't want to impose."

"Couldn't be surer."

"Thanks, Doc. See you soon."

Driving here first, then calling to see if I was free.

Something bugging Sean.

He'd been happy with Larry Daschoff, I couldn't see that going bad.

I stayed curious during the four minutes it took for my doorbell to ring.

When I opened the door he tugged at his tie and shuffled his Docs and said, "I really do hope I'm not intruding."

"Happy to see you, Sean. C'mon in."

I offered him something to drink.

"No, I'm fine, Doc, thanks a ton."

My battered leather couch hosted a new body without complaint. The one time I'd seen Sean since his return from vacation, I hadn't noticed that he'd lost weight. Always lean, he was now verging on bony. Slight hollowing of the cheeks, more jutting of the Adam's apple, new contouring of the boyish, freckled face. As if he'd submitted to a sculptor's blade.

He said, "Again, thanks . . . I don't want to cause any problems for you and I appreciate that you got me Dr. Daschoff and he's been super, really helpful. But are you also . . . wow, I don't know how to say this."

He puffed his lips. "I don't want to offend you . . ."

"No offense possible, Sean. What's on your mind?"

"Okay." Two deep breaths. "Do you and Dr. Daschoff talk? About me?"

"We don't, Sean."

"Sorry, then," he said. "So even though you referred me . . ."

I've learned to look at referrals as a form of foster-parenting. Do your best to find the right people, be available if you're needed, but otherwise let go.

I said, "When I didn't hear otherwise, I assumed everything was going well."

"Oh, it is, it's going great." His hands clenched. "Okay. Now I'm going to ask something else that I hope you don't take the wrong way."

"Do Milo and I talk about you."

He gaped. "Yes! Exactly. I mean if you do, I understand. You guys go way back and I know—I get that if you did, the reason would be to help me."

"We don't discuss you, Sean."

"You don't. Okay." He stood. "That was quick, huh? Sorry for wasting your time."

I remained in my chair. "What are you really concerned about, Sean?"

He flinched. Sat back down.

"Okay— I get that you're not my official therapist but could we talk and it would still be confidential?"

"Of course."

"It's not like I want to keep secrets from Loot. He's been great, I appreciate that he looks out for me. It's just that . . . I don't want to sound ungrateful . . ."

I said, "You feel he's being overprotective."

Wry grin. "You're reading my mind, today, Doc."

Easy with an open book.

He said, "Yeah, I do feel that way. Ever since the . . . no sense beating around the bush, when you saved my life, Doc. You know how I feel about that. We've talked about it."

I nodded.

"I could *never* repay you, Doc. I'm *eternally* grateful."

"I was happy to be there for you, Sean."

"Must've been terrifying for you."

"A lot more so for you, Sean. So, in terms of Milo . . ."

"Okay," he said. "Here's the deal. When the department cleared me to return, I figured I'd be back in the swing. But I haven't exactly been swinging, Doc. It's not like I've been discriminated against. Overtly. Loot's assigned me to surveillance and other stuff, at some level I'm doing the job. But there's been way more paperwork than before. Which is fine, if that's what's really needed. The problem is, and maybe it's my imagination, I don't think that's the reason. I think I'm being kept away from what the department calls potentially confrontational situations."

Nothing like bureaucratic verbiage.

I said, "You feel you're being shielded from danger. Like watching Conrad Deeb. Like getting actively involved in his arrest."

"Exactly, Doc, exactly! This guy is a violent psycho lunatic, so, sure, I can see where Loot's coming from. Because let's face it, the last time I got into a situation with one of those, I . . . but I learned from that experience, Doc, and the way I see it is nothing will rehab me better than *embracing* danger and doing a better job of handling it. I've thought it through a million times and I feel I'm ready. Dr. Daschoff agrees. He says no one knows the inside of my head better than I do and I say I'm ready."

"First of all, I don't think you did anything wrong, Sean, and neither does anyone else."

"Maybe," he said. "But let's face it, if you weren't there—okay, fine, whatever. The main thing is I learned from it. I'm on my guard and ready and I need to get back on the job a hundred percent. To be treated like Moe and Alicia. Like anyone else."

"I agree, Sean."

"You do?" he said. "Okay, so at least I don't have to worry about Loot talking to you and you saying something different."

"I doubt he'd do that, but on the off chance he does, I'd totally support you."

"Oh man." Sean's eyes got moist.

I said, "In terms of going forward, I see two approaches. I can talk to Milo and suggest he ease up. No guarantees, of course. And it might work against you."

He smiled. "Yeah, Loot can be . . . set in his ways. And to be fair, his ways are usually right. But this isn't about detective work, this is about what's in here. And here." Tapping his chest, then his forehead.

"Like Dr. Daschoff said, no one knows your experience the way you do."

He sighed. "Doc, you have a way of phrasing things . . . yes, that's it to a T. And I see what you mean by working against me. He'd see me as kind of . . . babyish. Needing someone to go to bat for me. So I guess I should talk to him myself."

I said, "Makes sense."

"I sure hope so."

◆

At the door, Sean shook my hand hard, made a slight move as if wanting to hug me but held back. "Doc, this has been super-helpful. I *really* want to be in on busting Deeb. The past is the past and my life has been fantastic, I wouldn't ask God to change anything."

This from a man who'd nearly been thrown off a twenty-four-story building.

38

I heard from Milo that evening.

"Nothing dramatic on Deeb. He left his apartment to jog, came back, didn't reemerge. Alicia and Moses got a look at him in a tank top and she said his arms are substantial."

I said, "Moe wasn't impressed."

"Godzilla might impress Moe. Apparently, the arms are minimally okay but Deeb's soft everywhere else, the arms were okay." He laughed. "Bottom line, Deeb looks fit enough to tote and toss Caspian. In terms of getting some DNA, nada. His pad's in a security building with the trash going into dumpsters out back. Unfortunately, the bins are kept in a gated area and pickup's by a private service, so the truck probably card-keys in. Meaning no curbside access to Deeb's gar-*baaahge* and so far he hasn't eaten, drunk, sneezed, spit, or discarded anything."

I said, "What's the undramatic part?"

"Always interpreting," he said. "Yeah, I was getting to it. Sean found his birth certificate, he was born in Rahway, New Jersey. Both parents are deceased. Mom because Dad killed her and Dad maybe because jail food for life ain't good for longevity. Though Manson did make it to eighty-three."

Undramatic. He probably saw Deeb's childhood as an ingredient for a defense maneuver and chose not to think of it.

I said, "How old was Deeb when it happened?"

"Twelve," he said. "Yeah, yeah, poor little kid was traumatized blah blah blah. It wasn't a huge story, couple of lines in a local newspaper article found by Sean. The lad does have a knack for paper. The only other bit of info has to do with the late Mr. Hoffgarden. His Mini Cooper showed up in Watts last night, minus tires, windshield, convertible top, radio, and seats. That came courtesy of Alicia via Al Freeman. Al does a daily check of every stolen vehicle in the county."

I said, "Any idea how it got there?"

"Al's guess, and I think he's right on, is that Hoffgarden parked on the street when he headed for what he thought was a hot night with Montag. That area of Venice is notorious for street robberies and GTAs. Either way, it doesn't matter, that one's closed, time to prioritize."

"When are you planning to get Deeb?"

"If his daily routine doesn't change, probably tomorrow. I caught Nguyen in a good mood and he's all for an arrest warrant. Though he did term the motive 'fucking bizarre.'"

"When tomorrow?"

"No idea. And alas, my friend, you won't be there seeing as Deeb has sat on your couch."

"Can't argue with that," I said.

He said, "Shucks, that was too easy."

39

I t happened at four a.m.

I learned about it at seven a.m. after I checked my email and opened the attachment from Milo titled *Case Closed* and garnished with a mass of happy, sun-yellow emojis.

Footage from the body cam worn by Detective Sean Binchy.

Entry to Conrad Deeb's apartment complex had come via a master key provided by GJS Properties, the owner/managers.

No persuasion necessary; Deeb was three months in arrears on his rent, eviction proceedings had begun, and per the company's attorney GJS was more than happy to *"cooperate with law enforcement provided the arrest be carried out as discreetly as possible with due consideration to other tenants."*

Milo had clipped and pasted that onto another email sent at six a.m. via his personal account. Followed by an emoji with a protruding tongue and, "Oh, sure, that was our main consideration."

I triggered the video.

Multiple footsteps amplified by the body cam's audio recorder sounded like a distant cattle stampede.

The screen bounced in time with Sean's rapid walk.

Sean's breathing was regular but rapid and a bit shallow, made raspier by the cam's speakers. Like the rhythmic whoosh that fills your head when snorkeling or scuba diving.

No conversation during the climb up three flights of stairs.

Long view of a hallway. Lit dimly. Thrifty owner/managers.

Milo's deep voice: "Three eleven."

Sean: "Got it, Loot."

More hoof-clopping, then silence.

Sean's left arm extended. Fist at the end of it.

Knock knock knock.

"Police. Open up."

Silence.

Sean, louder. "Police, Mr. Deeb. Open up."

Milo: "Do it, kick it ajar and wait."

Sean's right arm inserted the key.

Nothing for five seconds.

Milo said, "In," and a louder stampede punched through the cam's speakers.

Seven people, I learned later. Milo, Sean, Reed, Alicia, three uniforms, everyone in Kevlar vests.

Sean's right arm again. Stretched forward, now holding his black Glock.

Not the two-handed thing you see hundred-pound actresses do in movies. Confident, single-handed grip.

Steady, not a hint of shake. Good for you, Sean.

Tentative entry.

Flashlight sweep over a sparsely furnished living room.

No one.

Same for an open-view kitchen/dining area.

Several flashlights beaming, searching. A few books on the floor, a folding bridge table hosting additional volumes and a bottle of wine.

Two cheap folding chairs.

Acid-green beanbag in the corner.

Your basic lonely-guy setup. But I doubted Deeb had the capacity for loneliness.

Sean's gun-arm continued leading him through the front of the apartment then right.

Heading toward a closed door.

As he reached for the knob, the door swung open and the momentary shift in balance twitched the Glock.

When you're not prepared, bad stuff can happen.

Sean was ready. Motionless gun-arm, rigid as a length of rebar.

Aiming at Conrad Deeb. On his feet, wearing an Oxford T-shirt and sweatpants.

Positioned just inside the door.

Wide awake.

Smiling.

Not a trace of surprise.

Welcome to the party.

Sean: "Mr. Deeb, you're under arrest. Put your hands at the back of your head."

Deeb: "Of course, Officer."

"Turn slowly."

"My pleasure, Officer."

Deeb appeared to comply as Sean got close enough to cuff him. Then his right hand dove into the waistband of the sweatpants.

Out came something brown.

It rose, arced downward toward Sean's head.

Sean's left hand grabbed Deeb's wrist and twisted hard, evoking a cry of pain from Deeb.

Blur of scuffle as Milo and the others moved in.

Before they got there, the brown thing thudded on carpeting.

Wordlessly, his breath unchanged, Sean spun Deeb around and cuffed him.

Deeb said, "Very impressive, Officer. You must be a ninja. Or maybe a ninja turtle."

Then threw back his head and laughed.

A terrible sound.

40

Any experienced felon or intelligent rookie criminal knows enough to utter the magic words: "I want a lawyer."

Conrad Deeb made his request within moments of his arrest, sitting in the back of the cruiser that took him to County Jail and repeating himself for emphasis.

And that was it interview-wise.

The county rarely contests pleas of poverty and Deeb's plea led to the assignment of a public defender named Samantha Bowers. His arrest had led to his divorce lawyer dropping him and the custody dispute was settled a day later: full legal and physical to Antoinette McManus.

Bowers, eighteen months out of law school, stepped in full of zeal, creating paper-storms and dashing off aggressive emails to John Nguyen.

He told Milo, "You know that basket over my desk? My long shot's improving."

Then came the information sent to Samantha Bowers.

DNA from the kitchen at the Gannett/Delage crime scene matched to Deeb.

Milo sent shots of Cordi's wounds of "probable" to Rochester and Columbus and received appraisals regarding the murders of Christa Wurtz and Randi Walenska. No DNA existed in the Wurtz file, but detectives in Columbus had retrieved a mixed victim/offender sample from Walenska and expected results within six weeks.

The brown thing with which Deeb had tried to brain Sean was a hickory stick an inch and a quarter in diameter, hollowed out and filled with a steel core. No confirmation as to where Deeb had obtained it but Alicia had found something similar in a photo at Scotland Yard's Black Museum: one of several weapons in a stash taken from soccer hoodlums.

"So, maybe," she said, "he got it in Oxford."

Milo said, "Higher education."

The bludgeon had been polished and varnished but wood's rarely impermeable and microscopic bits of blood obtained in the center of the cylinder matched Caspian Delage's DNA.

Next: the findings in a Studio City storage locker rented by Deeb.

Five feet by ten, the smallest unit available at that facility, vacant except for an army-surplus footlocker.

Inside the locker were stacks of loose paper. Milo was hoping to find newspaper accounts of Deeb's crimes but found only Deeb's master's thesis, some Oxford-based ramblings praised by Deeb's tutor, and four drafts of Deeb's doctoral dissertation.

All of which he termed, "Gobbledygook."

Below Deeb's writings, stashed in a myrtlewood box with the sticker of a Portland gift shop on the bottom, was a fake pearl necklace Randi Walenska's sister was "pretty certain" had been Randi's, a pair of gold-framed eyeglasses confirmed to be Christa Wurtz's, and a turquoise bracelet identified as Cordi Gannett's by her mother, now, per her husband, emotionally shattered after getting in touch with her "true feelings" about her daughter.

At the bottom of the wooden box was a rainbow pride key chain minus keys linked to Caspian Delage.

Faced with all that, Samantha Bowers morphed from righteous indignation to damage control, informing Nguyen that she'd be "aggressively and assertively" pursuing a diminished capacity defense.

John said, "Go for it, I love comedy," and phoned me.

"You ready to help me dispel that bullshit? I'll even pay you."

"Always happy to help, John, but no can do."

"Why not?"

I told him about the custody case.

He said, "Oh . . . yeah, that could get messy. Were you directly involved in solving it?"

"Depends on how you look at it."

"Not really, Alex. What exactly did you do?"

"Had a thought and made a suggestion." I filled him in.

He said, "You really didn't actively *do* anything, you just intellectualized."

I said, "There you go."

"It could still get messy, though. The main thing is your name shouldn't appear in the murder book."

"I have no problem with that."

"I'll call Milo and make sure you're *persona invisibilia*. Meanwhile, who would you recommend to evaluate this asshole?"

"There're plenty of good people, John. I'm sure you've used some of them."

"Good point," he said. "Have a nice day."

Two good people, both of whom I knew, were contacted. But it never got to the point of a mental evaluation because Conrad Deeb was "utterly repulsed by the notion of being adjudged psychiatrically defective."

Normally, I'd assume that was lawyer-speak but in this case I suspected a direct quote from the defendant.

In the end, everything resolved as even the worst of crimes often do, after convoluted, legalistic horse-trading.

A ritual. Everyone knew the outcome but criminal attorneys are bred to paw the dirt and lunge for the throat.

In exchange for pleading to first-degree murder to Gannett and Delage, Conrad Deeb received the possibility of parole for each of two life sentences.

Simplifying matters, Nguyen got the D.A.'s in Rochester and Columbus to accept Deeb's Alford plea. Not acknowledging guilt on Wurtz and Walenska but admitting that enough evidence existed to convict him. Two additional life sentences to be served concurrently.

Deeb's primary goal: avoiding a trial in Missouri where the death penalty could still mean just that. Walenska's father objected initially but was won over by his wife, a former Quaker.

Deeb got sent to Pelican Bay where he began to file verbose appeals for himself and on the behalf of other incorrigibles.

Milo said, "He's gotta be smart enough to know it's futile."

I said, "He's probably concentrating on the other guys. They see him as useful, it's life insurance."

"Ah," he said. He laughed. "I say that a lot when I'm with you."

He tapped the shiny, scarred wooden bar of the Irish tavern where we'd sat for the past hour. A surface, I realized, not unlike the hickory stick.

He drained his beer and his shot, let out a satisfied breath. "Another Chivas on me?"

"Thought you'd never ask."

41

On a lovely, warm, clear L.A. afternoon, as Conrad Deeb sat in a high-power cell at County waiting for transport up north, Toni McManus called and asked for an appointment.

I said, "For Philomena?"

"No, just me. And could it please be soon? We're due to leave for Kentucky in a couple of days."

I checked my book. "How about four today?"

"Perfect. Thanks so much."

This time, she arrived early. I'd just finished a phone conference with a judge and was free to oblige her.

Same as other times I'd seen her, she wore all-black, but the flowing hair had been tied back carelessly with stray hairs frizzing, and her face looked raw and drawn.

I fetched her a bottle of fizzy water, popped it open, and handed it to her.

"You remembered." Wan smile. She drank greedily. "May I start by asking you a question?"

"Sure."

"When did you know? About *him*."

"When the police told me."

"Not before?" she said. "I'm not trying to be rude, I'm only asking because I just learned that you work with the police. My mother told me. She flew in, she's the one taking care of Philomena, which enabled me to come to talk to you. She's a crime buff, reads mysteries, watches I.D. She's on her computer all the time, thinking she can solve things. She looked you up and found out."

I said, "Flattered to merit your mom's attention."

"But you weren't investigating Conrad when you saw him."

"Not at all."

"That's what I thought," she said. "My mom has all sorts of ideas. Like maybe you're one of those Sherlock types."

Her posture loosened. "To be honest, Dr. Delaware, Mom would like nothing better than to meet you, so she can brag to her friends."

She turned grim. "I know she's doing it for my sake but she's making light of the whole situation. No trauma, just annoyance. He's getting his just deserts, she never trusted him. Which, of course, she never mentioned once to me. Anyway, that's not why I'm here. Mom brought the Citation and as soon as we're packed up, she's flying us back to Kentucky. Philly hasn't been told anything, she hadn't been seeing him very much anyway, so it's not a big change. But I figure eventually she's going to ask and I need to know what to tell her. Not just now, in the future. I guess it's the future that's freaking me out. What will come up and how do I handle it?"

I said, "The easy part first. Don't bring her dad up until she does, then tell her he has to be away for a while."

"Technically honest."

"And compassionate, Toni. No way Philly should be dealing with homicide. If he really wasn't a big factor in her life, he'll fade."

"He wasn't," she said. "I swear. What's the hard part?"

"As she gets older, she'll get curious and will need age-appropriate answers. I'm not going to cookbook those in advance. Your best bet will be to find a local child psychologist or psychiatrist and explain the situation. If their guidance makes sense, go with it."

"If not?"

"Get someone else, Toni. Trust your instincts."

"They're good?"

I nodded.

She said, "That means so much to me. Will you help me find someone?"

"No problem."

"Thank you, Dr. Delaware. I guess the main thing that's eating at me—besides what he did, besides the fact that I lived with a monster and was too obtuse to know it—besides all that, I need to honestly know if my baby is destined to be screwed up emotionally?"

"No."

She blinked. "No?" she said. "Just like that?"

"You'll provide her with love and attention and work on developing her resilience. There'll be challenges but with support, she'll learn to deal with them."

"You sound pretty sure of yourself."

"I'm not minimizing the situation, Toni. There'll be bumps along the way. Adolescence may prove especially tough because that's when teens wrestle with their identities. But I've found clinically, and there's research to back me up, that people do better than experts predict. With proper support there's no reason to think Philomena will be crippled psychologically."

"How do you define proper support?"

I said, "If I gave you a pat answer, I wouldn't be doing you a favor. The main thing will be to treat Philomena like a regular kid and be available when she asks questions. I'll get you a couple of referrals and if they don't work out, let me know. If you need to reach out to me at any time, I'll get back to you."

She tugged at her ponytail. "By regular kid you mean . . ."

"Don't over-shelter her or over-indulge her. Basically, do what you were doing before this terrible thing."

"Terrible thing," she said. "I knew he was a jerk but . . . no sense thinking about that—okay, got it. This helps, I really appreciate it. And I probably will want to reach out."

At the door, she said, "Oops, I almost forgot." Pulling a checkbook out of her purse, she tore off a check and handed it to me.

I said, "This is way too much."

"Doctor," she said, touching my hand, "please let me be the judge of that. I need to feel autonomous."

Before I could argue, she'd flung the door open, run down the stairs and into her Range Rover.

Revving up toward the redline, she peeled out, tires squealing in the gravel, setting off a miniature dust storm.

Seconds later, the dust had settled.

Like any silence that follows noise, especially sweet.

Back to a gorgeous day.

About the Author

JONATHAN KELLERMAN is the #1 *New York Times* bestselling author of fifty crime novels, including the Alex Delaware series, *The Butcher's Theater, Billy Straight, The Conspiracy Club, Twisted, True Detectives,* and *The Murderer's Daughter.* With his wife, bestselling novelist Faye Kellerman, he co-authored *Double Homicide* and *Capital Crimes.* With his son, bestselling novelist Jesse Kellerman, he co-authored *The Burning, Half Moon Bay, A Measure of Darkness, Crime Scene, The Golem of Hollywood,* and *The Golem of Paris.* He is also the author of two children's books and numerous nonfiction works, including *Savage Spawn: Reflections on Violent Children* and *With Strings Attached: The Art and Beauty of Vintage Guitars.* He has won the Goldwyn, Edgar, and Anthony awards and the Lifetime Achievement Award from the American Psychological Association, and has been nominated for a Shamus Award. Jonathan and Faye Kellerman live in California and Israel.

jonathankellerman.com

Facebook.com/JonathanKellerman

About the Type

This book was set in Garamond, a typeface originally designed by the Parisian type cutter Claude Garamond (c. 1500–61). This version of Garamond was modeled on a 1592 specimen sheet from the Egenolff-Berner foundry, which was produced from types assumed to have been brought to Frankfurt by the punch cutter Jacques Sabon (c. 1520–80).

Claude Garamond's distinguished romans and italics first appeared in *Opera Ciceronis* in 1543–44. The Garamond types are clear, open, and elegant.